FALSE FACES

FALSE FACES

Seth Jacob Margolis

St. Martin's Press New York

Design by Glen M. Edelstein

Library of Congress Cataloging-in-Publication Data

Margolis, Seth.
    False faces / Seth Margolis.
        p.   cm.
    "A Thomas Dunne book."
    ISBN 0-312-05818-7
    I. Title.
PS3563.A652F35   1991
813'.54—dc20   91-7394
                                                                   CIP

First Edition: June 1991

10 9 8 7 6 5 4 3 2 1

For Carole

and for Karl Margolis
and in memory of
Marjorie Margolis

Away, and mock the time with fairest
    show:
False face must hide what the false
    heart doth know

—*Macbeth*

FALSE FACES

Chapter

CRANE'S is about motion, about never stopping long enough for a conversation to ignite. Crane's is about talking to as many people in as short a time as possible. Crane's is about drinking. Crane's is about music playing so loud you feel it as much as you hear it. Crane's is about dancing. Crane's is about deep tans and incandescent burns; the sun's heat escaping from bodies as they move around adds a charged dimension to the place, a glow. Crane's is about crowds that make meeting people not merely a possibility, but unavoidable. Which is just as well, because more than anything else, Crane's is about sex.

Caught up in the Friday-night swirl of Crane's were Alison Rosen and Linda Levinson. Saturdays might be more crowded at Crane's, but there was an air of hysteria on Friday nights that generally subsided by Saturday, baked out by the hot summer sun. The sense of release, of sudden unwinding, was almost audible. Alison and Linda drifted from one end of Crane's to the other, from the packed terrace overlooking the bay to the packed bar area to the packed dance floor, where they swayed abstractedly to some unfamiliar music with a strong beat. Two guys moved in on them, assuming the invitation. Alison and Linda looked them over and retreated to the bar.

"Another weekend on Fire Island," said Linda after they'd gotten their drinks. She twirled her finger listlessly in the air. "Hip hip hooray."

"You're a lot of fun," said Alison, surveying this section of Crane's with bird-furtive eyes that matched her hair: brown with gold highlights. Her neck was long and graceful, and at thirty-two her skin retained a youthful, fragile quality. A hint of freckles covered her thin nose, so perfectly straight she was sometimes asked if she'd had it fixed (she hadn't). She was tall, with a figure maintained by constant dieting and daily exercise. Her friend, even taller, with long, glossy black hair and an angular, sultry face that looked like a perfectly realized photograph of itself, made a more striking first impression. Alison was not unaware of this fact—how could she be in Crane's, which was all about first impressions?—but Alison projected a quality of intelligence and complexity that, while it may have done her little good in Crane's, made her appearance in the long run the more rewarding. Problem was, she was having a hard time lately finding men willing to stick around for the long run.

"Sorry," said Linda. "I'll pick up once this drink takes effect. Still, don't you ever think you'd rather spend the weekend in your apartment, pull down the shades, turn up the air conditioner, pretend it's not summer, forget that you're supposed to be out having a good time?"

"When I do that I also consume large quantities of Moo Shu Pork and Häagen Dazs, which is one reason I always manage to make it out here weekends. Anyway, what's up? Sounds like you had a shitty week."

2

"Actually it was a difficult week, but a good one, in a way. I mean, I made some decisions I feel good about. Long-overdue decisions."

"Don't tell me. You're going to look for a new job?" Alison's voice perked up.

"Not really. These decisions are more important."

Alison rolled her eyes and took a sip from her gin and tonic. "More important than your career? You hate your job—you've been saying so for years."

"Maybe it isn't as bad as you think. Besides, I don't have a *career*. What should I do, join the Bloomingdale's training program? You were twenty-two when you did that. I'm thirty-two—a little old for that kind of thing."

Alison shrugged. She was fond of Linda, but felt that her friend sometimes held back on her, and that this prevented them from being truly intimate. Though they saw each other occasionally during the winter, it was on Fire Island that they were together most often.

She'd met Linda seven years ago when they'd shared their first house on Fire Island. They'd both answered the same ad in the *Village Voice*. Linda was in many ways still a mystery, however. She had a dreary job at a law firm but made no effort to leave it. She took a share every summer in Seaside Harbor, yet never tried to meet men, which in Alison's opinion was the real reason most women their age went to Fire Island. That and the beach.

"I don't understand you, Linda. Why bother coming out here if you're not going to try to meet people?"

"*Meet people.* You mean meet men."

"Of course I mean men! I just gave you a twenty-minute blow-by-blow on my social life—no pun intended—and all you do is stand there and dole out advice. What about you?"

"Look at all the good your *social life* has done you." It stung, but Alison chose to ignore this rare display of defen-   **3** siveness. "I *said,* are you seeing anyone?" Other than The Nowhere Man, Alison continued to herself, which is how she thought of Linda's unnamed, unseen, and undiscussed boyfriend. Linda had only mentioned two things about The Nowhere Man: he was married, more or less permanently, and he was nuts about keeping their relationship a secret from everyone, including Linda's friends.

"You'd be the first to know."

Somehow Alison doubted this. She trusted Linda, but there was another dimension to her that Alison simply couldn't fathom. Linda rarely mentioned her lover directly (*"We* went to the movies on Tuesday," she'd say, or *"We* had Chinese food in bed last night"), and something about Linda, a skittishness, prevented Alison from inquiring further. ("What's his name, at least?" Alison had once asked; "What difference does it make?" Linda had answered quickly, with a logic that was irrefutable, if maddening.) It clearly wasn't a relationship that made Linda very happy— how could it, when it relegated her to being a single person every weekend?—yet she seemed incapable of breaking away.

"Well, if it isn't Gloom and Doom."

As an opening line this left much to be desired, but it did serve as a kind of mirror, offering Alison a glimpse of herself and Linda, standing at the bar looking sullen and unapproachable. Chilled by this vision, she made a conscious effort to defrost. "You're Eric Farber, right?" she said brightly. "I knew I knew you. So go ahead, cheer us up."

"What'll it be, a threesome on the dance floor?"

"No thanks," said Linda quickly.

"Linda, you've met Eric Farber, right?"

"We've met."

"We go way back, don't we, Linda?" he said.

"Come on, Alison, let's check out the terrace."

4   Alison looked at Linda, then at Farber. "Well, Gloom would like to dance, even if Doom wouldn't." She took Farber's hand and led him to the dance floor.

Farber was the type of outrageously handsome man for whom Alison could never work up much attraction. He looked unreal, with the chiseled, bruised face of a male model. Still, he danced well, if unenthusiastically; Alison sensed he wasn't really interested in her, and when the song ended he thanked her stiffly—none of his earlier smoothness evident now—and disappeared.

"What was going on between you two?" she asked Linda, who hadn't budged from the bar.

"He's a creep."

An intriguing notion occurred to her: could Eric Farber be The Nowhere Man? He's not married, and surely there'd be no reason to sneak around, but even so . . . "I couldn't believe how cold you acted to him, Linda. He's not that bad a—"

"He's a creep, period. End of discussion."

If Linda were homely or boring, Alison might have had less trouble accepting her inability to break away from The Nowhere Man, her almost total unwillingness to venture beyond the apparent safety of her weekday romance. Sure, she had occasional one-night stands—God knows she had no trouble recruiting volunteers—but one night, or, more accurately, two or three hours, was as far as she went. She was extraordinarily sexy and also quite pretty, though men always seemed to use words like "knock-out" and "dyna-mite" rather than "pretty" in reference to Linda. And she had a friendly, generous personality, a fact, Alison knew, that was obvious to very few people, none of them men. What really baffled Alison was that Linda, who never made the slightest attempt to meet or hold onto a man (apart, of course, from her married friend), dressed in an undeniably feminine, sexy manner. As if her *only* aim was to attract men. Tight pants, sheer blouses, bathing suits that made jaws drop on a beach littered with beautiful female bodies. Linda's office clothes were no different—skirts slit high on the thigh, knitted dresses that clung to her for dear life, blouses always opened one button too many. She was tall and slender, wore her black hair long and perfectly straight. Her face was narrow, but her eyes, greenish brown, were large, almost too large for her head.

The whole look said, *Notice me, I'm available.* At least that's how Alison saw her. Yet her whole personality said, *Don't bother.*

"Linda." Alison nudged her friend, who was reading the labels on the bottles behind the bar with Talmudic intensity. "Look. There's that Rob guy from last weekend."

"Who's Rob?"

"You remember, the guy you were with last week."

"Oh yeah, him. That was nothing, an anatomical event. Or nonevent."

"Uh-oh."

"Rob What's-his-name was a washout. He came on so strong, here I figured he'd be good for half the night. Boy, was I wrong. I wouldn't have cared except he kept begging for a second chance. Lucky for you you weren't around. I think the whole house heard him. It was really pathetic."

"He's kind of cute, really," said Alison as she watched Rob, who stood in a noisy group, drinking a beer.

Linda appraised Rob from across the bar. "There was something sad about him. Lost. I didn't know how to make him feel better, though I knew another go at it wouldn't do either of us any good. He was too angry at that point . . ."

Just then Rob turned and caught the two women watching him. He jerked his head away as if slapped, and stared resolutely at the woman who stood across from him.

"Poor guy," said Linda. "He was so hard on himself and I really was just as happy nothing happened. Wasn't really into it."

6

"Great. No wonder he had trouble."

"That's not fair. I *acted* enthusiastic. At least I think I did. He didn't exactly strike me as the type who cared what I was feeling anyway. And I didn't complain at all afterwards." A few minutes later Rob (neither Linda nor Alison knew his last name; he shared a house, however, with a friend of Alison's cousin Eleanor) glanced quickly toward them and once again caught Alison eying him, though Linda had already drifted back to her bottles. Alison flashed what she thought was an engaging, come-on-over smile, but Rob, looking a little fierce, as if he'd been attacked instead of smiled at, turned and disappeared into the crowd.

Oh God, thought Alison. He must know I know.

Out on the terrace they leaned against the railing and watched the boats bobbing in the harbor. The evening air was rich with salty sea-smells and the promise of fair weather. A ferry glided silently toward Seaside Harbor, both decks crowded with Friday-night refugees from the city.

"Hard to believe five hours ago we were still in New York, working," said Linda.

"I love it on Fire Island. It always feels like a vacation to me, even if it's just a weekend."

"What I like best is that there aren't any cars." Alison agreed: the absence of automobiles was as soothing as the salt air—it was somehow evident even above the blaring music from inside Crane's.

Alison felt a tap on her shoulder. It was Larry, from their house, and Jason, his roommate. Larry worked in his father's lingerie business; Jason was an accountant somewhere. They were both impossibly young—on the far side of twenty-four, Alison estimated—and not at all comfortable to be with. The first weekend of the summer Jason had

7

jumped her in the living room. He was drunk, and she had had a tough time shaking him off, trying to be as gentle as possible—he was, after all, just a kid. Later that night he'd ambushed Linda, who'd sent him fleeing with a soft but firm "Get lost," a technique Alison made a point of remembering.

This year Linda and Alison had taken shares with people they didn't know. They'd found the house through an ad in the *Voice*, same way they'd met seven years ago. It was Alison's idea to branch out, meet new people. At thirty-two, she figured this would be her last summer in Seaside Harbor. Next season, she thought with a pessimism that she recognized as self-destructive but was unable to resist, it would be time to move on to a quieter, older community on Fire Island. Why not make the most of this last Seaside Harbor summer? Linda hadn't protested.

"How about a few lines for energy?" Larry offered, trying to sound casual; his shoulders, however, had begun to shrug uncontrollably. Alison and Linda looked at each other. Neither seemed anxious to make a decision: a little coke would certainly liven things up, but the price—indebtedness to Jason and Larry—seemed a bit steep.

The lingerie business must be booming, Alison thought as she and Linda, having finally made up their minds, followed the boys off the terrace. Larry seemed to have an unlimited supply of cocaine, and his generosity with the stuff was truly unusual. No skulking off to the bathroom for Larry: they estimated he went through close to two hundred dollars of coke a weekend.

At the door, Linda said she'd decided to head back to the house. She was tired—the cocaine would just keep her up.

"That's the whole point," said her friend.

"Honestly, Alison. See you all later."

"See you in the morning, Linda."

On a deserted dock they spooned half a dozen pinches of powder into their noses and tried without success to get a conversation going. Even the coke didn't help. Fifteen minutes later Alison shivered, said she felt a chill, and in no time they were back in Crane's, sniffling like three patients at an allergy clinic in the middle of pollen season.

Chapter

IT wasn't hard for Alison to lose her two housemates; it only took concentration to *stick* with someone in Crane's. Back in the swirl of Crane's at prime time, Alison happily succumbed to the flow as it carried her from one half-formed dialogue to another. She had the sensation of entering a theater after intermission, listening to conversations that made only partial sense to her but were nonetheless strangely compelling. Only standing still required real effort, and she was in no condition to expend any.

She found herself talking to a homely but, she concluded after a few minutes, oddly attractive guy who offered to buy her a drink. She accepted and he left for the bar, but she never saw him again that night. Perhaps he met someone else. Or maybe she had moved and he was unable to find her. She really couldn't remember.

The cocaine was working like a shot of adrenaline; she felt full of euphoric energy, as light and free as a helium balloon. One moment she was wandering aimlessly but contentedly through Crane's; a moment later, unable to recall how it had started, she found herself in the middle of a conversation with a really good-looking guy, and when he offered to buy her a drink she not only said yes, but made sure he could find her when he returned from the bar with her gin and tonic.

Five minutes later the conversation hadn't progressed beyond the "Which house are you in?" and "Who's in it?" phase, but Alison didn't really care; she just enjoyed *looking* at this man, who possessed precisely the looks she liked: tall, lean, dark, not too handsome but with a confident attitude. It had been some time since she'd flirted with a guy; it was nice to know all the parts still worked.

"Crane's is really crowded tonight," she said for lack of anything better. He didn't seem to care whether they talked or not. "I guess the hot weather brings people out here—"

"So, uh, you want to come back to my place?" he interrupted, with an impatient edge to his voice that implied she'd been babbling for some time. "My roommate's not here this weekend," he added with the matter-of-factness of a car salesman rattling off the standard features of a new sedan.

Alison was startled by this and couldn't hide it. Perhaps she'd heard him wrong. "We just met five minutes ago," she said, and then regretted it, for the statement seemed rather obvious, and elicited only a puzzled look from her companion. She was shocked almost in spite of herself— after three drinks and a few hours of conversation, such an invitation would not have been too unusual, might have been expected, even, but this was stretching it.

"Sorry I asked," he said a minute later, looking genuinely surprised, looking, Alison thought, as if *she* were the one who'd done something strange. "I just thought we were hitting it off."

He sipped his drink coolly, his eyes lazily reconnoitering the crowded bar behind her, and Alison realized she couldn't remember his name . . . or hadn't he told her? She started to walk away when he stopped her.

"So, uh, listen, you know that girl you were with earlier, the one with the long straight hair? You think she'd want to come back with me? Like I said, I have my own room this weekend."

"I don't believe this," said Alison.

"You mean she wouldn't?"

Alison was glad Linda had left Crane's for the evening. It wasn't that her friend was undiscriminating, it was just that she could be lazy about these things, and Mr. Let's-Skip-the-Formalities might have done very nicely with Linda for a no-strings-attached anatomical event. "You won't know unless you ask her," she said, and started to laugh, for the whole scene—this guy, Larry and Jason, Crane's—suddenly struck her as unbearably funny.

It was warm for Fire Island, which is cool at night even in midsummer. Linda left Crane's and turned right, heading west. The house was only a short walk from Crane's—nothing in Seaside Harbor was ever more than a few blocks away.

On a map, Fire Island looks like the slip of a cartographer's pen: its entire expanse runs for forty miles parallel to the longer, thicker, more substantial mass of Long Island just to the north across the Great South Bay. A glorified sandbar at best, it pokes out from the Atlantic where Robert Moses State Park ends, continues east past towns with breezy, weekend names like Kismet, Saltaire, Seaview, the Pines, Fair Harbor, Cherry Grove, each with its own homogeneous constituency of summer residents, each with its own distinct flavor, before receding back into the ocean at Davis Park. There are no cars on Fire Island, a fact, along with the ocean and the long, wide beaches, that is responsible for much of the place's appeal. An armada of ferries links Long Island to its emaciated offshoot to the south, shuttling weekenders back and forth during the summer season like so many dinghies serving a cruise ship at anchor offshore.

Main Street was crowded—eleven-thirty was early by Seaside Harbor standards—and noisy. The distant sound of surf, only a few hundred yards away across the island, was punctuated by drunken howls, exaggerated laughter, and the all-pervasive rhythmic thumping from the sound system at Crane's. Weekends in Seaside Harbor have the feel of a college campus just after finals week.

As Linda walked along Main Street, she received a few slurred invitations from passing men. "No thank you," she replied politely in a sweetly girlish voice that didn't seem quite right coming from a body slipcovered in a little white T-shirt separated by three inches of exposed, tanned midsection from gleaming white pants tight as Saran Wrap. Her high-heeled shoes forced her to take little cha-cha steps, giving the impression that she was hurrying.

Linda turned left on Tupelo Road and found herself alone. While Main ran east–west the length of Seaside Harbor, Tupelo was one of several roads (paths, really) that cut across Fire Island north–south, from bay to ocean, forming a grid. The sky was speckled with stars, all but invisible in Manhattan, where they were no match for the city's neon glow.

Linda's house was three in from the ocean, about four blocks from Main Street. She was looking forward to being in her own bed, asleep. Shortly after turning off Main she heard someone walking behind her. Nothing unusual about this, except that when she turned around—just checking it

13

out, not really alarmed—nobody was there. Linda looked up and searched the sky for the moon. It wasn't there either.

A few minutes later she again heard footsteps. And again, when she turned around—nobody. A slight chill went through her, a feather tickling the back of her neck. She quickened her pace as much as her wobbly shoes allowed.

The music from Crane's could still be heard dimly as a pattern of deep, rhythmic explosions, as if blasting for construction were going on a few miles away. A group of noisy revelers crossed Tupelo heading west. After they crossed, Linda casually looked behind her. No one.

Good thing Al and Fran are probably back at the house, she thought. Al and Fran were the married couple in the house. Then: why am I so paranoid? This is Fire Island, not Manhattan.

Without the traffic sounds she was used to, the silence was a presence in itself. She heard the footsteps again. Now she was sure someone was behind her, following her. This time she also heard bushes rustling as she turned around. Still, the street was empty. Tupelo Road, like all the paths in Seaside Harbor, was elevated slightly from the sandy ground and bordered by dense bushes and small, arid trees, mostly pines. The vegetation formed high, almost solid walls on either side, so that the paths resembled corridors in a maze in which visibility is limited to straight ahead.

"Linda." She heard her name whispered, just barely heard it, for it merged with the wind that gently threaded through the thick brush.

"Who's there?" she said softly. She heard her voice waver; she was frightened.

No reply. It's just the wind, she told herself with little conviction. Her mind was clouded with gin, but the fresh salt air, so different from the stuff she inhaled during the week, managed to sharpen her senses, made her aware of soft sounds and slight movements, and heightened her sense of alarm.

She stopped. A person emerged from the side of the road, stepped up to the road, actually. The moonless night shielded the figure in darkness as it approached.

Linda instinctively backed up, still facing the man. She could tell it was a man from his figure, big and masculine and threatening even in the dark. Especially in the dark.

"Who's there?" she asked, her soft voice again betraying fear, the wind now blowing against her, carrying with it a faint odor of men's cologne. A familiar smell . . .

No answer. The figure continued to approach. Now Linda felt real terror, felt it deep inside her, like cramps. Running seemed out of the question, given her shoes and the condition of the path, but she continued to back away from the oncoming figure.

Suddenly he stepped into a beam of faint light that radiated from the porch of a nearby house.

"You!" Linda gasped, her relief tempered by extreme annoyance. "What the hell were you trying to do, scare me to death?"

He continued walking toward her until they were just a few feet apart. At this range Linda, still shook up, was surprised and not a little bit frightened to recognize in his face an angry but determined look, his mouth twisted, his eyes squinting against a light only he could see: it was the look of a boxer between rounds. He seemed transformed, a different person altogether. And he still hadn't spoken.

Linda had little time, however, to digest the implications of his silence, for as soon as he was within arm's length he grabbed her, brutally clasping his hand over her mouth, forcing her off the street into the brush. It happened so swiftly, and was so totally unexpected, that she didn't have time to cry out, didn't even think to cry out. They fell as he pushed her off the path, but his grip on her never loosened. Her face and arms burned from the sharp branches that scratched her as she fell.

They were now concealed entirely from the road, lying on the damp, sandy ground, his big, sweaty hand clamped viselike over her mouth, practically covering her entire face; her jaw ached from the pressure. She struggled, hitting him as hard as she could on the back and sides. It was like hitting concrete. He straddled her, the weight of him keeping her down. His left hand still covering her mouth, he placed his right around her throat. The size and strength of his hand and the thinness of her neck enabled him to cut off the flow of oxygen, so that he could safely remove his left hand from her mouth with no fear of her shouting for help.

Both hands were now employed in strangling her. "Bitch," he said softly, the hatred in his voice more than compensating for the lack of volume. The dense foliage, having parted when they tumbled into it from the path, now engulfed them in almost total blackness.

Linda's eyes bulged wildly from their sockets. She continued to pound at him without effect; he didn't seem to feel a thing, it was like hitting a marble statue. Close to death and unable to speak, let alone shout for help, her eyes were her last repository of life—they seemed to plead with him, as if arguing her case one last time. *You're wrong, you're making a horrible mistake!* her eyes were saying. *You don't have to do this! It's not like you think!*

But if her eyes communicated anything, it did nothing to weaken his resolve.

"Die, bitch," he hissed, and a minute later she complied, her body going suddenly limp with a slight shudder, like a car stalling. Her attacker—her murderer, now—kept his grip around her neck for a full minute longer, making sure she really was dead. He let go, then clasped his hands around her once more, taking no chances. When he released his hold for a second time, he noticed that his left hand, the one he'd held over her mouth, was covered with saliva. "Cunt," he said, wiping his hand on her pants, as if this were the most distasteful part of the whole episode.

He stared at her for a few moments, still sitting on top of her, then grabbed her T-shirt and gave it a violent yank that tore it across her chest. He pulled angrily at it a few more times until it was completely off her. Slowly, as if fearful of awakening her, he unzipped her jeans. Moving down toward her feet, he started to tug at the pants, but they were too tight—he got them over her hips but no further. She was wearing white panties dotted with small yellow and blue flowers. He ran his hand over the panties, surprised at their smoothness, their thin delicateness. Then he pulled them down below her hips and gazed at her intently, as if her nakedness startled him in some way. Slowly, almost cautiously, he leaned forward and ran his hands over her breasts, up and down, up and down. Her body was still warm—hot, really—and she seemed to come alive under his caressing hands. He felt his breathing grow heavier, felt himself giving in to the lifeless body beneath him.

Suddenly he pulled back and slapped her across the face. Linda's head jerked to the side, as if she were still alive. "Goddamn cunt," he said hoarsely, his chest heaving.

He stood up quickly and peered out from the brush. Tupelo Road was deserted. He began walking leisurely toward town.

Alison bought herself a gin and tonic and resumed her pleasant ramble through the crowd, first in the bar and then on the terrace. One drink later and she was feeling awfully good. The cocaine was wearing off but the gin was filling in nicely: she felt impervious, as if a protective aura sur- **17** rounded her as she wandered among hostile beings. The sound system blasted "I'm So Excited"—an exaggeration, but she did feel good.

She spotted one of her housemates, Ronnie Amron, standing amid a ring of beer-enlivened men, and when she got close enough to overhear them she could tell they were teasing her, their jibes full of sexual innuendo and thinly disguised put-downs. Ronnie seemed to enjoy it, though, even egged them on as if her only concern was that they have a good time, even at her own expense. Ronnie worked for an ad agency in some vague capacity that she made much of but which Alison suspected was glorified secretarial. Her roommate in Seaside Harbor was her sister, Tracy, a research biologist for a pharmaceutical company. Ronnie was pretty in a hard-edged way that men seemed to like, and outgoing; her sister was less pretty and less outgoing. Alison found them both difficult to know. Tracy, the younger one, seemed to relate only to her gregarious older sister, who related equally well to everyone, never varying her behavior, her level of familiarity. Whether she was with old friends or new acquaintances, Ronnie was perky, enthusiastic, solicitous, inquisitive; at first she had made Alison feel special, as if all this enthusiasm were directed at her alone. But after watching her in action for seven weeks, Alison realized that Ronnie was this way with *everyone,* guys she met once on the beach, girls she'd gone to high school with, people she'd been sharing the house with for half a summer. Ronnie tried Alison's patience, not one of her strong suits to begin with.

Her attention still held by the spectacle of Ronnie surrounded by a small circle of male detractors, it occurred to Alison that Ronnie's younger sister couldn't be far away, and sure enough she spotted Tracy just outside the ring, looking lonely and tired, like the ticket-taker at a high school basketball game, always on the fringe of the action, never a participant. She'd bet her life Tracy would sleep on the living-room couch tonight, and tomorrow night too, a victim of her sister's insatiable appetite for pleasing.

"Hey, babe."

An inauspicious opening, if a common one. Alison turned and found herself facing a not unattractive guy—not her type, but not too far off either. His face had a jutting, almost cubist quality, as if he'd been assembled without the proper instructions. It was a face, she could tell, that would take some getting used to, but its unexpected shading, its tanned angularity, was undeniably appealing.

The conversation that ensued was actually rather promising, as they managed to skip the "Is this your first time in Seaside Harbor?" "Which house are you in?" "Who are your housemates?" phase and still find something to talk about. Inevitably the conversation turned to jobs.

"What do you do?" she asked, bowing to the inevitable.

"I play basketball. I jog. I'm famous for my kisses. Sometimes I even read." He said this with a serious, unsmiling expression.

"I hope not too much, I hear it's bad for the eyes."

"Kissing?"

"No, dummy, reading. Anyway, I'm serious. What do you do for a living?"

"Seriously, I'm a mayor."

For a moment Alison didn't realize she was being had. Flirting often involved a kind of gentle, sassy teasing, but it generally ended after a few minutes or so.

"Mayor of what?"

"It's a little town in Idaho, you probably haven't heard of it." He paused, gauging the depth of her gullibility. "It's called Spuds. Like I said, you probably haven't heard of it."

Uh-oh, she thought, one of *those*. There was a species of man in Seaside Harbor that wouldn't be serious for even one conversation, let alone get caught in a relationship. Alison knew the type well: over the course of an evening a man of this species will tell the most outrageous stories to the women he meets. Eventually—and this is what always astounded Alison—he finds himself a member of a symbiotic species of woman, a species of woman that falls for this type of banter, the more outrageous the story the better. There were guys who would tell women they had a month to live but gained an extra week each time they had sex. Alison had actually heard this once, and heard a woman fall for it, or, more likely, pretend to fall for it. Who, if anyone, was fooling whom was a question she could never satisfactorily answer.

"I'm here in New York for a potato convention. I thought I'd check out Fire Island as long as I was close by." Still the serious, unsmiling expression, his shoulders angled earnestly forward.

"What do you talk about at a potato convention?" she asked in her most solicitous voice.

"Oh, there's lots of things, really. I hardly have a moment to myself. Growing techniques, fertilizers, pesticides, competition . . ."

Alison spotted a gleam in his eye: another bimbo falls for a truly outrageous story—wait till I tell the guys about this one.

"Competition? For potatoes?"

"Oh," he said, his voice now turning deadly serious. "It's a major concern. It used to be just Maine and Long Island we worried about. But now the Japanese are into potatoes and we're being undersold right and left. First TVs, then cars. Now it's potatoes. It's a national disgrace."

Alison giggled. "That's really very good. Potato competition from the Japanese. I like that, I really do." She turned and walked away from the now openmouthed mayor of Spuds, Idaho. He really had thought she believed him, and before the night was out, she knew, he'd find someone who did, or pretended to.

Alison bought herself another gin and tonic, drifted in and out of a few conversations, felt good that men wanted to meet her, felt bad that they all seemed younger than her. She didn't have the energy for lengthy conversation. The first few minutes you could chatter away, by rote almost, about the usual topics—any longer than that took real effort, real concentration. This is what frightened Alison sometimes: how was she going to meet a man, form a lasting relationship, when she lacked the enthusiasm even for a five-minute conversation? It was the conundrum of getting older: getting married was now more important than it had ever been before, but after years of bars and blind dates and lonely mornings-after, she didn't have the necessary energy or stamina or patience. It was so much easier hanging out with Linda—sweet, familiar, unthreatening Linda.

Alison recalled their earlier conversation and regretted the way she'd treated her friend. If Linda wanted to keep her private life private, so be it. There were other levels on which a friendship could thrive.

She continued to thread her way though the crowd. Crane's was still in high gear at one in the morning. She spotted Rob and decided to ask him to dance. She felt bad that he thought she had been taunting him earlier that evening.

"Hi, my name's Alison," she said in her most upbeat voice.

He said nothing.

"Pleased to meet you too," she said with somewhat less enthusiasm.

Still no response.

Alison decided to give it one last shot. "I know how you feel, I'm all talked out too. How about dancing instead?"

He shot her a truly hostile glance. "Cunt" was all he said   **21** before walking away. The word, or rather the intense hatred it carried with it, hit Alison like a punch in the stomach: it literally took her breath away.

"Hey, don't take it too hard. I'll dance with you." Alison turned. Her white knight grinned at her through a moustache that completely covered his top lip. He had a big nose, a stomach that drooped over his belt, almost obscuring it, and bad breath.

"Sure, why not?" she replied, still stunned.

He was a good dancer, it turned out, and Alison *loved* to dance. They went at it for the longest time. She began to feel tired, then felt herself cross the line separating exhaustion from overexhaustion; in the former state she had longed to call it quits, in the latter, even calling it quits seemed a tall order—*that* would take energy, more energy than she had at the moment. So she danced some more, feeling as if she were tumbling down a hill, an enjoyable sensation, but dizzying. This music, with its uninterrupted beat: sometimes it got a hold of her and wouldn't let go. The songs merged seamlessly, one into another. Even when she finally managed to pull herself off the dance floor, she felt her body still pulsing to the music, responding not to her own need to rest but to the music's exhortation to dance. Walking home at last, navigating the crisscrossing paths unconsciously, she wondered if she'd thanked her partner with the big nose and bad breath. He'd at least guaranteed that she'd have no trouble sleeping tonight. Had she said good night? Or had he left her first, there on the dance floor? She really couldn't remember. She was awfully tired. After all, it was only Friday—well, Saturday, technically—and she'd been up for over twenty hours straight.

Chapter

ALISON woke up Saturday morning at eight with a gin hangover. She felt a tiny, tiny marble rolling freely inside her head; sudden movements forced it against the raw inside of her skull, causing isolated spasms of pain. Another two hours of sleep and that marble would dissolve like a gumdrop, but Alison had a thing about sleeping late; she couldn't do it no matter how tired she was. Puritan ethic, some might say, but Alison was Jewish and knew that the Puritan ethic was, comparatively speaking, child's play.

So Linda has slept out, she thought, glancing at the empty bed next to hers. Good for her. She remembered Linda telling her she was going home. Must have changed her mind, or met someone on the way. First affair of the summer—second if you counted Rob. Let's hope this one lasts. She pulled herself out of bed with some difficulty, thinking: fat chance.

By ten-thirty Alison was lying on her back on a towel on the beach. These were the prime tanning hours, and Seaside Harbor's serious tanners were already greased up and supine. Like a herd of cattle, all grazing in one direction, every tanner on the beach was facing the sun, an awkward position, since it required that they lie with the ocean on their right, their bodies on an uncomfortable slant.

The wide beach stretched for miles in either direction, lined with all variety of summer houses: small, shingled cottages weathered to the color of driftwood; boxy, glassy, modern affairs, some of them with pools sunk into decks that jutted out over the dunes; large, older homes with French doors opening onto broad terraces, gauzy white curtains fluttering from inside like spirits from a more elegant, less crowded past. Most of the houses in Seaside Harbor were divided into shares, generally with two people to a room, so that the typical four-bedroom house might contain eight unrelated people on a given weekend, plus guests willing to put up with damp, musty couches or hard, sand-sprinkled floors. Other towns discouraged sharers, but not Seaside Harbor, where a modest, even run-down house rented for fifteen thousand a summer.

Alison was listening to the new Springsteen album on her Sony Walkman. Lying absolutely still, the hot sun and morning breeze conspiring to delight her body and soul, isolated by the crushing, all-encompassing music—it was worth it, Alison thought: five sticky days in the city, the race for seats on the LIRR, the creeps at Crane's, conversation with her housemates before coffee, being the oldest female for miles (an exaggeration, but Alison liked to dramatize her plight to herself). All of it a small price to pay for the privilege of lying on this beautiful beach under an unobstructed sun, baking in heaven.

24   She lapsed in and out of sleep, waking only to shift her towel position to follow the sun's westward path or to turn over the Springsteen tape, and then turn it over again. When Alison liked a new album she played it over and over, listened to little else until she could stand to hear it no longer and never listened to it again. This process usually took a month.

Occasionally she thought of Linda, wondered when she'd come down to the beach and tell her all about last night, whom she'd been with. They always hung out at the same place on the beach, along with most Seaside Harborites. She was still thinking about Linda, and about that Rob fellow from the night before, when sleep once again overtook her. The morning breeze began to fade with the approach of noon.

The tape ended with a loud click, but it was the absence of sound that awakened her. She reached into her beach bag and brought out her watch, placed it between her face and the sun, now directly overhead: 12:15. The beach would be crowded now. And yet, something was wrong. She felt it. Where were the standard beach sounds she knew so well: the voices muffled by the sound of the surf, the radios, also muffled, the crunch of sand as people walked by?

Something was wrong. She could feel it.

Abruptly she sat up. The beach was curiously empty of people, though it was littered with blankets, towels, beach bags. For a moment, dizzy from sitting up too quickly and from two hours of direct sun, Alison was truly terrified: where *was* everyone? It looked as if a neutron bomb had hit, obliterating every living thing but leaving their belongings eerily intact. Then she saw. At the edge of the beach, at the bottom of the white stairs that led from the sand to the end of Tupelo Road, were assembled a hundred or so people, mostly silent. Standing a few steps up, in khaki

25

shirt and pants, was Seaside Harbor's sole officer of the law.

A few feet away from the crowd, Alison knew her instincts on waking up had been correct: something was wrong. There was an aura of alarm over the crowd—she could almost see it.

"Does anyone know of anyone—a female—who didn't come home last night?" the officer was asking as Alison approached. Four hands went up. There was an awkward pause before four or five more hands were raised.

The officer's mouth, never entirely closed, opened wider. "You mean to tell me . . . five, six, seven, eight of your friends never made it home last night? Jesus Christ," he mumbled under his breath, shaking his head. "Hasn't anyone here heard of AIDS?"

"What's going on?" Alison asked someone.

"They found a body. A female body."

"I don't believe it. Here? In Seaside Harbor?"

"Believe it. Strangled to death. No ID."

"Who. . . ?"

"I said, no ID."

"You girls who raised your hands, you're saying your girlfriends didn't show up last night, is that correct?" asked the officer, sounding skeptical.

They nodded. Alison looked for Linda in the crowd. Not spotting her, it occurred to Alison to raise her hand, since Linda hadn't come home last night either, but it seemed indiscreet, potentially embarrassing for Linda, so she refrained. "My girlfriend slept out last night," volunteered one woman. "But she always does. I mean, she sometimes does, you know what I mean? Oh shit, she'll kill me. I mean, if she's still . . . oh shit, I don't know what I'm saying."

"You haven't seen her this morning?" asked the officer, a clean-cut man of about forty with long sideburns and dark green sunglasses. Sweat stains were growing around his armpits like puddles in a rainstorm.

26

"No."

"Can you tell me what she was wearing when you last saw her?"

The entire crowd now focused on this one person, who seemed uncomfortable as the center of attention. "Sure. At Crane's last night she had on a red mini-dress. By Perry Ellis, I think. Yeah, Perry Ellis. Red shoes, slippers really, with red laces that—"

"Okay, okay, I get the picture. It's not your friend," interrupted the officer. "How about you, you say you haven't seen your girlfriend today either?"

All eyes turned on a small, pretty girl in a black one-piece bathing suit with hips cut so high and neckline so low that it looked as if she had put on a modest suit that morning, stood in front of a mirror, and then simply torn away those parts of the suit she didn't absolutely need. She shook her head. "I haven't seen her since last night, at Crane's."

"And what was she wearing?" asked the officer, unabashedly ogling the object of his interrogation from his elevated vantage point.

"Black Norma Kamali skirt, a pink top, T-shirt really. Moccasins, I think, or maybe—"

"Not her," he interrupted, and the crowd heaved a sigh of mixed relief and disappointment.

The third no-show that morning, according to her roommate, had last been seen in a white mini-dress ("either Vittadini or Calvin—she has both"). Not the victim, concluded the officer. Number four had also been wearing a white mini-dress, and there was some discussion as to whether this was the very same dress worn by number three until the officer interrupted and declared that the victim absolutely was not wearing a white mini-dress, he didn't care who the designer was.

"Hey, why not tell us what she was wearing and then

maybe we'll know who it was?" someone ventured. A grunt of agreement erupted from the crowd.

Alison thought: they'd know if it was Linda—Linda always has a pocketbook full of identification. Then she realized with a slight shudder that Linda never brought her pocketbook to Crane's, couldn't dance with it, just brought a few bills in her hip pocket for drinks.

"Look, I'd tell you what she was wearing, but I don't want to start a panic here."

"What panic?" said a male voice from the back of the crowd. "Yeah, what panic?" chimed in a few more people.

"All right, all right. Calm down. She was dressed kind of ordinary, like, uh, well, like a lot of girls here and I just thought, well, if I was to tell you she had on this or that, you'd all—"

"Tell us!" the crowd exhorted him, like the congregation of a fundamentalist church. "Tell us!"

"Okay, okay," he relented, clearly not pleased that his original strategy had to be abandoned lest he lose control of the situation entirely.

Even before he spoke, Alison knew it was Linda, knew with certainty. The fact that Linda had left Crane's alone last night and then hadn't shown up had something to do with her premonition, but it went deeper. She knew Linda was gone as clearly as if a loud radio had suddenly been turned off. The absence of Linda was almost palpable.

"The victim was wearing . . . is wearing . . . white pants, jeans, I guess, a white shirt . . ."

"Linda," Alison murmured. She might just as well have shouted, for all heads turned her way. The crowd backed off from her, as if from a leper. "Linda, my roommate," she said softly.

"Young lady," the officer said, though he couldn't have been more than seven or eight years older than Alison, "do you think you know who the victim is?" Alison heard him, but didn't quite realize he was addressing her.

"Linda," she repeated.

"She says it's her roommate, Linda something," said someone in the crowd.

"I know her roommate," said a female voice. "Linda Levinson." The voice paused. "Oh my God," it resumed, "it's Linda Levinson, I can't believe it."

Now the crowd became vocal. "Who's Linda Levinson?" someone asked. "I thought it was Robinson, Linda Robinson."

"No, Linda Levinson. You know, the pretty one, great body?"

"Oh yeah, with the long hair."

"Brown hair."

"No, black. Long and straight."

"I'm telling you it's brown. With black highlights maybe."

"Really pretty-looking chick."

"Did you know her?"

"Knew *of* her."

During this exercise in group recall, attention had momentarily strayed from Alison, who stood, like the heroine of a Greek tragedy, alone and silent amid an agitated chorus.

The officer tried to quiet down the crowd, gave up, then worked his way through it to Alison. He reached her with some difficulty. When he took her elbow to escort her through the crowd, she felt herself collapsing into his arms. Suddenly, walking, even standing, seemed unbearably difficult, and her head pounded as it tried to absorb the news. He caught her before she hit the sand, and with the help of two men carried her up the stairs and off the beach.

The crowd said nothing at first, the silence not a true silence but a held breath, the restraint practically audible, and when at length they began to talk, they embarked on a frenzy of speculation that was to last all summer.

Chapter

JOSEPH DiGregorio, known as Joe D. to his friends, sat on the roof deck of the Seaside Harbor ferry smoking a cigarette, his first in two weeks. He'd bummed it off a fellow passenger. Joe D. only smoked when he was nervous, and he was not a nervous person. It was Saturday morning, three weeks after Linda Levinson's murder.

Joe D. was a Waterside, Long Island, native, a Waterside resident, a Waterside cop. Twenty-nine years old, he had been on the police force for eight years. His assignment this morning was to do what a whole squadron of cops had so far been unable to do: find Linda Levinson's killer.

Nobody brought cars to Fire Island; walking and bicycling were the only ways to get around. If you brought your groceries from Long Island, where prices were lower, you moved them in the kind of low wagon little boys used to have, so the ferry was not large, and it moved at a fast clip once it left Waterside Harbor behind. Like several other passengers that morning, Joe D. was listening to a portable cassette player, though he was probably the only one listening to Bach's Second Brandenburg.

Joe D. was infatuated with Bach, had been ever since he was thirteen. That year a pianist had visited his junior high school as part of the administration's attempt to inject culture into the students' lives. The pianist had played a selection from the Goldberg Variations, and that had clinched it. To Joe D. it sounded as if there were two or even three people playing at once, and the more he tried to untangle the various strands of the music, the more caught up in it he became, until he felt literally *inside* the music, surrounded by it, at its mercy.

After school that day he ran downtown and bought his first Bach album: the Goldberg Variations, of course. At home he removed a Rolling Stones album from his record player, put on the Goldberg Variations, and once again felt himself a captive of the music, as if Bach were casting out from three centuries back and reeling him in with themes and variations so seductively and intricately beautiful he was powerless to resist. Over the years he had tried other composers, Bach's contemporaries, even Bach's own sons, but Johann Sebastian Bach was his first love, and like all first loves it made subsequent affairs seem pale and tepid in comparison.

Joe D. continued to enjoy rock and roll, continued to go to bars and clubs and parties with his friends, but in his room, in his car, and now, with the Walkman, virtually anytime he was alone, it was Bach he listened to, only Bach.

On the ferry to Seaside Harbor he tried concentrating on the Second Brandenburg, which he had selected for its high-spirited drive, but even Bach let him down this time, even Bach was no competition for the Linda Levinson case.

Waterside had jurisdiction over much of Fire Island, in- **31** cluding Seaside Harbor. During the summer one full-time cop was assigned to Fire Island—Officer Harrison, the one who had gotten the identity of the body on the beach—but otherwise there wasn't much police work called for on the island. Linda Levinson had the posthumous distinction of being the first person ever to be murdered in Seaside Harbor. She was also Joe D.'s first murder case.

This was perhaps the third or fourth trip to Fire Island Joe D. had ever made, though he had grown up only a few blocks from the ferry landing. The local Waterside kids hung out at Robert Moses State Park or Jones Beach. Fire Island was for "New Yorkers" (meaning people who lived in New York City), not for Long Island kids like Joe D. and his friends. Hell, you weren't allowed to eat on the beach at Fire Island, and even a hamburger there was unaffordable for most of them. Besides, they had never felt welcome on Fire Island. It may have been only a few miles away from Joe D.'s home since childhood, but it might as well have been halfway around the world, so great was the psychological distance separating it from Waterside, a quiet, mostly middle-class community on the outer edge of suburbia. Fire Island was *fancy,* or so it seemed from Waterside, and fancy was not what teenage boys looked for in a beach. On Fire Island you didn't find girls any younger than twenty-two, unless they were with their parents, so what was the point, anyway?

Even today, at twenty-nine, Joe D. sensed he was crossing a border of some kind. Fire Island, especially Seaside Harbor, was like no other place he'd ever been. He'd gone out to the Hamptons. To Long Island's posher North Shore. Seen the big houses, the Mercedes and Jaguars. But Fire Island was different. Weird. Shit, they didn't even *have* cars on Fire Island. He really wished he hadn't been given this case.

But an order was an order. It was three weeks since the body had been discovered by an early-morning jogger, and the pressure was mounting. A group of Seaside Harbor realtors paid regular visits to the mayor, always with the same message: find the murderer, and find him fast, or this could be a calamity. Fire Island was a series of open communities, with few locks on the doors and a comfortable air of homogeneity that induced people to trust each other on weekends in a way that would be unthinkable during the week in the city. Let a murderer loose in this kind of atmosphere and you have the makings of a true disaster—with the rental market an early casualty.

There was an even more pressing reason to wrap up the case soon. In five weeks the Fire Island season would be over and the Seaside Harbor community would disperse to Manhattan, bathing suits and T-shirts replaced by suits and sweaters and the warm, reassuring anonymity of urban life. True, the likelihood of a second attack would diminish after Labor Day, but so would the likelihood of apprehending Linda Levinson's killer.

Saturday, the day the body had been found, half a dozen Waterside cops descended on Seaside Harbor. They went from house to house, searching for information. They learned two things. First, nobody, but nobody, had a motive for killing Linda Levinson, not according to her fellow Seaside Harborers. Linda was a "nice" girl, like all the rest of them; only a maniac would kill a person like Linda Levinson, a sexual maniac, probably. The fact that she had not been sexually abused, a fact that was already common knowledge in Seaside Harbor, did not put a dent in this theory, which was widely accepted. Second, the killer was not, was definitely *not*, a Seaside Harbor resident. Seaside Harbor people didn't kill each other, it was that simple. Now, on Long Island or back in the city such things happened all the time, but not on Fire Island. Thus, it was

33

widely believed that some maniac (see theory one) had taken the ferry over from Waterside, picked off the first unescorted female to have the misfortune to cross his path, and simply hopped back on the ferry once his dirty business was over with. The well-known fact that the nefarious deed had taken place after the last ferry had departed in no way weakened the appeal of this theory, which the police encountered frequently that Saturday.

By Sunday night, when the vast majority of residents had left Fire Island, the police didn't have a clue. Literally. Chief of Police Louis Castiglia watched one ferry after another fill up and depart, and thought: the killer is on one of those boats, and he's just slipping away from us like water through our fingers. Castiglia was a short, stocky man so incredibly gruff and irritable that many people assumed he had a heart of gold—nobody could be that gruff and irritable inside and out. But they were wrong. He was.

That week Chief Castiglia himself visited Linda's parents in Brooklyn and called her boss, Jonathan Golland. And learned nothing. Maybe they were right in Seaside Harbor, maybe no one did have a motive for killing her. And yet it just didn't look like a random killing.

"I'm telling you this Linda Levinson was straight as an arrow," he'd shouted at Joe D. last Tuesday afternoon. "No drugs, no boyfriends. Only thing she did wrong was get herself killed."

They were in Castiglia's office in the Waterside police headquarters building. It was a large square room with large rectangular windows on two sides. At least Joe D. had always assumed there were windows: Castiglia kept the venetian blinds down and closed tight—not a ray of sunlight was allowed to enter. A ceramic lamp, more appropriate for a living room than an office, its shade badly yellowed, was the sole source of illumination. It sat on a distant corner of Castiglia's massive metal desk, on which no more than two sheets of paper were ever, ever allowed to rest simultaneously. Castiglia was a fanatic about keeping his desk free from clutter, and whenever a third letter or memo or file threatened to sully his clean slate, he'd summon his secretary, a frail, nervous, sparrow of a woman, with a booming "Gladys!" and demand that the offending paper be removed at once. It was a joke among Waterside cops that Castiglia had modeled his office after one in a James Cagney movie—it looked tailor-made for late-night, smoke-filled interrogations of bootleggers and gangsters and hit men. But the truth of the matter was that the movies were as close as Castiglia ever came to a gangster, though in all fairness to the man he certainly didn't need this setup to intimidate—his bulk and his notoriously short fuse and, above all, his reputation for never, not once, cracking a smile, ensured that no visitor to his office would ever feel entirely at ease. Just outside his office, which was accessible through a heavy wooden door directly across from his desk, was a large, noisy room where most of the activity of the station took place: a center, if not a hive, of activity. But inside Castiglia's office it was always quiet and dark, always slightly cooler than elsewhere in the building, a cave of a room in which visitors were inclined to speak in hushed tones, if they were inclined to speak at all.

"It was probably just a psycho, Chief," ventured Joe D. softly.

"Psycho my ass. It was a killer."

"Yeah, but a psycho doesn't need a motive. It could have been anyone, but it just happened to be Linda Levinson."

Castiglia shook his head. "All I know is I got the mayor on my back telling me to find this killer fast. After Labor Day we won't have a prayer. The killer's there, in Seaside Harbor, I know he is, but he'll be gone in September, back to the city and out of our reach. And if he hits again . . . Shit, those girls over there run around in their bikinis all **35**

day, get laid by a different stud every weekend, none of
'em bother locking their doors at night. What do they expect?"

"Chief?"

"What I'm saying is sooner or later something was bound
to happen over there."

Joe D. readied himself for the *there's no morality left in
society* lecture that Castiglia was wont to deliver at the least
provocation. The fact that the Chief was putting it to a
waitress from the Waterside Diner every Tuesday and
Thursday night in no way lessened his indignation. Or perhaps it added to it, Joe D. considered, enduring the lecture
until the Chief got to the point.

"Our guys are getting nowhere. The kids clam up the
minute they see a cop. Even if one of them knew something they wouldn't tell us, because if they were wrong
they'd be ruined over there. Shit, they're living eight, ten,
twenty to a house, it's like a fucking orgy twenty-four hours
a day, breakfast, lunch, dinner—"

"Chief—"

"All right, all right. So let's say a guy thinks one of the
people in his house might be the killer, a weirdo, say. So he
tells the police, we talk to the guy, find out he's not the
murderer. So what happens to the guy who informed on his
roommate? He's finished, kaput. Unless of course the guy
really is the killer, a kook. But it's too big a risk, talking to
the police in a place like Seaside Harbor. When push
comes to shove, they stick together. I'm figuring it this way.
If the killer is a nut case, no motive or anything, just gets
his rocks off killing some babe, then we got trouble, 'cause
if he had fun once, he'll want a second shot. And if he kills
again my butt's in a sling."

The Chief paused. "Shit," he said angrily, most likely,
Joe D. thought, thinking of his waitress and how he probably would not be able to see her that night, the murder

having cut into his plentiful free time. Thinking also that this case had aimed the spotlight of local and even New York City attention squarely on Castiglia's inflated self, and the Chief did not, definitely did not like attention, not when it shed light on his twice-a-week afternoon golf games and two-hour lunches of equal parts bourbon and linguine, followed by siestas at home from which he rarely awoke early enough to return to the station. No, all this attention was not appreciated, not one bit, and the sooner the case was wrapped up, the sooner he could hunker back down to the routine he had grown so fond of, the routine he had perfected so lovingly over the years.

"If he's a not a nut case, then he had a motive. But Linda Levinson is as clean—was as clean as a whistle. So I'm thinking we have a creep on our hands. He stripped her practically naked, DiGregorio. And forensics thinks he did it *after* she was dead."

"Jesus, I didn't know that."

"We kept it out of the papers. Sounds like a lovely guy, don't he? That's why I'm putting three guys on duty over there from Friday to Sunday. One guy on weekdays."

Castiglia reached under his desk and astonished Joe D. by producing a copy of the *Village Voice*. "Ever see this before?" he said, as if issuing a challenge.

Joe D. had seen it before, plenty of times, but simply shrugged. Saying yes seemed risky, like admitting he was a member of the Communist Party or something.

"This, Lieutenant DiGregorio, is the *Village Voice*." He held it awkwardly, at arm's length, as if fearful of contamination. He thumbed quickly to the classifieds in the back and handed the newspaper to Joe D.

Circled in red were two notices for midseason shares in Seaside Harbor. "You, DiGregorio, are going under-cover."

"You're kidding, right?"

"I'm kidding? When was the last time I kidded about anything?"

Joe D. honestly couldn't recall an instance.

"These kids won't talk to cops. So they'll talk to you."

"Why me, Chief? I've never been on a murder before."

"You think any of us has?" The Chief wrinkled his face, regretting this bit of candor. "Recently, I mean. I'm sending you because you're young, you're good-looking, or at least you're not too bad-looking, and you'll fit in."

The assignment held no appeal for Joe D. Honest-to-God investigative work he might enjoy, but pretending to be someone he wasn't—it just wasn't something he wanted to do. "Any chance of giving it to someone else? DiRosa, maybe. He's only thirty-two, and he's had a lot more experience than me."

"DiRosa is a fat slob. They don't let you off the fucking ferry over there if you're fat, take my word for it. Don't you think I'd like to send someone with more experience? Three fucking weeks and we got a big fat zero to show for all our hard work. That island's crawling with cops and still not one fucking clue. They're tripping over each other and it's still not enough. Fear, DiGregorio. There's fear over there and it's like a plague that's getting worse every weekend. One of our guys, I'll spare you this particular individual's identity, he got a kick in the balls last weekend from some babe thought he was jumping her. Which maybe he was, the guy's scum from day one, DiGregorio, immoral, if you know what I mean, running around from morning till night, and his wife shut away with all those kids . . . what was my point?"

"Fear, Chief."

"Yeah, fear. My guys tell me they don't talk about nothing else but this murder over there in Seaside Harbor, even after three weeks. I wish they'd all stay away, stay back in the city where they come from. I can handle the real estate brokers, DiGregorio, but what I can't handle . . ." He paused for a moment. "What I can't handle is my own fear that there'll be another murder, DiGregorio. Why don't they all just stay away? Why don't they all stay in the city?"

"They've paid for their places, Chief. And it's hot in the city, and I guess they figure as long as they stay in groups they won't—"

"All right, all right, so they won't stay away. So that's why we're sending you over. You'll have plenty of backup—I'll have three guys on duty at all times—but we need someone on the inside, someone that'll fit in. So you get on the phone, DiGregorio, and call about those houses in Seaside Harbor. Say you're a lawyer or something, all the ads want professionals. Say your sister's Brooke Shields and she has a thing for her big brother's friends. Say whatever you fucking like but I want you on the island by Saturday."

"Chief—"

"And another thing, don't tell anyone where you're going. Nobody, not even that girlfriend of yours, what's her name?"

"Marie."

"Marie. Not even her. Just tell her you're on duty weekends for a while and to keep her legs crossed until you get weekends off again. We'll cover for you here at this end if she calls. Which I sincerely hope she doesn't."

As the ferry pulled into Seaside Harbor, still wrapped in morning mist, Joe D. reflected that lying wasn't really all that hard after all. His first lie had been on the phone with a guy named Mark Silver, who was advertising in the *Voice* for a share. (Apparently two women in the house had fled Fire Island after the murder and only one of the vacancies had been filled—by a man, Joe D. was told, since few **39** women not already committed to Seaside Harbor were willing to do so now.)

Joe D. told Mark he was an accountant in private practice on Long Island. He figured nobody would bother to ask for more details as long as he stuck to something like accounting.

"Well, you sound like a nice guy, Joe," Mark had said.

"Great, so I'm in?"

"Sure, but don't you have any questions, like what kind of people we are?"

"Uh, yeah, what kind of people are you?"

"We're all professionals in our twenties and thirties. A bunch of us know each other from the Vertical Club."

"The Vertical Club?"

"Yeah, you know, the health club on the East Side. It's where the girls go to work out after they've whipped themselves into shape at the New York Health and Racquet Club." He paused for effect. "Just to give you an idea of what you have to look forward to in *that* department."

The second lie was to Marie. "I thought you had weekends off for the rest of the summer," she protested plaintively.

"I thought so too, but you know Chief Castiglia, once he makes up his mind . . ."

No, he thought, getting off the ferry, lying wasn't so hard after all. Walking to his house, his summer share, he was struck by how familiar it all looked, even though he'd only been to Fire Island a few times. With its web of sidewalks and closely packed houses, Fire Island was hard to forget. The sun was still low in the sky but had already managed to warm the island. He could hear the ocean a short walk away; the crashing waves sounded ominous rather than inviting, as if issuing a warning.

Chapter

"**E**VERYBODY, meet Joe DiGregorio," announced
Mark Silver.

"Hi Joe," they answered in unison.

"Joe, this is Janet."

"Hi Janet."

"And this is Cindy."

"Hi Cindy."

"This is Stu."

"Hi Stu."

"Stacy."

"Hi Stacy."

"Marsha."

"Marsha."

"David."

"David."

"And Alan."

"Alan."

"Coffee, Joe?"

"Please."

He joined the group at the large round table in the house's common room. If his life depended on it, he couldn't recall a single name.

"I told Joe all of our rules," said Mark. "Guest fee is twenty-five bucks, no guests on holiday weekends. We add up household expenses Sunday afternoon, split them evenly, no questions. Maybe you should handle that chore, Joe, being an accountant."

"Yeah, sure," said Joe D., who still had trouble with the multiplication tables.

"Anything else he should know?" asked Mark.

"My only question," said one of the women (Joe D. guessed it was either Stacy or Cindy), "is does he have any diseases we should know about? You know, what with his coming in midseason, we didn't have time to do the usual tests."

Everyone smiled mirthlessly at this. A half-hour later Joe D. began to relax. It felt good being accepted so readily, like he had passed a test of some kind. He even had to remind himself he was working, that he was a fake, not really one of these people.

The house was a small, rectangular structure raised off the sandy ground by cinder blocks. It had obviously endured too many summers filled with too many uncaring tenants and their even less considerate guests. The ground floor consisted of two large rooms: a kitchen dominated by a large picnic table, and a living room with furniture right out of an "I Love Lucy" rerun, complete with a turquoise vinyl couch with matching chairs and a wooden coffee table shaped like an artist's palette. This lap of luxury, Joe D. had calculated, based on his own portion of the rent, was costing the group seventeen thousand dollars for the summer.

42   "We do have a new rule, Joe," said one of the women, speaking slowly and seriously. "Since the murder, you guys have to escort us to and from town after dark. Once we're there we're on our own, but there's no way we're walking alone after dark. All the other houses here have the same rule."

"Was the murdered girl someone you knew?" Joe D. asked as offhandedly as he could. A chorus of male groans greeted the question. "That's not something we want to talk about a lot," said Mark.

"That's not something you *guys* want to talk about."

"Like AIDS," said someone else.

"Yeah, like AIDS."

"It doesn't do any good, all this speculation," said Mark.

"You mean you can't get laid this summer. For all we know, *you're* the Fire Island killer."

"And you're my next victim, Marsha."

"*Was* it someone you knew?" Joe D. asked Marsha, happy just to be able to attach a name to a face.

"Stacy knew her."

"I knew her," said Stacy, a petite redhead wearing, Joe D. felt, just a bit too much makeup for ten in the morning. "We went to college together. Albany."

"Were you close?"

"No. I really don't think anyone was too tight with Linda. Except maybe Eric Farber." She giggled for a second, then caught herself and resumed in a more serious tone. "I shared with him last summer. He took her out, Linda I mean, a few times last summer and a few times this summer, I think. Slept with her once a couple of weeks ago . . ."

"Stacy, really," interjected someone, either Janet or Cindy—Joe D. was totally confused now.

"Well, she's dead now. I mean, what harm can it do?"

"How do you know?" asked JanetorCindy.

"Know she's dead?" asked Stacy.

"No, asshole, know that she slept with Eric."   **43**

"I know because I was visiting Eric's house a few weeks ago. We all teased him about it, which is why I laughed. We all figured it was the first time Eric ever got laid. He keeps pretty much to himself, like he can't be bothered with women."

"Was it serious?" asked Joe D. casually.

"Are you kidding? Serious for Linda is—was—spending the whole night with a guy. With Eric she left after . . . you know, *after*. We had come back from Crane's, it was about one in the morning, and she was just leaving his room. She was real embarrassed, hardly said a word to anybody, just rushed out of the house. Funny thing, I wouldn't have given it a second thought it it weren't for her being killed."

"Was Eric shook up about the murder?" Easy, Joe D., he warned himself.

"Are you kidding? Only three things turn Eric on. Money, money, and money. I saw him that day she was found, Saturday, at Crane's at happy hour. I said to him, 'So Eric, can you believe it, about Linda?' And he says to me, like he never met her, 'Sure, I believe it.' Just like that, and then he asks me to dance. Not what you'd call a compassionate guy. But a hell of a dancer."

"And rich," volunteered someone female.

"And gorgeous," volunteered someone else, also female.

Why haven't they thought of name tags? wondered Joe D.

"Debbie told me he pulls in high six figures."

"I heard seven."

"With or without bonus?"

"Is his house near here?" Joe D. asked.

"Yeah, two houses down on Cranberry. The white house with blue shutters. Why, you want to meet him or something?"

Joe D. was preparing an answer when he was rescued by Mark. "What the hell are we talking about Eric Farber for? He's a creep."

There was general agreement from the men in the room, and that was that.

As the morning wore on, people migrated to the beach, alone or in pairs. Joe D. realized as he and Mark arrived at the beach that his housemates reassembled in a group once they got there. He was easily the palest person around, though he was naturally dark-skinned. He carefully covered himself with sunscreen: what would Marie say if he showed up Monday with a tan when he was supposed to be working all weekend?

The beach was wide and stretched as far as the eye could see to the east and west. This section was also crowded, though fifty yards or so in either direction the beach was nearly deserted. This puzzled him.

"Why does everyone stay so close together when there's so much room down the beach?"

"Be my guest," offered either Alan or Stu. "Less competition." And then Joe D. understood. Bunching together like this made socializing much easier, and socializing, apparently, was what going to the beach was all about. He'd already lost track of where his group's turf left off and the next group's began, so crowded was this small patch of beach. There *was* a lot of mingling, and no one was swimming, in spite of the blazing sun.

"Doesn't anyone swim in this place?" he asked, revealing his naiveté a second time.

"The girls don't," replied AlanorStu. "If they did, their makeup would wash off."

Joe D. pondered this a bit, then leaned back on his towel and closed his eyes. Fragments of conversations drifted his way like cirrus clouds across an otherwise blue sky.

"Pass me the number four," said a female voice.
"I thought you were on oil."
"Only for my body. For my face I'm on four."

*   *   *

A male voice: "I met her at the Shark Bar Thursday night. She was with a friend. Nice girl, I really liked her."

"D'you shtup her?"

"Jesus, Harry, cool it, will ya?"

"I think you're ready for number two on your face."

"You think so? On my nose too?"

A new voice, female: "My mother begged me not to come back here this weekend. She's afraid I'll be next."

"Did you know her?"

"Not well. You?"

"Not well. My brother was once fixed up with her."

"Anyway, she's in Westhampton this summer. But it's a half-share, so I think I'll invite her out one off-weekend."

"And shtup her then."

"Harry, you're an asshole."

"How long have I been on my back?"

"Twenty minutes."

"Twenty minutes! I told you I only wanted fifteen minutes on my back."

"Cute suit."

"From Loehmann's. Guess what I paid."

"I give up."

"Thirty."

"No! I hate you."

"You watch the Yankees last night?"

"Yeah, must be the masochist in me."

"You believe Mattingly in the eighth?"

"Yeah, I'll bet he's crying all the way to the bank."

*   *   *

"Two girls in my house didn't show up this weekend.
Third weekend in a row."

"The murder?"

"Of course the murder. I guess I should have been
happy, since I got my own room for a change, but I got
creeped out, all alone when maybe the murderer is still
here, maybe he's in my house, who knows? So I tiptoe into
Sharon's room, she had it to herself too on account of the
no-shows, and who should poke his head up from her bed
but Barry What's-his-name. You know, from your house?
With the moustache? Or maybe it was Stanley. Which one
is with Goldman Sachs?"

"How long on my front?"

"One minute longer than the last time you asked."

"What I hear is she never had any boyfriends."

"That's what I hear too."

"So who could have done it?"

"I know? My mother said it must be some *schwarze*."

"That's a laugh, a black in Seaside Harbor."

"He bought it last summer for sixty thousand. It's on the
market now for two hundred."

"Insiders' price, right?"

"He's in his father's fur business."

"Nice."

"Man, this murder talk is getting on my nerves."

"Tell me about it. You touch a girl, she thinks you're
about to strangle her."

"It's always something in this town, the hot topic of the
summer. Last year it was AIDS. Now it's Linda Levinson." **47**

"If only I could stand to look at him."
"You can get used to anything."

"Trade you my chair for your towel."

"What're you reading?"
"Cultural Literacy."
"Any good?"
"It's all right. I think I've read the first page six times today."

"I mean, I thought about not coming out here anymore, but I figure I already plunked down twelve hundred dollars for a half share and I'll be damned if I'm going to let some creep spoil my summer."
"Let's face it, what were we going to do in the city this weekend? The place is a fucking ghost town."
"Like I told my mother, look, it's no picnic in Manhattan. Last month the penthouse in our building was picked clean by these guys who swung from the roof and kicked in a window. Seriously. Like fucking gorillas."

"I told him, I can deliver two hundred dozen in assorted sizes but only as a favor. I'll make *bupkis* on the deal."

"You see her roommate this weekend? Wouldn't surprise me if she never came back to Seaside Harbor."

"Do you see what I see?"
"I think I'm in love. Those tits . . ."

"Jesus, this sun is strong. I'm switching to number six for my face. Anyone got any number six?"

*   *   *

A few hundred yards away on the same beach, Alison sunbathed by herself. She was glad she had come back to Seaside Harbor this weekend. At first she had sworn never to return: the very thought made her shudder. But a week passed, and then another, and finally a particularly hot Friday rolled around and she realized she had no plans for the weekend. Her friends would all be on Fire Island or in the Hamptons, and, besides, what was the point of sitting around in the hot city all weekend with nothing to do but think about Linda? Sooner or later she'd have to go back. Might as well be sooner.

Thinking about Linda, her head would start to spin. Other times she felt it in her stomach, the injustice of Linda's death, the tragedy. Linda, murdered: she still couldn't quite wrap her mind around the idea. For two weeks she'd gone to work at the usual time, but by noon she'd have to leave, making half-baked excuses to her boss, exhausted by the effort of fighting off grief, of coming to terms with Linda's . . . Linda's disappearance.

For that's how Alison thought of it. Linda had disappeared—poof!—from the face of the earth, from her life. Murder? She'd deal with that aspect of it later, after she'd accustomed herself to the absence of her friend. And what made it even harder to understand was Linda's remoteness, that quality she'd had of being only half present even when the two of them, Alison and Linda, were alone together. Now she was entirely gone, and there were moments when Alison wondered if she'd ever been there in the first place.

She thought about Linda's parents, whom she'd seen a few weeks ago in Queens at the funeral. About having to pack all of Linda's beach things and hand them over to the police. About having to answer a thousand questions from Officer Harrison, and later from other cops, all with Italian last names she couldn't remember. About being known for **49** the rest of the summer as the murdered girl's roommate. Already, on the ferry the night before, she had seen a few people whispering as she walked by, noticed a few averted glances as well.

Panic had coursed through Seaside Harbor like a current, and the people who had returned these past weekends (all of the men, apparently, and about half of the women) seemed charged with something other than the usual, frenetic Fire Island energy: a sense of anticipation crackled everywhere, adding creases to faces already etched and browned by the sun. Alison recognized it in frightened glances cast over bare shoulders on the sidewalks that cut through the thick, brittle underbrush, the uncharacteristic standoffishness of people, particularly women, in Crane's. And, most of all, a certain nervous hysteria, almost sexual in its hot intensity, its raw, physical menace. It infected every conversation, regardless of the topic. These Fire Island summers, for all their seeming hilarity, could be tediously predictable, particularly for those, like Alison, who returned weekend after weekend, year after year, less drawn to the beach itself than afraid of long, lonely weekends in the hot and deserted city. For many people, the murder had imposed a curious but welcome structure on the summer, a purpose or meaning, the way a fatal disease can galvanize and unite a once apathetic, loose-knit family.

Coming back was hard for Alison—sleeping in their room, now hers alone for the first time, facing the crowd at Crane's. But she'd gotten through it all and now, three weekends later, the sun was having the restorative effect it always had. For a few minutes at a stretch she would almost forget all about Linda, and then she'd remember, and sit up, and look around the beach and think:

One of you killed Linda.

Over breakfast they all carefully avoided mentioning the murder, though Alison noted this morning that the sisters, who usually had coffee in their room, joined the group in the kitchen, the better to catch any information on the summer's biggest story.

Larry was the first to broach the subject. "We're really sorry about Linda," he said awkwardly to Alison. His eyes, the color of a strawberry milk shake, betrayed a night of coke-fueled sleeplessness.

"Yeah," said Jason, "we really don't know what to say. It's kind of weird because we've been sharing this house with her but we really didn't know her."

"So it's like someone we were close to died," Larry continued, "but also like a stranger died, which makes it—"

"I understand," Alison interrupted, and she really did understand. This sort of communal living gave the impression of intimacy, yet it was only proximity they shared.

Tracy, the younger sister, spoke for the first time that morning. "You don't think it was anything to do with the house or with us, do you? I mean, do you think we might be next, just because we shared a house with her? Like we know something we may not even know we know?"

"Don't be stupid," Alison had said in an angry voice. "Linda was killed by a psychopath, so none of us is safe, none of us. It had nothing to do with Linda, she was just . . . unlucky."

"She was only asking," said Ronnie in defense of her sister. "No need to attack her."

"I was *not* attacking her. And I'm sure Tracy can speak for herself." With that Alison ran to her room, changed, and walked alone to the beach.

She *had* been unfair to Tracy. But since Linda's . . . *disappearance* she'd had a hard time dealing politely with anyone who wasn't as affected by the loss as she was. It was strange, she thought, heading down the stairs to the beach: only Linda's parents seemed truly grief-stricken. Other friends of Linda's had attended the funeral, but they had

51

been surprisingly dry-eyed, given the tragedy that had brought them all there. Had Linda been as distant with them as she'd been with Alison? Even so, Alison felt the loss intensely . . . Surely there was someone else, somewhere, who also mourned Linda deeply. Then she thought of Linda's married lover—unnamed, unseen, undiscovered. The Nowhere Man. For the thousandth time she wondered if she'd been right not to tell the police about him. At first, during the initial questioning, that awful Saturday when she'd first heard the news, Linda's lover hadn't even crossed her mind. Linda had so rarely mentioned him, and she'd made it clear that he had nothing to do with Fire Island, that she spent her weekends in Seaside Harbor precisely because the place had no associations with him. It was a random thing, the killing—this had been Alison's first reaction, and revealing that Linda had been seeing a married man seemed like a final betrayal . . . and totally unnecessary.

Still, she'd been tempted to call the police, had come close a few times. And then she'd think of Linda's parents, what news of a married lover would do to them. She'd think too of the newspaper articles saying that Linda's murder was the work of a psychopath, not someone the victim knew, and she wouldn't call the police, was relieved, in fact, not to have to talk to them again.

The sand felt warm and yielding underfoot when she removed her sandals. Instead of the usual spot, she turned left and walked until she found an area she knew wouldn't get too crowded later in the day.

Joe D. was feeling restless. The afternoon sun was oppressively hot, there was no breeze, and the beach was so crowded around him, so noisy, that he could barely hear the surf just yards away. Raising the subject of the murder was out of the question; last night's Yankee game was about as serious a topic as this crowd could bear.

"Listen, Joe," Mark had said earlier in the day. "Try not to bring up the murder again. We have enough trouble with the girls buzzing on about it all the time. You'll scare them away."

Joe D. regretted his haste. Be patient, he told himself. Get into the rhythm of the place.

"Think I'll take a walk down the beach," he said aloud, but nobody seemed to hear him.

Restlessness was half of his motive for taking a walk. The other half was to look for Alison Rosen, Linda's roommate. He'd talked with Harrison last night on the phone and gotten a description: tall, light brown hair, good figure. So far he'd spotted only a dozen or so women who *didn't* fit that description. Fortunately Harrison had also described the bathing suit she had been wearing when he'd come down to the beach to learn the identity of the body: a one-piece suit with blue and white diagonal stripes. "Real sexy," Harrison had added. Joe D. couldn't tell if he was referring to the suit or to Alison Rosen.

He wasn't even sure that Alison was on Fire Island, let alone on the beach. He'd called her apartment in the city first thing this morning and there'd been no answer—a good sign, but she could be visiting friends for the weekend, or her parents. And of course there was no guarantee she'd be wearing the same bathing suit.

He walked the length of the crowded area and still hadn't spotted a blue and white diagonally striped bathing suit. With little hope of finding her he kept walking along the edge of the water. The beach suddenly became much less crowded, and the effect on Joe D. was like walking from direct sunlight into shade, so soothing was this relatively empty stretch of sand compared to the bedlam in which he'd spent the morning. The surf splashed around his ankles, sharply cold; he dug his feet into the water-cooled sand as he walked, and felt himself relaxing after a tense morning.

And then he saw her. Or, rather, saw the blue and white diagonally striped bathing suit. He felt as if he'd stumbled onto an old friend and had to resist the impulse to shout her name and run over to her. In fact, running into an old friend would have been a relief, for Joe D. was feeling out of his element, a new sensation for him.

He approached her before realizing that he needed a line, something to start up a conversation. "Uh, hi," he said, his conversational skills deserting him at the last moment.

Standing at the edge of the water, she smiled thinly.

"Are you going in or just standing here to cool off?" he asked.

"Just standing."

"My name's Joe DiGregorio. People call me Joe D. Or just Joe."

Another thin smile.

"And your name is—"

"Look, I'm not in the mood for company, okay? That's why I'm here and not there." She pointed to the section of the beach he'd just come from, as if ordering him back there.

"Yeah, it can be a drag over there. Not relaxing at all. And competitive, everyone trying to say just the right thing. I like it better here too."

"Then you understand why I'm not in the mood for conversation."

Joe D. was at a loss. There just didn't seem to be a way to start a conversation with her. "Sorry if I disturbed you," he said, and continued down the beach.

"It's Alison," she called after him.

"What was that?" he shouted, turning around.

"Alison. My name is Alison Rosen."

"Pleased to meet you, Alison Rosen," he said, walking back toward her.

"I'm sorry I was so rude. I'm not in the best shape right now. It's not you."

"No problem. Anything I can do to help?"

She shook her head.

"Your first summer here?" he asked for lack of anything better.

"Seventh."

"Seventh! A real veteran."

"Look, Joe. I'm just not in the mood to talk right now. It's not your fault. Really."

"Okay, I'll be on my way. But maybe we could get together later?"

She cocked her head, as if she didn't understand.

"What I mean is, are you doing anything later?"

"Going to Crane's for happy hour, of course. Aren't you?"

"Of course."

"Well, then . . ."

"Can I pick you up at, say, six?"

Alison laughed and Joe D. noticed for the first time how really pretty she was. "What's so funny?" he asked.

"This must be your first time in Seaside Harbor."

"How did you guess?"

"Because everyone just *goes* to Crane's for happy hour on Saturday. I mean, you don't usually *take* someone there, like on a date. You just sort of meet there. It's kind of hard to explain."

"Yeah, I'll say."

"Anyway, it's not important."

She turned and headed back to her blanket. He resumed his walk. "Happy hour begins around five!" she called out after him. He smiled and waved and felt like a million bucks.

"So what do you have?" asked Chief Castiglia. Joe D. was at a pay phone on Main Street. Nearby, a small pizza restaurant with a few outdoor tables was doing a brisk late-afternoon business.

"Chief, I've only been here less than a day. Give me time."

"I'll give you shit, DiGregorio. We don't have time. There may be a maniac on the loose over there."

"Well, I met her roommate."

"Yeah?" he said hopefully. "The Rubin girl? What does she have to say?"

"Chief, I can't just interrogate her. I'm supposed to be undercover, remember? Anyway, it's Rosen, Alison Rosen, and I have a date with her tonight . . . sort of."

"*A date*. I didn't send you over there to make dates! And all expenses paid, I might add."

You might think he'd sent me to Vegas, Joe D. thought, and not a lousy ten miles away to the beach.

"I'll try to find out something tonight. Anyway, they all seem to buy my cover story. At least that's something, right, Chief?"

"Your cover story? Some big shot I've got working for me over there."

"Listen, Chief, I really have to go get changed for happy hour. I'll call tomorrow."

"Happy hour!"

"Oh, and listen, see what you can find out about a guy named Eric Farber. Not a suspect, just a name at the moment."

Chapter

IT took Joe D. half an hour to find Alison in Crane's that evening at happy hour. He'd see her, through layers and layers of people, a drink lifted to her mouth, a smile half-formed on her lips, and then she'd be gone, like a deer spotted for an instant in a thick forest.

"Alison!" he greeted her enthusiastically.

"Joe," she replied with somewhat less enthusiasm. He reminded himself that her friend had been strangled recently. It explained her coolness, the way her whole face sagged when she uttered his name. Or at least he hoped it did.

"Can I buy you a drink?"

She lifted her glass to indicate she already had one.

"Oh well. Mind if I get one myself?"

"Be my guest."

Joe D. worked his way through the crowd and got a beer. When he returned Alison was gone.

He spotted her, ten minutes later, on the dance floor. For the second time since meeting her he realized how attractive she was. She was the type you didn't notice at first, he thought, and then it hit you—she's beautiful: even with seven weeks' worth of tan she still had a delicate look that contrasted pleasantly with the leathery brown faces to which most women in Crane's aspired with considerable success. Perhaps it was her nose, unexpectedly thin and lightly freckled, that lent her an appealingly vulnerable quality, or maybe it was her wide brown eyes, so pale they looked like they were hiding from something. She had what Joe D.'s father would call a *shape*; most of the other women here had dieted away their shapes.

A few songs later she left the dance floor without her partner.

"Alison, what happened?"

"What do you mean, *what happened?*"

"I mean I left to get a beer and you just disappeared."

Alison looked at him like he was crazy. "Look, whatever your name is—"

"You know my name. It's Joe D."

"Joe D. I don't know what you think is going on, but this isn't the high school prom." Her voice had a hard edge to it that struck Joe D. as forced—her mouth twisted slightly as she spoke, as if her lips were resisting the words that were being forced through them.

She started to walk away. Joe D. was inclined to let her go, but reminded himself he was on a case and getting to know Alison was part of the job. "How about dinner later?" he called after her, feeling like a jerk.

She turned and looked at him like he was not only a jerk but dangerous.

She just shook her head before disappearing into the crowd.

58

Alison bought herself a gin and tonic and wandered onto the terrace. Looking out at the marina, simmering in a deep orange glow from the setting sun, she regretted her rudeness. Maybe he was naive, she thought, and a little awkward, but he seemed nice enough, and he was handsome. God, was he handsome. He had the darkest eyes she had ever seen, set deep in his face; they seemed to pull her in, insisting on a closer inspection like warm, dimly lit rooms at the end of a long cold hallway. His hair, too, was dark, so black it almost looked blue in parts. It was thick and curly and just tousled enough to look attractive. He had a crooked, shy smile and dark, rugged skin. Alison figured he stood about six feet. He was almost irresistible.

So why, she asked herself, had she resisted him? God knows she was lonely enough. And frightened. Still, being with strangers, no matter how good-looking, only made her feel worse. What she wanted was to be with old friends, good friends. True, in Seaside Harbor she was surrounded by people she knew, but they were acquaintances, nothing more. Linda's death had put a wall between her and everyone else; it was a transparent wall: she could see other people, watch them trying to get through to her, but real contact was impossible; she felt she was in a different, isolated realm.

She followed the path of a sea gull as it glided around the marina in a wide, proprietary circle. Why am I always alone when I most want to be with somebody? she thought. And why am I always with somebody when I most want to be alone?

Joe D. fought his way up to the bar and bought another beer. As he plotted a strategy for establishing a rapport with Alison Rosen—kidnapping her was beginning to look like his best bet—he consoled himself with the thought that

59

at least he didn't have to worry about being a successful single person, what with his being practically engaged to Marie.

He wondered what Marie would make of Crane's. They went out Saturday nights a lot, to clubs on Long Island mostly, but this place was different. For one thing, the clubs he and Marie went to didn't really get going until after ten or eleven; here it was only half past six and the place was in full gear. At the places he was used to, people really dressed up, not formally or anything, but dressed so they looked like they were out for the evening. These people dressed like they were sitting around a pool somewhere, especially the women. He didn't know what to make of women in shorts and T-shirts who wore sandals with four-inch heels. It was like they were all in a contest in which the winners were the ones who spent the most money and looked like they spent the least—except, of course, that everyone knew to the penny what every article of clothing cost. Also, where he and Marie usually went there were some single people, but mostly it was couples. Here in Crane's it was just the opposite; there was no feeling of belonging or stability. Everyone just drifted from one conversation to the next, from one part of the bar to another: it was like being in the bumper cars attraction at an amusement park; you just banged up against other people, sometimes on purpose, other times accidentally, but the most important thing, the unavoidable thing, was to keep moving. Joe D. found himself caught up in this swirling, incessant motion; it was easier to go with it, to keep roving, than to resist it by standing still. The happy-hour crowd spilled out onto the nearby dock, lured by the warm, clear evening. He wandered outside, spotted Long Island across the bay, drifted in and out of a few conversations, wandered back in.

60   "Joe D.!"

Hearing his own name was a pleasant surprise. He turned: it was Alison. Fifteen minutes had elapsed since he had last seen her.

"I thought it over. Dinner, I mean. Does the offer still stand?" Gone was the harsh voice, the aggressiveness. She seemed softer, more relaxed. It suited her.

"If I had any pride, I'd say no."

"I know, and I'd deserve it."

"Maybe I don't have any."

"Any what?"

"Pride."

"God, I hope not. It's a very unattractive quality in a man."

He paused a few moments for effect. "What the hell. Sure."

"Let's go!"

"Now? But I just started on this beer."

"Now." She grabbed his arm, and he was barely able to put his glass down before she pulled him out of the bar. She seemed to have an urgent desire to get out of Crane's.

"Where to?" Joe D. asked outside Crane's.

"Seaview."

"A restaurant?"

"No, silly, it's a town. About two towns over from here. We'll take a taxi."

"Why not the subway while we're at it?"

She laughed. "A *water* taxi. A boat."

"I know, I know. I grew up a few miles from the ferry landing. But why Seaview? There are a couple of restaurants right here in Seaside Harbor."

"I just want to get out of Seaside Harbor for a change, that's all."

"You're the boss," he said.

"You catch on quick, Joe DiGregorio."

61

*   *   *

The taxi ride lasted ten bumpy minutes. The warm evening turned suddenly cool as the small boat sped into the wind. Talking over the din of the engine and the thump-thump of the boat hitting the choppy water would have been futile. Alison snuggled up to Joe D. for warmth, and he put his arm around her, a little surprised by her gesture of intimacy and his own response. Or at what seemed like a gesture of intimacy to him.

The restaurant in Seaview was a small, rustic place with a folksinger.

"A carafe of house white," Alison told the waiter once they were seated. She polished off a glass as soon as it arrived.

"Why the rush to get out of Seaside Harbor?"

"Claustrophobia."

"Claustrophobia? I don't get it."

"Seaside Harbor can seem like a really small town sometimes. Suddenly I feel like I know everybody, everybody knows me. It just felt claustrophobic tonight, that's all, and I had to break out."

"Why tonight?"

"Listen, no questions, okay? It's not that important."

Not that important, she thought, unless her hunch was correct, unless someone *was* watching her. The whole town was watching her, of course, the murdered girl's roommate, a kind of widow, in a way. But this was different. This was specific: two eyes staring hotly at her, isolating her amid the crowd at Crane's. She'd turn, and it seemed as if every head in Crane's swiveled away from her, every gaze averted from the dead girl's best friend. It was probably her imagination, her paranoia, this specific pair of eyes that she could feel on her back like the burning sun. Unless her hunch was correct, unless there *was* someone watching her, not just another rubbernecker looking to catch a glimpse of the wreck of Linda Levinson's life, but someone else, something else. Watching her.

They ordered lobsters. And then a second carafe of wine. "You from Manhattan?" he asked her at one point.
She nodded. "Seventy-third and First. You?"
"Waterside."
"Waterside!"
"Yeah," he said, feeling defensive.
"Sorry. It's just that everyone in Seaside Harbor is from the city, and I guess I think of Waterside as the place where you catch the ferry to Fire Island. Period."
"Well, it's also a place to live. I was born there. Were you born in Manhattan?"
"No. I was born in Brooklyn, but we made the big move to Westchester when I was seven. Scarsdale High. Then Boston University. Very typical. Very uninteresting."
"I think you're fascinating," he said, feeling the effects of the wine. What am I doing? he thought. What am I saying?
"Yeah, real fascinating. I'm a type, don't you see." Alison was feeling the wine too, judging by her voice, which had developed an uneven lilt. "Jewish girl from the suburbs gets okay grades in school, goes to B.U. with a thousand other suburban girls with okay grades, somehow manages to get through four years of college without meeting a Jewish doctor, or at least without marrying one—I met plenty. So I get an apartment in New York with a roommate at first, subsidized by my father, of course, start on a career, date as often as I can. A few years and a few promotions later I get an apartment of my own and things seem just great until I wake up one morning and I'm thirty and my career is just fine, only I'm alone most of the time and I'm **63**

not happy about that." She paused to catch her breath. "In fact, I'm real depressed about that."

Alison emptied her wineglass and gestured to Joe D. for a refill.

"So I tell myself it's time to get serious, time, well, time to think about having children."

Another deep sip from her glass. "You can leave now," she said. "I'll understand."

"Leave?"

"Come on, Joe. Don't you hear what I'm saying? Loneliness? Children? I mean, I'm not proposing marriage, no need to worry about that, but most men would be back on the ferry by now."

"Maybe that's what you want, for me to run away."

"Not bad. My last shrink said when things get sexual I chase men away. Including, as it turns out, my last shrink. But tonight's different. I've had a really awful week, you see, and I'm just too worn out to filter my thoughts."

"Then don't. I won't run."

She studied him for a moment, her expression wary. "Suddenly there's a whole new pressure, this pressure to have a child before it's too late. One day I never gave it a thought, and the next day it's all I think about. What ever happened to a transition period? I thought these things happened gradually, over time. Is it possible to go from young and carefree to middle-aged and anxious overnight?"

"I wouldn't exactly call you middle-aged, but I agree with you on one thing: life takes you by surprise. We may think about the future a lot, but I don't think we're ever ready for it. I'm not exactly the morose type, but every birthday I feel a little cheated, like something's been taken away from me."

She smiled to show she understood, that she was glad he **64** was on the same track, and with the smile, her whole face took on a radiance that had been absent earlier in the evening. He found himself leaning toward her, his elbows resting on the small table.

"So I promise myself I'm going to look for the positive in the men I go out with instead of always finding the negative. Problem is, you see, just when I decided that Alison Rosen was coming down off her high horse and giving the men of New York a second chance, the men of New York decide Alison Rosen is past her prime and not worth a second glance. Hey, that rhymes. Second chance. Second glance."

Joe D. shook his head. "I'm sure lots of men would—"

Now Alison shook her head. "Okay, so I was exaggerating again. And I'm also a little drunk. But the fact is I'm thirty-two now, getting a little old for Seaside Harbor. A little old for you too, Joe DiGregorio, from the looks of you."

"Sorry to disappoint you. I'm exactly your age," he lied.

"Funny, you look about twenty-five," she said. "No offense intended."

"None taken," he replied.

On the water taxi heading back to Seaside Harbor, Alison again snuggled up to Joe D., but this time the gesture seemed entirely natural. Alison closed her eyes and he pulled her even closer.

At her house on Tupelo he turned to her. "That was really great."

Alison looked amused. "Aren't you coming in?"

"Well, sure, for a few minutes." Jesus, he thought, I shouldn't be doing this.

The front door opened directly into the living room, where Al and Fran sat watching television. They were both Wall Street lawyers with short, squarish haircuts and matching horn-rimmed glasses. Both wore beepers that summoned at least one of them back to Wall Street every weekend.

"Al and Fran, meet Joe. Joe, Al and Fran."

He barely had time to say hello. She took his hand and led him across the room and up a flight of stairs. Music seeped through a closed door as they passed—Springsteen, he thought. He detected another, equally rhythmic sound—hoarse, choppy gasps, male and female. "That's Ronnie," said Alison, nodding toward the deep breathing. "She's always got Springsteen on when she has a man in with her. Alone, it's Ronstadt or Stevie Nicks."

"Hey, Alison, I don't know . . ."

"What don't you know?" she asked as they entered the twin-bedded room. She pulled her cotton sweater over her head.

Was it the wine he'd had earlier or was it simply being in the room with her, alone, that interfered with his attempts to consider his official responsibility? Not to mention Marie. For a split second he realized whom one of the twin beds must once have belonged to, but this thought vanished instantly and all he could think of was Alison, standing there before him, suddenly—and infinitely—desirable.

"If you stand there fully dressed for much longer, I'm going to feel embarrassed," said Alison, who was now naked. He crossed the room and they kissed with a warmth and intensity he was totally unprepared for.

He started to undress while Alison watched intently, as if each movement were critically important. Finally, after a slow-motion minute they embraced a second time, then fell onto the bed holding each other.

Later, Jason and Larry returned from Crane's, drunk and frustrated, and heard the unmistakable sounds of lovemaking from Alison's room.

"Maybe it's my breath," whispered Larry.

"Yeah, sure," said Jason.

"No, I'm serious. Did I use the Lavoris earlier, before we left? Maybe if I'd used the Lavoris . . ."

Alison knew as soon as she opened her eyes, without even looking out the window, that the weather had turned sour. On nice days the sun found its way around the drawn curtains and sprayed prisms of light on the walls and ceiling, warming the room, luring her out of bed with the promise of another perfect Fire Island day. On cloudy mornings like this one the room was uniformly gray, damp, and chilly. There's nothing like salt air to recharge the senses, but without the sun filtering through, it has the opposite effect, sapping energy and dulling desire.

She rolled over to check the time, careful not to disturb Joe D., which wasn't easy in a twin bed: 7:30. The long, sunless day stretched before her like a challenge she wasn't up to.

Alison glanced at Linda's bed, as perfectly made up as a hotel bed waiting for the next guest. For a few hours last night, with Joe D.'s unwitting help, she had been able to put Linda—Linda's murder—out of her mind. That's why she'd broken her own rule and slept with him so soon after they'd met. He'd felt strong and protective; desire had driven out fear and sadness for a few delicious hours. And now, like symptoms of an illness which only last night was in temporary remission, both were back in force. She felt depression growing inside of her and wanted desperately to talk to someone familiar, an old friend, certainly not Joe D. He was sleeping soundly, a day's growth of beard on his face, the length of time she'd known him. She thought of calling someone, but everyone she knew would be sleeping at this hour, and the truth was, here in Seaside Harbor it would have been Linda she'd have talked to . . .

The terrible irony of this thought, the injustice of Linda's **67** death, overpowered Alison. She began to cry, trying to do so quietly so as not to wake Joe D., her resistance causing the tears to flow even more intensely. The last thing she wanted was for him to wake up: this seemed critical. After five minutes of crying she forced herself out of bed and dressed quickly and silently.

She walked over to the bed to rouse Joe D., but held back a moment to observe him. Even sleeping, his mouth opened ungracefully, his whole face fluttering when he inhaled; she found him beautiful. His black curly hair, his dark eyes that turned down slightly at the outer edges, his long, long eyelashes that brushed against his cheeks: these were his best features.

"Joe," she whispered, shaking him gently. His eyes opened, and for a second he didn't know where he was.

"I'm leaving," she said.

He grinned, not hearing her but realizing suddenly, with pleasure, where he was. He lifted his arms toward her, gesturing for her to join him in bed. She started to weaken but turned away.

"No, I'm going back to New York. It's a really shitty day and I can't stand to be here when it's not sunny."

"To hell with the sun. We'll stay in here all day. How about it?"

She shook her head.

"At least let me walk you to the ferry," he offered, his voice registering his disappointment.

"No time. If I leave now and hurry I'll make the eight o'clock ferry. See you . . ." Before he could say another word she was gone.

As she walked to the ferry under the low, gloomy sky, Alison ran through her mind the trip back to her apartment: ferry to Waterside, taxi to the train, train to Penn **68** Station, IRT to Times Square, shuttle to Grand Central,

IRT again to Seventy-seventh Street. It reminded her of a dream she often had in which she was trying to go somewhere (to school, to a departing ship, to her apartment) but was prevented from getting there by an endless series of mishaps. She'd wake up from these dreams tense and frustrated, the way she felt now.

Alison began to run, though she had plenty of time to make the ferry. It was back, that feeling of being watched. The sidewalks were far from empty—other people were heading for the ferry, and there were some joggers—but this was that same sense of being watched by a *specific* pair of eyes, following her every move with owl-like omniscience. Still running, she spotted the ferry already at the dock and thought perhaps she'd take a cab from Penn Station.

Joe D. fell back to sleep and awoke a few hours later. To his considerable embarrassment, the living room of Alison's house was full of people when he came down from her bedroom still buttoning his shirt. Johnny Carson making his entrance never felt more in the spotlight than Joe D. did at that moment.

"Uh, hi, folks," he said, shrugging.

Everyone smiled—Al and Fran, Tracy and Ronnie, Jason and Larry.

"Shame about the weather," Joe D. ventured, making his way to the front door.

They nodded.

"Well, see you," he said on reaching the front door, which, mortifyingly, was stuck.

"Give it a kick at the bottom," someone offered. He did, with a bit more force than was absolutely necessary, finally got it open, and left.

Chapter

7

JOE D. took some ribbing when he returned to his house that morning.

"Who's the lucky girl, Joe?"

"Not bad for the first weekend!"

"The Italian Stallion returns."

That sort of thing. He still couldn't remember their names, couldn't even recall seeing some of them before. Did they all actually live in the house, or were some of them just visiting?

He reminded himself he had a job to do. True, he'd have happily spent the day in bed with Alison, but she had other ideas, and just as well, because, after all, he was practically engaged (that's how he always thought of him and Marie, *practically engaged,* a state of limbo in which they'd drifted, by his choice, not hers, for three years), and he wanted to be able to report something to Chief Castiglia on Monday.

Eric Farber was the one lead he'd come up with so far.

Not a lead, really, just a name. One of the few names he was actually able to remember and the one name definitely linked to Linda Levinson. Something to go on, at any rate. Alison had told the police that Linda had had no boy-friends that summer.

One of his housemates—Stacy, he thought, or else Marsha—had told him otherwise.

By the time Joe D. set out for Farber's house, the white one with blue shutters on Cranberry, it was pouring. The rain had rinsed Seaside Harbor of its charm. It reminded Joe D. of an enormous men's locker room, damp and chilly and smelling of decay. He stopped to look at the ocean. It churned angrily. One big wave, he thought, and all of Fire Island, a glorified sandbar at best, would be completely submerged. The place had a temporary look to it anyway, as if it had been built only yesterday and could recede back into the Atlantic any moment.

Joe D. took off his high school ring just before arriving. He rapped on the screen door but there was no answer. He could hear the television, and voices, so he opened the door himself and entered the house.

The living room was full of people. An air of languor suffused the room; it was almost visible.

"Does Eric Farber live here?" he asked the group, his clothes thoroughly soaked.

All eyes momentarily shifted to observe the new arrival. No one moved.

"Yeah, you a friend of Eric's?" someone replied.

"No, not really. My name's Joe DiGregorio. I found a ring in Crane's last night and someone told me it was his."

"Oh, sure, come in. Some day, huh?"

This house was somewhat nicer than the one he was rent-ing. It was modern and glassy and surrounded on four sides by dense green brush that gave it the feel of an off-season

71

ski house. It was furnished with sturdy, modern pieces and bright, colorful fabrics. The rain, however, didn't do much for the decorating scheme, casting long shadows over the bare wood floors and clean white walls, and adding an earthy, mildewy smell. People were reading the *Times*, playing cards, watching television. Just like his own place. Nobody looked very happy, and some even looked angry, as if the rain were not an act of nature but a personal affront.

Someone shouted upstairs for Farber. A few minutes later he appeared, wearing blue jeans and nothing else, the better to display a muscular build, the kind of body forged in a gym. He had perfectly straight brown hair, thin, pale lips and cold, cold blue eyes. A gold chain glistened around his neck. There was nothing soft about Eric Farber, thought Joe D. His body looked steel-plated and his eyes promised more steel inside.

"I found a ring last night. Someone said it's yours." Joe D. handed it to him. "Yours?"

"Who told you it was mine?" The voice matched the body: aggressively tough, unyielding.

"Don't remember. Someone named David. Or Peter maybe."

Farber shook his head; these names meant nothing to him, he seemed to say. "I never went to Waterside High. Who'd think a thing like that?"

"Sorry to bother you," Joe D. said defensively and loud enough for everyone in the room to hear. It did the trick.

"Hey, Eric, lighten up."

"You could thank him, you know."

"It *is* raining out."

"Okay, thanks, but I still don't know why anyone would think it was my ring. You say a guy named David—"

"Look, I really don't remember," interrupted Joe D.

"How about a Bloody Mary?" someone offered. "We're drowning our sorrows in them today."

He accepted and then faced the dreaded introductions.
"Joe, this is Jackie."
"Hi Jackie."
"And Amy."
"Hi."
"And Lonni."
"Hi Lonni."
"That's Jim."
"Jim."
"Stacy."
"Hi Stacy." (Uh-oh, he thought, is this a new Stacy or the same one I met yesterday?)
"The guy glued to the tube is Bobby."
"Hi Bobby."
"And I'm Marty Lawrence."

They chatted for a while, asked him who he was sharing with, what he did for a living (Marty, it turned out, was an accountant, which worried Joe D.: what if he wanted to talk accounting? Mercifully, he didn't), if this was his first summer in Seaside Harbor, whether he was at Crane's last night.

Lucky for Joe D. someone else, Amy, he guessed, brought up the murder. "I overheard some guy at Crane's saying he heard the police think the murderer wasn't from Seaside Harbor. They figure some lunatic came over for the evening, couldn't get any action at Crane's, met Linda Levinson on her way home, and tried to rape her. When she struggled, he killed her."

"Of course it wasn't someone from Seaside Harbor," said one of the men.

They all agreed it couldn't be someone from Seaside Harbor, a thought they seemed to find comforting.

"Probably some sicko from over on the Island," said Bobby, which Joe D. found annoying: who did these people think they were? Why was it so impossible for them to imagine that the murderer was one of them? The general

73

assumption seemed to be that if you had a college degree and lived in Manhattan and worked for a law firm or an accounting firm and spent summers on Fire Island and wore the right little symbol on your polo shirt (neither a polo player this summer, as a matter of fact, nor an alligator), you were automatically above suspicion. You couldn't possibly do anything dishonest, let alone commit murder.

"Did any of you know her?" he asked.

"*Of* her," said someone. "She was a secretary with a law firm."

"An M and A firm. I forget the name."

There was a pause. "Eric knew her."

Everyone turned to Eric, who flinched at the sudden attention. "I knew her," he said, shrugging, "but not well."

"Yeah," said Bobby, "he knew her well in the biblical sense."

"Not funny, Bobby," said Eric angrily.

"Sorry, but the fact is you knew her as well as anybody did." He turned to Joe D. "She was a good-looking chick but cold, real cold. Nobody made time with her. Except Eric."

"Can we just drop the subject?" Farber blurted. "It gives me the creeps."

After a moment's pause the conversation turned to the Yankees, drifted to the weather, and wilted with the stock market. Joe D. asked for the bathroom and was directed upstairs.

There were two bedrooms on the second floor. He figured one of them had to be Farber's, as Farber had been upstairs when he arrived. The first room was occupied by two women, judging by the clothes on the bed and the cosmetics on the bureau top. In the second, much neater bedroom he saw a wallet lying on top of a dresser. He entered the room and casually, as if someone were watching, he **74** picked it up. It contained a driver's license for Eric K.

Farber, credit cards, about two hundred dollars, and some business cards which revealed that Eric K. Farber was an account executive with Fried & Sons, "members of all principal exchanges." He pocketed one.

There was a suit in Farber's closet, blue pinstripe with a Paul Stuart label, and a briefcase on the bed. He must have come directly from his office. His heart pounding (for this was something Joe D. had never done before—following up on burglaries long after the fact was more his speed), he opened the briefcase. Inside he found some papers and forms, none of which made much sense to him. Also an appointment book. He scanned the three or four weeks preceding Linda's murder. Farber was a busy guy from the look of his datebook. Every day was filled, and all entries were in the same telegraphic style, though the initials and the restaurants changed: "Lunch, KR, Le Cirque," "Drinks, PL, Melon's," "Dinner, PC, McMullen's," "Lunch, RV, Four Seasons." A series of notations caught his eye. He flipped back through June and recognized an obvious pattern: every Saturday in June and July, until four weekends ago, contained the same entry: "LL."

Joe D. replaced the datebook and returned to the living room after flushing the toilet for effect. He waited until Farber left the room and then turned to the woman sitting next to him. "Hey, I'm sorry I upset Eric by asking about what's-her-name, the girl who was killed . . ."

"Linda Levinson."

"Right. I guess he knew her well."

"Depends what you mean by well. I know they saw each other a week or two before she died. We all have full shares here, so it's hard to tell one weekend from the next. Anyway, we all saw her leave his room. I don't think a good time was had by all, if you know what I mean.'

"That was, uh, four weeks ago, wasn't it?" he asked, trying to nail down the date without sounding like a cop.

"Right. That Saturday night was the last time he saw her. To my knowledge."

"Did they have a date?"

"No. They must have met at Crane's because we all went together that night. And came back together, except for Eric, who left Crane's early. That's when we ran into her—Linda—coming out of his room."

Someone, either Jim or Bobby, announced that it was time for a little vitamin C and left the room, presumably to fetch some. "A pick-me-up" was how he described it.

A moment or two later, JimorBobby returned and plunked a small container and a hand-held mirror on the coffee table. He tapped a small amount of what Joe D. assumed was cocaine—vitamin C, now he got it—onto the mirror and began mincing it with a razor blade, forming it into thin white lines an inch or two in length.

Joe D. observed the process closely, having never before witnessed the cocaine ritual, let alone participated in it. One by one the housemates got down on their knees, leaned over the table, inserted a small, thin straw into one nostril, pinching the other shut with a finger, and sniffed a line of cocaine up through the straw like a vacuum cleaner, moving the straw along the table as the line evaporated up their noses. He became so absorbed in observing this process that, when the straw was offered him, he had no excuses handy. Trying the drug was out of the question; apart from the fact that he was a cop, the stuff scared him. Smoking pot he had no problem with; it was just like smoking cigarettes, only harsher. But cocaine . . . the whole process was alien to him, it looked sinister. He never even used nose spray, and getting down on the floor and shoving a straw up his nose in front of all these strangers . . . no way.

"I'll pass," he said as nonchalantly as possible.

They looked at him queerly for a second but quickly resumed the ritual, alternately getting on their knees before the coffee table as if taking turns at an altar. His refusal meant more of the precious stuff for them, so he was not surprised when encouragements to dip in were not forthcoming.

He left the house as soon as he could without appearing rude. He had to say this about cocaine, it had succeeded, despite the dreary weather, in lifting the spirits in that room. It wasn't anything he could put his finger on, it wasn't as if they had all started giggling or anything, symptoms more typical of pot or even liquor. The drug hadn't changed their behavior in any obvious way, it had simply brought to the room an aura of unreflective, abstracted pleasure. Joe D. felt it as strongly as if the temperature in the room had suddenly dropped. His head heavy with the Linda Levinson case, he envied them their cocaine high. But he was on a job . . .

So Linda had had a . . . a meeting with Eric Farber the Saturday before she had been killed. Considering how matter-of-fact Farber was about his relationship with Linda Levinson, he was awfully methodical about noting their dates in his appointment book. Assuming, of course, that "LL" *was* Linda Levinson.

In Joe D.'s clue-hungry mind, however, there was no doubt at all as to the meaning of those two letters.

Chapter

"W E assumed it was random, Lieutenant DiGregorio,"
said Linda Levinson's mother, a plump woman in her sixties with grief etched on her face. "We never considered it
was someone she knew."

"Linda was a good girl," added Linda's father, the first
words he'd spoken since Joe D. had arrived at their house
in the Flatbush section of Brooklyn. He was a short man,
younger-looking than his wife, with a full head of wavy
white hair. They both spoke in accents that were equal
parts Old World and New York.

The Levinsons lived on the first floor of a two-story, two-
family house. The interior looked like an illustration from a
1960 Sears catalog, except for the brand-new, oversized
color television that was the focal point of the living room.
It was a freestanding model, with its own oak cabinet. On
top of it was a framed photograph of Linda. It looked as if
it had been taken back in the late Sixties, when Linda was

in high school. Her long straight hair was teased on top, her face was cocked slightly, as if she were mildly, but not unpleasantly, confused about something. A gold heart hung from a chain around her neck.

"We're not sure it was someone your daughter knew, but we haven't found any evidence of sexual abuse, for example." (Actually, this wasn't, strictly speaking, true: her T-shirt had been torn off her, and her pants pulled down below her hips, but this was, according to the autopsy, as far as it had gone. Of more concern was the fact that she'd been stripped not during a struggle but *after* she'd been killed. This sordid detail, however, had been withheld from the Levinsons and from the press, for which Joe D. was, at this moment, very grateful.)

"Thank God," uttered Mrs. Levinson.

"Or robbery. Your daughter wasn't even carrying a pocketbook at the time." The Levinsons nodded; this was not news to them. "Which is why I'd like to ask you a few questions."

They exchanged glances, their sad and heavy but suspicious eyes reassuring each other that there could be no harm in answering a few questions. "We spoke already to your Chief Castiglia, but go ahead," said Mrs. Levinson softly.

"First, can you think of anyone who had a motive?" An obvious opener, Joe D. thought, but after all this was a first for him (talking to parents of teenagers caught driving without a license was as tough as his job got) and he was very uncomfortable. No doubt the Levinsons had already answered this question for the cops who'd visited the day their daughter's body was discovered, but Joe D. wanted to hear for himself, *learn* for himself.

Mrs. Levinson shook her head. "Her life was *too* quiet. Alison Rosen was the only friend she ever mentioned, and we only met her at the funeral." She began to cry softly, her body vibrating. Joe D. wanted to get up and leave.

He charged ahead. "Boyfriends?"

Again she shook her head. "She never talked about boys. Not that I didn't bring up the subject. Thirty-two she was and single. We were worried."

"Was she close to anyone in the family?"

"You don't think—"

"No, of course not, Mrs. Levinson, I'm just trying to get a complete picture of your daughter."

"She was our only child." She spoke these five words slowly and deliberately, pausing between each one as if understanding them now for the first time. "She had a few cousins, an aunt in Astoria, but mostly just us. We're from Hungary, Lieutenant. Most of our family . . . we don't have much family. Linda and my husband and me, we were very close. So you see, Lieutenant DiGregorio, why it had to be some crazy person. Who would want to harm her? Who?"

She was sobbing now, and Joe D. felt further questioning would be cruel. Truth was, he didn't know how much longer *he* could take it. Their grief permeated the room, depleting it of air. He felt he was choking and wanted desperately to leave. He decided to get to the real point of his visit.

"One last question. Have you removed your daughter's things from her apartment?"

"Couldn't bear to do it," replied Mrs. Levinson, wiping her tears with the back of her hand. "I know I'll have to do it soon. Certainly we can't afford to keep paying rent. Do you know what her rent is? Was? One thousand seven hundred and forty-five dollars. For two rooms! And we pay just three-fifty for all this. We had no idea she paid so much until her landlord called to ask us where was the rent. I told him he should be ashamed charging that kind of money, I can't imagine how Linda afforded it, and then calling us now, after . . ."

She must suddenly have realized the purpose of his question. "Oh my," she interrupted herself, "you want to go through her things." She looked at her husband, who nodded gently. "The police have already been there once, but if you think it's necessary . . ."

"I've just been assigned to the case. I'd like to take a look myself."

Mrs. Levinson looked distressed. "I just can't stand the thought of a stranger going through her things again."

She paused and glanced at her husband, who again nodded. "But if you have to . . . I'll get you a set of keys. Your Chief Castiglia returned them last week."

The moment she left the room Mr. Levinson came to life. He jumped to his feet so suddenly that Joe D. too stood up, ready to defend himself. Mr. Levinson, however, looked like he wouldn't—couldn't—hurt a fly. He quickly crossed the room until he was just a few inches from Joe D.

"There was a man," he said, almost whispering.

"Mr. Levinson?"

"A man. A boyfriend. My wife doesn't like to talk about these things, especially now. Sometimes she would call Linda in the evenings for this or that and a man would pick up the phone. The same man every time. She would hear Linda in the background, shouting at the man for answering the phone."

"When you say the same man, Mr. Levinson, do you mean the same man two days in a row?"

"I mean for a couple of years the same man. My wife, she recognized the voice."

"Did she ask Linda about him?"

"Sure she asked. But Linda just said he was nobody. That's what she said, he was nobody. I used to ask her too. 'So Linda, any boyfriends?' I'd ask, expecting her to say

'Yes, Daddy, there is somebody.' But she never did say yes." His voice was thick and unsteady; he was trying hard to stave off tears.

He took Joe D.'s arm and grasped it with unexpected strength. "Find him, Lieutenant. For me. Find her killer. For my wife it's too late. Nothing will help her get over this. For me, it will help. Not much, but it will help. Find him."

Out on the street, Joe D. inhaled deeply, the first real breath of air he'd had since entering the Levinsons' house.

There was a motel-like orderliness to Linda's apartment on Sixty-second and Second: every object in its place, and every place deliberately, cleverly designed for the object. All the decorating schemes recommended by popular magazines were employed here faithfully—mirrors to make the small bedroom seem larger, plants in big pots on the floor and hanging in baskets from the ceiling, art posters in chrome frames, vertical blinds, a sectional couch, glass coffee table, bentwood rocking chair, Oriental rug. It felt lifeless, Joe D. thought. And now it really was.

He was going through the closet next to the front door, which was full of Linda's coats, a few dresses, and dozens of shoe boxes neatly piled on a shelf, when he was struck for the first time by the reality of Linda Levinson. Until now she had been just an assignment. Even meeting her parents hadn't made her any more real for him—she was their daughter, now dead, and though he sympathized with them he couldn't, until now, bring himself to feel pity for Linda herself, the person, after all, who had lost the most. God knows this apartment didn't bring her to life for him—he'd been in Howard Johnsons with more personality. Going through her closets, however, brought her instantly, powerfully into focus. Feeling her clothes, the clothes she'd

selected from all the other clothes available, smelling the

distinctive personal odor that her closet gave off: he could almost see her, could almost sense the person who had once chosen these clothes, who had worn them, who had hung them neatly in this closet expecting to put them on again. Suddenly he felt sorry for Linda Levinson. Suddenly he felt like an intruder in her apartment. It was an uncomfortable, eerie feeling.

Something caught his eye: a mink coat, hanging all the way at the back of the closet. Nothing unusual about the coat itself, but Joe D. wondered how Linda, a legal secretary, could have afforded such an extravagance. And the apartment itself: $1,745 a month came to over $20,000 a year. Either legal secretaries are better paid than Joe D. imagined, or Linda Levinson had been living well beyond her means.

Next he searched her bedroom. On top of her dresser he found a large, wood-inlaid jewelry box. Inside were a pair of expensive-looking diamond earrings and a long strand of pearls. If these are real, thought Joe D., they're worth a fortune.

A moment later he heard something in the living room, the sound of a door closing. He drew his gun from his shoulder harness and went back into the living room, where the sound had come from. Finding the room empty, he realized it must have been the front door he heard closing: someone had been in the apartment with him, probably hiding in the bathroom, which was off the small hallway between the living room and bedroom.

Joe D. rushed out of the apartment in time to hear a second door close. He raced down the hall and opened the emergency-stairway door. Someone was running down the stairs at a furious pace, at least three flights ahead of him. Linda's apartment was on the seventh floor. Joe D. plunged down the stairs, taking the steps three at a time, but when he got to the ground floor the lobby was empty.

Panting heavily, he asked the doorman if he'd seen someone leave. He shook his head. "Could've used the service entrance. It's not locked from the inside." He pointed to the rear of the lobby.

Joe D. ran to the service door and poked his head out to the alleyway: it was deserted.

He returned to the doorman. Had anyone entered the building today asking for Linda Levinson? "The murdered girl? No way. Course, tenants have keys to the service door, so if someone had keys to her apartment he could have come in that way."

Joe D. resumed his search of Linda's apartment but, as expected, found nothing of interest: whoever had been hiding in the bathroom had probably taken any evidence worth worrying about.

Obviously, the first team of cops had overlooked something. But what? And why had the intruder waited until now to remove it?

Joe D. sat down on the end of Linda's brown velvet sectional couch, still feeling like an uninvited guest, and consoled himself with the thought that he had learned four things from his visit to Linda's apartment. One: Linda had lived beyond her means, or had had a rather rich source of income apart from her salary. Two: someone was afraid of what the police—or anyone, perhaps even Linda's parents—would find in her apartment, and apparently this someone had successfully removed whatever it was that worried him (or her). Three: whoever it was, he had a set of keys to her apartment. This Joe D. knew because there was no evidence of forced entry and the intruder clearly had entered the building through the service entrance, which was accessible only to those with keys.

The fourth was the most important discovery. Linda had been murdered by someone with a motive, someone she knew. Not by a lunatic whose path she happened to cross one Saturday night in July.

Chapter

THE next day, Wednesday, Joe D. again drove into the city. This time he visited Linda's boss, Jonathan Golland of Strickman, Cohen, Allen & Golland. He'd asked a few of his weekend housemates if they'd ever heard of Strickman, Cohen, Allen & Golland. They all had. Apparently it was the fastest-growing law firm in New York. While very much a "white shoe" firm, it was looked down upon somewhat by the legal establishment (but not by his housemates) as being just a bit too aggressive (*slippery* was the word some people used in reference to Strickman, Cohen). Nevertheless, it had grown from the four original partners to over a hundred and fifty lawyers in just ten years, and the firm represented some of the biggest corporations in the country.

Joe D. had never heard of it. He was impressed to find that Strickman, Cohen occupied no fewer than nine floors of a skyscraper on Park Avenue just north of Grand Central Station.

The receptionist looked bored and surly, the way they always do in New York, Joe D. thought. Then he identified himself as a cop and she became animated, squirming in her chair as she tried to lean across her pristine desk.

"Are you here about Linda Levinson?" she asked in a soft, conspiratorial tone. Joe D. estimated it would be ten minutes max before the entire firm knew about his visit.

He was shown to a corner office roughly the size of his childhood home by a pretty young secretary—Linda's replacement, he figured. He caught a glimpse of Park Avenue forty-three stories below and understood what was meant by a breathtaking view. Watery waves of heat radiated from the crowded sidewalk. Joe D. touched the window; it was reassuringly hot despite the air-conditioning. A remarkably handsome man, with the square jaw and open, weathered face of a politician, got up from behind the desk and extended his hand.

"I've been in this office for years and I'm still not used to it," he said, gesturing toward the floor-to-ceiling windows. There was something proprietary about the way his arm swept across the view. "I'm Jonathan Golland. You must be Lieutenant DiGregorio. Very pleased to meet you." This guy *must* be a politician, Joe D. thought: he really does seem pleased to meet me.

"I guess you know why I'm here."

Golland nodded solemnly. "Terrible, terrible business. She—Linda—was such a nice girl, too. And a terrific secretary. The best. I've been following the case in the papers. In fact . . ." He produced a copy of the *Times* and handed it to Joe D. There, on the front page of the Metropolitan section, was an aerial shot of Seaside Harbor under the headline: "Fear Mounts in Wake of Unsolved Fire Island Killing."

"Can you think of anyone who might have had a motive?" asked Joe D. halfheartedly, the headline having deflated him somewhat.

"For killing Linda? I can't believe anyone would want to kill Linda. She was quiet . . . sweet . . . didn't go out much. As far as I knew."

"She talked about her social life with you?"

"Not with me," he said with, Joe D. thought, a hint of urgency. "But then of course she wouldn't have confided in her boss, would she? And she kept pretty much to herself as far as the other secretaries were concerned. I encouraged her to make friends here, get more involved with the other girls . . . it makes it easier to get things done, to ask for favors, that sort of thing. But she never made the effort. I'd say that was her only flaw. As I said, she was a quiet girl."

"And very pretty, I hear."

Golland nodded. "Correction: she was beautiful," he said. His voice had turned wistful.

They were interrupted by a buzzing sound so reverently hushed Joe D. couldn't place its source until Golland pushed a button on his phone.

"Your wife's on the line," said a woman's voice, also reverently hushed.

"Tell her I'm in a meeting," said Golland curtly and then nodded at Joe D. to continue.

"What were you paying Linda?" Joe D. was dismayed to detect a slightly reverential hush in his own voice and made a point of losing it.

"Linda made about thirty-two thousand dollars a year. Plus overtime."

"Overtime?"

"Yes. You see, I specialize in mergers and acquisitions, and when I'm involved in a big deal I sometimes work around the clock. So I'd keep Linda here to type, handle the phones, and so on. She was paid time and a half for it. It's standard policy here."

"How much overtime did she make in the past year or so?"

"Oh, I'd say seven thousand. Maybe eight."

Joe D. thought: Jesus, she was making thirty-eight grand a year, more than I do. Maybe making the police force wasn't such a big deal after all. Maybe he should have listened to his high school guidance counselor. She'd urged him to apply to college, had even talked with his folks about it, told them that their son's grades and board scores would get him into any school he applied to. But the only board score his father had ever heard of dealt with runs, hits, and errors. And the fact was, the only thing Joe D. ever wanted to do was become a cop. Maybe he was good at school work, but that didn't mean he liked it. Besides, his father had been a cop, would still be a cop if a drunk teenager driving on the wrong side of the Sunrise Highway ten years ago hadn't forced him into very early and very bitter retirement. No encouragement to go to college—and no financial help either—had been forthcoming from either parent, and so he'd joined the Waterside police force the day after graduation. It had looked like a good deal at the time, but now, when it seemed like everyone and his sister made more than he did . . .

"Lieutenant, you were asking about Linda's salary . . ."

He'd been off somewhere, in the past. "So she made, uh, how much did you say?"

"Forty thousand or so, overtime included."

"Sounds generous," he said, thinking it still wasn't enough for that coat and the pearls and that apartment. "Did Linda have any source of income other than her salary from Strickman, Cohen . . ."

". . . Allen and Golland. No, I believe she was from a

modest family in Brooklyn or Queens or someplace like that. Why?"

"Just curious."

The buzzer intruded again.

"It's your wife," said the reverential voice.

"I told you I'm in a meeting."

"Yes, but she insisted . . ."

Golland picked up the receiver. "Yes," he said with some bitterness, then "No," also bitterly. "Yes. Yes. No. I'll try." He hung up, and again nodded for Joe D. to continue. Joe D. held back a moment, though, interested in what had happened to Golland. He seemed ever so slightly deflated now—a beach ball with perhaps ten percent of its air let out. He lost much of his charm and good looks in this reduced state, but it took him only a second or two to pump himself back up, a process that Joe D. watched with fascination. When Golland nodded a second time Joe D. obeyed.

"Did Linda ever mention boyfriends, anyone regular?"

Golland shook his head vigorously. "She was a shy girl, old-fashioned in a way. I don't believe she dated very much, and I know there was no one steady."

Then who, wondered Joe D., answered Linda's phone when her parents called?

"Is there anything else about Linda you think I should know, Mr. Golland?" he asked, abdicating responsibility for the remainder of the conversation. At this point Joe D. felt he had gotten out of this interview all that he had expected, which is to say not very much.

Golland considered the question for a while, nodding slightly. He even rubbed his chin. "No," he said after what struck Joe D. as an uncomfortably long silence. "No, Linda was an open book, Lieutenant. Open for all the world to read. A truly guileless, charming individual. Perhaps it was her openness that ultimately caused her downfall. In these times it simply doesn't pay to be too generous, too un-suspecting. But people like Linda can't help the way they are, they're just naturally, inherently trusting. She'll be sorely missed."

Golland seemed genuinely moved, but not excessively so; his words seemed to overreach his emotional grasp. Joe D. paused briefly to make sure the eulogy was finished, then thanked Golland for his time.

Chapter

10

"IN other words, what you're telling me is you got zilch. *Zilch!*"

Chief, that's not true at all. I told you, I now know for sure it was someone she knew, and that someone was in her apartment with me. This is no serial killer we're up against. At least we know it's not going to happen again. Linda was the target, and now that she's gone, there won't be any more killings."

"Who, then?"

"Chief?"

"Who killed her?"

Joe D. shook his head. He glanced around Castiglia's dimly lit office, looking for something to focus on other than his boss, but the room was almost entirely flat and one-dimensional, perhaps deliberately so, totally void of anything to distract the visitor from the hulking, irritable presence behind the desk.

"What was the motive?"

"Chief, it's only been a week."

"Only been a week! Do you realize that Labor Day's less than a month away, DiGregorio? If we don't get this creep by then, we'll never get him."

Joe D.'s search for a distraction was over: he'd discovered the Chief's nose. Why hadn't he noticed it before? It was enormous, as out of proportion to his face as his bulbous stomach was to his otherwise slender body. The tip of this nose jiggled slightly when he got excited, the way a dog's tail wags when it's happy. Glazed with perspiration, the nose caught the light from the desk lamp and glowed. Joe D. concentrated on the nose rather than the diatribe. It helped.

"Have you seen these?" He lifted a stack of clippings from his desk. Joe D. scanned the headlines. From the *New York Times,* the article Golland had shown him: "Fear Mounts in Wake of Unsolved Fire Island Killing." From the *Daily News:* "Police Report No Progress in Fire Island Slaying." From the *New York Post:* "Terror Island."

"Things were going just fine until this here murder. People left me alone and I did likewise. I want to see some progress by the end of this weekend, DiGregorio. Understand? Progress."

Thursday night, Joe D. went over to Marie's house. She lived with her parents in a two-family house just outside of downtown Waterside. Marie worked as a secretary at Grumman, the big aerospace company on Long Island. They watched television for most of the evening in the living room. Marie's parents watched in their bedroom upstairs.

"Listen, Marie, I got some bad news. I'm working this weekend. Orders."

92   "Not again," she said, pouting.

"Yeah. We're shorthanded and there was no way I could get out of it."

"Well, at least stop by when you can. Not like last weekend."

"That's the problem. I don't think I'll get many breaks and if the Chief sees my car outside your house he'll blow a gasket."

They sat in silence for a few minutes.

"You've changed," said Marie softly.

He turned to her, took her hands in his. Pouting was Marie's least attractive state. Other girls he'd known became kind of sexy when they were unhappy, like all they needed was a little tender loving care. Not Marie. She had a round, full face, sweet-looking most of the time, and young; she was twenty-two but was often mistaken for sixteen. Pouting made her face fleshy, made it droop; Joe D. could practically see the tears welling up behind those big fluffy cheeks. She had a tendency toward plumpness that she managed to control through periodic dieting and twice-a-week sessions at an Elaine Powers Figure Salon. Joe D. always figured she'd give up the battle of the bulge once they got married. Which was one reason he put off marrying her. Of course he *planned* on marrying her; it just seemed wise to put it off for a few years.

"What are you talking about? I haven't changed one bit. I've just been busy lately, that's all."

Instead of defending himself further, he tried to kiss her. She resisted at first, then gave in.

"See, that's what I mean," said Marie a moment later.

"Huh?"

"In the old days" (by which she meant two weeks ago) "*I* had to pull away from *you*. Now you're the one who stops first. Kissing, I mean."

"But Marie, your parents are upstairs . . ."

"That never worried you before. Besides, we could have

93

gone to your apartment, but you insisted on coming over here."

Which was the truth. He'd insisted on Marie's house tonight because he knew that without privacy he wouldn't be expected to get too romantic with her. He thought of his long, persistent, and ultimately successful struggle for her virginity—and now he was the one backing off. Since he'd been assigned to the Linda Levinson case he hadn't really been able to think about much else, including Marie. And to be honest, he found himself thinking a lot about Alison. She was the first woman other than Marie he'd slept with since they'd begun dating three years ago. He remembered how Alison had practically forced him into her room Saturday night, and then how she'd left him stranded there the next morning. He hated the dishonesty of having to deceive his weekend housemates about what he was doing on Fire Island, but the truth was he really couldn't wait to get back there. Not so much back to Fire Island as back to Alison.

At the door Marie pulled him to her. "Joe D., do you love me?" she asked sweetly.

"You know I do, babe," he answered.

"Tell me you love me."

"I just did."

He kissed her on her forehead and left.

Chapter

11

"**J**OE!" Alison looked surprised but not especially pleased to find him at the door. It was Friday night. Joe D. had walked directly from the ferry to her house.

"I thought we'd go to Crane's together or something."

"How about we just meet there later? I'm not even dressed yet . . ." Alison was wearing two towels, one around her body, the other around her hair on top of her head, turban-style. She smelled of baby powder.

She still hadn't let Joe D. in, so he opened the screen door himself. "I'll wait," he said.

Looking annoyed, Alison let him pass. "Everybody," she announced to the six people in the living room, "this is Joe Gregorio."

"*Di*Gregorio."

"Yeah. This is Tracy."

"Hi Tracy."

"And Ronnie."

"You two must be sisters," he said, pointing to Tracy.

"And Jason."

"Jason."

"And Larry."

"Nice to meet you, Larry."

"And Al and Fran."

"I think we already met," said Al, grinning.

"I'm going up to dress," announced Alison with more resignation than enthusiasm. The television was tuned to a Mets game and it was clear to Joe D. he was no competition for it. He joined Tracy in the kitchen. An impressive configuration of dirty dishes sprouted from the sink and spread across the counter, jutting out over the edge in a few places.

"Going to Crane's tonight?" he said. Tracy was a tiny thing—Joe D. guessed she weighed no more than a hundred pounds. Her face was pretty in a sweet, childlike way; Tracy could easily pass for sixteen.

"Of course," she replied. "Isn't everybody?" She was going through the refrigerator, picking at different foods, apparently not very interested in starting a conversation.

"Say, isn't this the house that girl lived in? The one who was killed?"

She turned around, looking suddenly very serious. "Linda Levinson. That's right. She was Alison's roommate. Didn't Alison mention her?"

"I guess she was too upset to talk about it."

Tracy shut the refrigerator. "We were all devastated."

"Did the police question you about it?"

"The whole day. It was a Saturday. Course, none of us knew her very well. We just shared this house with her."

"Does anyone here have any idea who did it?"

"Nope." She folded her arms across her chest, as if the room had suddenly turned cold. It hadn't: Joe D. realized she was scared. "You're frightened."

96

She nodded. "I just keep thinking he . . . the killer . . . will come back and try to . . . harm us . . . the rest of us here in this house. I didn't want to come back here to Seaside Harbor after that day but my sister said I was being stupid. So here I am, but I still don't sleep well in this house. Can't wait till Sunday night, to be honest."

"Why would the killer be interested in the other people in the house?"

"He probably isn't. At least that's what Ronnie says."

"But you don't agree."

"I shouldn't say anything," she said, practically whispering. She moved closer to him, disturbing an unwashed plate and setting off a chain reaction that flung several dishes to the floor. Fortunately, they were plastic; Tracy ignored them. "But I'm just so scared. You tell me if you think I'm overreacting. There was this guy, Rob something, who Linda brought back with her the weekend before she died. Friday night. Nice-looking guy. Well, anyway, all of a sudden we hear him talking real loud, sort of complaining. I don't know how to explain this, it's kind of embarrassing." She hesitated.

"Don't be embarrassed."

"Well, he couldn't get it up with her was I guess the problem." She smiled nervously. "No big deal except he went crazy, he was so upset. Kept saying he was sorry. We could all hear, you see. These walls are like paper, they really are, even with my sister sometimes . . ." She finished this thought silently. "And he was so loud. Ronnie and I just sat up in bed and listened. She giggled but I felt awful for both of them. Such an ugly scene."

"What was ugly about it?"

"I guess he wanted to stay the night, maybe give it another shot, but she insisted he leave . . . in this cold way she had of talking sometimes. Like she wasn't angry or any-

97

thing, just didn't care. Well, he didn't like this one bit, started shouting at her."

"Shouting what?"

Tracy thought a moment. "Just, you know, cursed her out, called her really horrible things. I was frightened for her, I really was. I asked Ronnie if maybe we shouldn't wake up Al or the boys—Jason and Larry—but she said they couldn't have been sleeping through it anyway and if they thought it was getting rough they'd do something on their own. It was real ugly. I remember closing my eyes and wishing I could open them and be somewhere else. Wishing I could close my ears, too." Tracy's pale face was flushed from the memory of that night and the fear that remained with her.

"Where was Alison during all this?"

"Not here."

"Not here in the house?"

Tracy nodded. "She never came home that night, lucky her . . . oh my God, I can't believe I just said that! She'll kill me if she finds out I told you that. You *are* seeing her, aren't you?"

"No problem, we only met last weekend," said Joe D., pinching the disappointment out of his voice. "What was this Rob guy's last name?"

"I can't remember. But the funny thing is, Alison knew the guy, or knew of him. He shared with her cousin or something. I think she was with Linda in Crane's when she met him. Maybe she introduced them. So when the police were questioning us that Saturday I thought maybe I should mention all this, but Ronnie said not to. She said I'd ruin his reputation—he's an attorney, you see. Ronnie said if every man who can't get it up is a murderer there wouldn't be any women left alive. Besides, she said that the other people in the house would bring it up with the police if they thought it was so important. But you know what? They didn't. I think everyone's too afraid of ruining someone else's precious reputation. Though I suppose it does seem impossible, what with his being an attorney and all. He's with Stone and something or other. Or is it something and Stone? Anyway, Ronnie was sure it was Paul, Weiss but I told her that was ridiculous because Paul, Weiss is in midtown, Park and Fifty-first, and this Rob fellow definitely works downtown, I heard him mention it one time in Crane's. Not that Ronnie changed her mind, she still insists he's with—"

"Why do you think you might be in danger?"

"Oh, well, it's silly, really. But if it *was* this Rob guy, and I'm not saying it was, in fact I really don't think it was, but let's just say he was the killer, then maybe he'll want to kill everyone who knew about what happened that night. Everyone in this house. I mean, if he killed one person, then he's capable of—"

"I wouldn't worry about it."

"Really? You wouldn't?" She sounded eager for reassurance.

"Really. What kind of guy was this Rob? You say he's a lawyer . . ."

At that moment Ronnie walked in and Tracy, who'd started to answer, clammed up instantly.

One glance at her sister and Ronnie knew she was upset. "You've been talking about Linda, haven't you?" she said to both of them in an accusatory tone. Her voice had an unpleasant, almost metallic edge. It was obvious that Ronnie thoroughly dominated her younger sister. They looked very much alike, with their oval faces and round, light blue eyes, but Ronnie was easily twenty pounds heavier; the additional weight was attractive, the difference between a fully realized painting and a preliminary sketch.

"Actually we were talking about law firms. I'm partial to Strickman, Cohen. You?"

She flashed him a skeptical look. "It's getting impossible to have a conversation about anything other than Linda Levinson these days. Linda Levinson this, Linda Levinson that. Frankly I find it unhealthy and boring. If people can't think of anything more constructive to talk about then they should keep their mouths shut."

"They're afraid," said Joe D., in awe of this woman, wishing he were as sure of one thing as she was, apparently, of everything. Tracy was simply dissolving beside her older sister. "People are afraid and it helps to talk these things out."

"Bullshit," said Ronnie. "People are gossips and they're ghouls and they thrive on bad news. I think a second murder would make their summer, I really do. This place is beginning to get on my nerves. Tracy, I told you we should have gone to East Hampton this summer."

"You never—"

"Come on, Tracy, let's go," she ordered. Then, to Joe D.: "My sister is a very nervous person. Please don't upset her by talking about this business."

Joe D. stifled the urge to salute her as she took Tracy's arm and yanked her from the room.

It looks like Linda Levinson had had a busy time the weekend before she died, he thought, idly picking up the dishes from the floor and placing them atop the pile on the counter. Friday night with this Rob fellow, Saturday night with Eric Farber. Neither of the encounters had been particularly satisfying, from the reports he was getting, but like the song says, you can't always get what you want.

Alison was silent on the way to Crane's; Joe D. could feel her pulling back from him. He promised himself he wouldn't confront her on it. After all, he was a cop on an assignment and was practically engaged (that phrase again, *practically engaged*—it was beginning to annoy him), so he didn't have much right demanding things from her. Like a little consideration. And some attention.

Still, less than a week ago they had spent the night together. A really incredible night, he thought. At least it had been incredible for him. Maybe Alison was used to this sort of thing, but he certainly wasn't. Sex with Marie was okay, but more of a release than anything else. With Alison release had been only the beginning. It was the difference between taking a bath and diving into the ocean.

So maybe he felt guilty about using her to find Linda Levinson's killer. But she didn't know he was on a case.

The setting sun cast a softening glow over the island. They passed several groups of people on their way into town, their faces full of enthusiasm for the weekend just beginning.

The truth was, Joe D. felt hurt by Alison's rejection. And he liked her. A lot.

He bought her a gin and tonic at Crane's, danced with her, then turned around and she was gone. It took him nearly an hour to find her in the crowd that overflowed, drinks in hand, onto the adjacent dock. When he did, he confronted her in spite of himself.

"I thought we were, you know, together." He saw her eyes widen at this and quickly added: "For tonight."

"Last weekend I was afraid to be alone. Tonight . . . tonight I'm afraid *not* to be alone."

"But last weekend—"

"I'm sorry, Joe. I can't." She shrugged and walked away.

He reminded himself he was only on a case, that none of this was real, but it didn't help. He felt he'd let her down in some way. He sensed a struggle taking place inside her that had a lot to do with her friend's murder but even more to do with something else that he only partially understood— an unwillingness to get too close, a fear of losing control. **101**

Last weekend, over dinner, and later, in her bedroom, she'd let down her guard and now, a week later, she was running scared. He believed he could actually see the two opposing forces at work on her face, the need for intimacy and the dread of it, pulling her skin tight, tensing her lips, creasing her brow. How much better she looked when she allowed herself the luxury of letting go.

He tried convincing himself he didn't care, that his only interest was solving the case. Getting involved with Alison Rosen would have been a big mistake, he told himself. For starters, it's all a lie—you're a cop and a fraud and you'd have hurt her. You'd never have known where you stood with her, never known when to back away lest she head for the hills. She's part of a different world, this Fire Island world of lawyers and doctors—*professionals*. You don't belong here and you never will. Just as well she'd called it off.

But it did no good. Something about her intrigued him, something had grabbed hold of him and held fast no matter how hard he tried to shake it off.

He bought a beer and joined a group of guys from his house. At least he *thought* they were from his house; Joe D. was beginning to have trouble with faces as well as names.

"Why the long face?" one of them asked. Joe D. shrugged and tried to smile.

"Woman trouble, it looks like," said someone.

"I know your type," volunteered a third guy. "You're too nice to the girls. Which is not what they want. Believe me. If they wanted to be treated nice they wouldn't be here. This place is a fucking zoo, and the only people who come here are animals."

"Yeah, like us."

"You said it. Like us."

Joe D. laughed uncomfortably. "You guys are too much," he said weakly.

"Oh yeah? Ask Steve here about last Saturday night."

"Steve?" he complied, turning to a big guy with the exaggerated physique of a gym addict.

"Funny you should ask. I spent the whole evening here in Crane's trying to make time with this one girl. We go out back there and do a few toots, I spend practically a whole paycheck buying her these fucking milk shakes she was drinking. Sombreros, they're called. So at around one-thirty, what does she do? She says she's tired and would I walk her to her house? Need I say how happy I was to oblige? Turns out she lives practically in Seaview, and the whole way she jabbers on and on about how happy she was having someone to escort her on account of the murder. Then, whammo, at the door she practically breaks my nose slamming it in my face."

Steve paused for an infusion of beer.

"Anyway, I'm feeling real pissed to put it mildly. So back at Crane's I go up to this other girl at the bar, not bad-looking, either. We make small talk for maybe five minutes, she starts telling me about her job—she's a VP at an ad agency or something—and then I just say to her, 'So, we going back to your place together or aren't we?' And you know what? She says yes. Just like that she says yes, like what was I waiting for, anyway? Before I know it we're back at her place humping away, and I'm telling you her face wasn't much to look at but her body went into overdrive. *Jesus*. The girls in the next room pounded on the wall, then the couple upstairs started pounding too. *Jesus*. It just goes to show you. It doesn't pay to treat them nice."

There was a murmur of agreement. "Nice is not what they're looking for," said someone.

"It's a waste of time," said someone else.

"What's there to talk about with them, anyway? They don't know shit."

Another murmur of agreement greeted this observation. "Take politics for example. I bet you ten bucks you ask ten **103** chicks here who the vice president is, no more than three'll know."

"Vice president of what?" asked Steve.

"Of the country, asshole."

"Oh yeah, I don't think any of them would know that."

They continued discussing the limits of the female intellect for some time. Joe D. found the conversation depressing and quickly disengaged himself.

Alison took a Tab from the refrigerator and sat at the kitchen table. She opened the can, took a sip, then stared at it intently, as if it contained not just soda but solace.

"Hey there, are you okay?"

It was Al, with Fran at his side.

"Thanks, I'm fine," she lied. In reality, a quick dip in the Atlantic with rocks tied to her ankles seemed just the ticket.

"You're sure there's nothing we can do?"

Looking up at them, so obviously comfortable with each other, more like brother and sister than a married couple, she thought: there is something you can do—you can tell me how people learn to trust each other.

"No thanks. It's been a rough day, that's all."

"Well, call us if you need us," said Fran, and they left her alone in the kitchen.

She thought about her performance in Crane's—for it *was* a performance—and felt not only lonely but guilty. Loneliness and guilt—twin sisters who shadowed her unrelentingly. She had chased away Joe D. with her own special brand of man-repellent, a noxious combination of dry ice and boric acid, and her reward for this unnecessary act of self-defense was utter loneliness, a sensation of hollowness so vivid she could practically feel the chill winds gusting inside her.

104 The other reward, of course, was guilt, for she had responded to Joe D.'s kindness with cruelty, and now, hours later, her behavior seemed unforgivable.

If only he hadn't been so *nice,* she thought. His niceness challenged her in some irresistible way, the way a "wet paint" sign all but demands that you touch the paint to prove it dry. It was a question of not trusting. It was a question of fear.

One thing about fighting people off, she thought as she headed up to her room. You always win.

Joe D. started to leave Crane's but changed his mind. The prospect of a long night in a bed as soft and lumpy as cottage cheese was grim indeed. Sharing a room with a guy whose name he had trouble remembering didn't help. A few beers might.

"A Miller," he told the bartender, "and a Jim Beam." He needed cheering up and he needed to fall asleep, and he figured a boilermaker would facilitate one or the other.

"Depressed?" piped a little voice to his right and down a good foot and a half.

At first he didn't realize he'd been addressed.

"I *said,* depressed?"

He noticed her now, a tiny thing under a mass of loose brown curls.

"Excuse me?" he asked, and he could tell by the clutching look she gave him that if he weren't careful he'd soon be entangled in a conversation.

"You look depressed, and you ordered a boilermaker. I thought maybe you wanted to talk to someone, that's all." She shrank from him as she spoke, as if she weren't really prepared to follow through on her initial foray.

"No, I'm fine," he said sharply, and she shrank some more, her thin body collapsing into itself like a folding lawn chair. "But thanks for asking," he added, unable to send her unencouraged back into the fray.

105

She smiled sourly, her thin, straight lips widening without curling. "Just call me Florence Nightingale."

"Hey, listen, all I did was order some booze."

"Sure, sorry I snapped."

He turned away.

"Another member of the Farber Hall of Fame," she sighed and started to walk away.

He turned back and tapped her shoulder. "The . . ."

"Farber Hall of Fame. Named in honor of the first brush-off I ever had the pleasure to be on the receiving end of." Alcohol was evidently interfering with whatever mechanism it was that controlled her speech volume; she wavered randomly between a shout and a whisper, her body pitching forward as the sound amplified.

"You said his name was—"

"Farber. Eric K. Farber. Numero Uno. The boy who broke my first heart."

"The name's Joe DiGregorio."

"Rachel Garvin," she said, expanding a little, regaining some of her earlier presence.

"What're you drinking, Rachel?"

"Stoli with a lime," she said, then added: "And tonic. Stoli with tonic." He relayed this to the bartender and quickly plotted his strategy. The crucial thing was not to lose her at any cost, though that cost, he thought as she downed most of her drink in a single gulp, might be steep.

"I haven't seen you around before, Joe DiGregorio. Where you been hiding?"

She was pretty in a diminutive way, with a long, thin nose that came to an abrupt, perfectly rounded end that no assortment of genes had ever combined to produce. Her eyes were large circles that lent her a quality that was equal parts innocence and sadness. Her body looked well-proportioned, also in a diminutive way—she couldn't be more than five-one or -two. He found her absolutely unappealing and guessed other men had the same reaction. The whole of Rachel Garvin was simply not equal to the sum of her parts, each of which, taken individually, was rather pleasing. He tried to figure out what it was that didn't quite click about her while she, encouraged by vodka, reviewed aloud the highlights of her life from birth to the present moment.

Interrupting her proved difficult, but at length he steered her monolog to the subject of Eric Farber.

"Oh, him. Forget it."

"No, I'm curious. I think I know him from somewhere."

"Eric? You might, he was here tonight. You can't miss him, the golden boy with everything going for him."

Her tone intimated that one thing he *didn't* have going for him was Rachel's undying respect.

"What's so special about him?"

"For starters, his looks. If he wasn't doing so well on the street, he'd have no problem making it as an actor. Or maybe a model. He's beautiful, that's all. Beautiful."

"You said he's doing well on the street . . ."

"Yeah, Wall Street. He's a broker with Fried and Sons. One of their top producers. A girlfriend of mine in personnel there says he pulls in close to two hundred a year, and he's just a lousy broker. Me, I'm a lousy vice president with only the second largest bank in New York and I barely pull down seventy grand."

About twice my salary, Joe D. thought, trying to picture this increasingly drunk urchin behind a vice president's desk. It was a picture that simply wouldn't focus.

"How does a guy like Farber make that kind of money? He can't be much older than, what, thirty."

"He's thirty-one, my age exactly. We were in the same class at Great Neck North. We're both great neckers, you see. Well, not Eric, he's just a big prick, or maybe not so big, I never had the pleasure of a first-hand inspection, sorry to say. But me, I'm a great necker from way back, a **107** card-carrying great necker." She had nuzzled up to him, her breasts pressing against his abdomen. "You wouldn't by any chance be a great necker too, Joe DiGregorio?"

The loud music, her slurred speech, and the fact that she was pressing herself against him with surprising force made it increasingly difficult to carry on a conversation. He bought her another drink, himself a beer—sans brandy this time—and led her out of Crane's. She followed him unthinkingly, oblivious to the change in venue.

"How about we sit on the dock and talk?" he asked. Her answer was another rub against his midsection. He headed for the dock which jutted out from Crane's, aware that one wrong step and she'd end up floundering in the Great South Bay. He gingerly helped her down onto the dock, positioned her legs over the side, and sat down next to her. She rested her head against his arm, and for a moment they stared silently out into the darkness. He thought he saw a flickering of light in the distance, perhaps from Waterside, and felt momentarily homesick, sitting there beside this disintegrating stranger, uncomfortable in his new role as tonight's designated hedge against loneliness and regret.

"So Farber makes two hundred grand," he said casually, feeling like a shit. "What's his secret?"

"No secret. He makes money for his clients, so they keep investing with him, and his commissions just keep going up and up and up and up and . . . Oh, I feel a teeny bit dizzy. Hold me, John, or I'll fall."

"You're already sitting."

"So I am. Hold me anyway and I'll tell you the secret of Eric K. Farber's success."

Putting his arm lightly on her shoulder, he reminded himself that this was all in the line of duty. She was wearing a white sweatshirt; it felt as soft and damp as a just-used towel.

108   "Takeovers," she murmured as if it were a sweet nothing. "Takeovers." He could feel her warm breath on his chest. "All the guys in my house this summer say Eric picked more hot takeovers than almost anyone else on the street. Course, they say it was all luck, you know, you throw enough shit against the wall some of it's going to stick, but I think they're jealous, don't you? If they had picked the takeovers they'd be rich like Eric the K., right?"

Joe D. was uncomfortably aware of a kind of osmosis taking place: Rachel Garvin was merging into him, opening up the borders of her vodka-soaked body to engulf him. He felt her on all sides of him, like a tight-fitting sweater, and shifted uneasily, which only caused her to collapse into him ever further. He pressed on, however, his self-esteem diminishing all the while.

"Did Eric know Linda Levinson?" he asked, figuring he had about five minutes left to work with before she passed out or sent them both tumbling into the Bay.

"The dead girl? Maybe he did, maybe he didn't. Eric's only interest is money, Jack. He's so busy making it and spending it, he doesn't have time for girls, dead or alive. His father went bankrupt, you see."

This last sentence was whispered moistly in his left ear.

"Oh?" he said.

"And then he killed himself. His father, I mean, not Eric. Eric's still alive, at least from the neck up. He was here tonight, in Crane's."

Her grip on reality was clearly loosening.

"Oh yes, the Farbers had this great big house with a three-car garage. Honest, three cars. Eric had a red Camaro. Ooooh, he looked so gorgeous in that red Camaro, so handsome and popular and admired. And tan, always tan, twelve months of the year—the Farbers went to Florida, oh, it seemed like every other week. He had these blue eyes that just about drove me crazy and he'd wear these tight Levis, always perfectly faded, not too much, you **109** know, but just enough, and those blue eyes, they melted me, and he had the thickest hair, sandy-colored, and the longest eyelashes and the bluest eyes and a smile that always seemed like a gift, like he was giving you a gift of his smile, and blue eyes to die for and a great body, you should have seen him playing tennis, he moved like he was in a dream, *your* dream, and a voice that was so sure of itself it made you feel better just to hear it and eyes as blue and bright—"

"Rachel, maybe it's time—"

"He was my first love. It still hurts a little."

Reminiscing about the teenaged Farber burned through the vodka and touched something deep and raw inside her. Too bad she and Farber were still in the same orbit, Joe D. thought. Otherwise his golden presence might have melted from her memory, freeing her.

She continued in a more sober voice. "But then it all fell apart, you see. The business, his father's business, collapsed, and one day he started his car but didn't open the garage door. They had to move out of that house—it was a Tudor, big and beautiful, I used to look for him in the second-story windows, wondering which one was his bedroom. They moved to a garden apartment, nothing so terrible but I think Eric never got over it, having to come down like that. I think that explains his obsession with money, don't you? We had our tenth high school reunion a few years ago and he invited the whole class back to his house. Can you believe it, he bought a house in Great Neck, just a short way from the house his father gassed himself in? I hear he kept his place in the city, spends most of his time there. So it just goes to show, doesn't it?"

"Show what?" Joe D. asked.

"What?"

"You said it just goes to show."

"Oh, Jim, I feel so sad all of a sudden. Nothing ever

works out the way we want it to, does it?" She reached into her jeans pocket and pulled out a thin vial attached to a key chain. Mechanically, as if applying lipstick after a meal, she dipped a miniature spoon into the vial, scooped out a pinch of cocaine, and lifted it to her face. Half of the tiny mound blew off into the darkness, but the other half made it into her left nostril. She repeated the routine, losing even more of the stuff this time to the southerly breeze, before she remembered her manners and offered him some. He declined.

"At the bank the SVP's secretary supplies us all," she said, repeating the process.

"The SVP?"

"Senior vice president. My boss. Hey, let's get on one of these and take a ride." To Joe D.'s alarm she pointed to one of the nearby motorboats. When he shook his head she began to pout. "Oh, please, James. I feel so much better now."

"I think maybe I better take you home, Rachel."

"Just a itty-bitty cruise? Here, snort a little of this and you'll feel just as good as I do."

"Rachel."

"You don't want coke, I may have a lude somewhere. Let me look." She plunged her hands into her pockets and came up with a pill. He shook his head, at which point she shrugged defiantly and started to pop it into her mouth. He caught her hand and took the pill away from her. She didn't seem to notice.

"Come on, Rachel, I'm taking you home." He stood and pulled her up carefully. She felt heavy in a dense, compact way, like a small child. The liquor and coke had relaxed her face, robbing it of its best feature, its sharpness. She looked pouty and tired.

"Can I ask you something, Jim?" she said as they made their way down the dock toward Crane's. "When you say

111

'take me home,' do you mean to sleep with me, or just to take me home?"

"Rachel."

"No, really, which one?"

"Take you home, that's all."

"I was afraid of that. You seeing someone?"

He thought of Marie and Alison; he felt as if he hadn't seen either in a million years. They merged in his mind into a blurry, uncomfortable composite. "Yeah, I'm seeing someone."

"Well, that figures, it just figures." She stopped in front of the entrance to Crane's. "Time to say nighty-night. I'm going back in." She sounded remarkably sober all of a sudden; her effort to pull herself together for a second stab at Crane's was visible in a forward thrust of her shoulders, a lifting of the chin.

"Maybe you'd better let me take you home, Rachel."

"Thanks, but no thanks. I'm fine. You could do me one favor, though."

"Anything."

"Kiss me.

He bent over, aiming for her cheek. She took his head between her hands and directed his lips to hers, holding him against her with a force that startled him. He felt her tongue against his lips, sliding across, pushing them apart. Before he pulled back he became aware of a momentary stirring deep within him. He felt her need, her longing, felt it radiating from her but also from inside of him, warm and familiar and irresistible.

"Good night, Rachel," he said.

"Thanks for the drink, Joe," she said.

Chapter

JOE D. felt the earth shake and then, still only partially awake, realized that the earth was stationary but he was shaking. Or being shaken.

"Joe, wake up." A woman's voice.

"Marie," he said groggily, his eyes still closed.

"Who the hell's Marie?"

Joe D. sat up. "Alison! What time—?"

"It's eight-thirty. Time to jog."

"Eight-thirty? Jog? But last night you . . . I thought you didn't want—"

She put her hand over his mouth. "Get dressed. I'll meet you in the living room."

"But I don't jog."

"Nonsense. Everybody jogs."

Joe D. got out of bed with some difficulty; last night's beer weighed heavily. His roommate, Mark, growled from the next bed. "Shit" was all he managed before sinking back to sleep.

Fortunately (or maybe unfortunately) Joe D. had a pair of running shoes with him, but he wore them as walking shoes, not for jogging. Apart from occasional games of basketball with his high school buddies, Joe D. didn't exercise. He never understood the point of running without a destination, or climbing mechanical stairs, or lifting useless weights. There were too many places in life you *had* to run to, too many stairs you *had* to climb, too many things you *had* to lift. But if Alison wanted him to run with her, he certainly wasn't about to refuse.

After all, he was on a case.

"You jog often?" he asked Alison. They were running east along one of the footpaths that connect Seaside Harbor with neighboring villages.

"Five days a week," she answered. "You?"

"Never," he gasped; it was beginning to show.

Joe D. had never seen so many joggers. Though still early, the paths were teeming with runners, some in perfect shape, others in no shape at all. What really surprised him was how many people passed them, some talking as easily as if they were on a leisurely stroll. He thought he and Alison were running about as fast as two people could run and still communicate beyond grunts, but he was wrong. A few joggers even carried hand weights—apparently running a string of seven-minute miles offered insufficient challenge.

"Let me know when you want to turn around," said Alison.

Left to his own devices he would have turned around that instant. Would have *walked* back, in fact. "Sure. Not yet, though. We're just warming up." Joe D. spoke haltingly in short clumps of words, gasping for air in between but trying not to show how breathless he really was. "I was talking with Tracy. Last night. While you were dressing. She seems pretty upset. By your roommate's. Murder."

"How should she be, delighted?"

"Well. You don't seem. All that disturbed. I mean. You never. Even mentioned. It."

Alison stopped suddenly and turned to him. Joe D. was grateful for the chance to catch his breath, though he knew he was in for it.

"Look, no one here was more upset by Linda's death than I was. It's just that I decided I was going to enjoy my summer as much as possible in spite of it. Not that it's been easy. No one wants to talk about anything else with me. I've never been so popular."

It was true: Alison was practically the only person he'd met in Seaside Harbor who didn't willingly bring up the murder, which peppered nearly every conversation he'd had. A month without violence had only intensified the speculation and fear; an aura of anticipation shrouded the island, which held its collective breath as it grew increasingly impatient for round two to begin. That there might not be a round two was a possibility that seemed not to have occurred to anyone, and Joe D. sensed that this very expectation of a second murder might in fact give birth to one, an act possibly unrelated to Linda Levinson's death.

Much to his disappointment, Alison started to jog again, faster than before, as if propelled by anger.

"Sorry. I brought it. Up," said Joe D., who hadn't managed to catch his breath during the brief respite. They had jogged into an area in which the houses were spread farther apart and set amid dense greenery that almost completely obscured them from passersby, though no house was set back more than ten yards or so from the footpaths. Blue and white and yellow wildflowers shone through the thick undergrowth; birds flickered, almost unseen, from branch **115** to branch. In places the short trees formed a bower overhead, blotting out the sun; it felt much cooler in this neighborhood, as if they had crossed from midsummer to early autumn. At its very center, equidistant from ocean and bay, the island looked less like a beach resort than a rural cabin community. This area struck Joe D. as much more peaceful and relaxing than Seaside Harbor.

"I like. It here," he panted.

"I'm not sure they'd like you, though," she replied, still not winded in the slightest.

"Thanks a lot."

"Or me either. This is Point o' Woods. Very expensive and very exclusive."

As if on cue they passed a tall fence with a locked gate. Through the gate he could see Crane's in the distance and just behind it the Seaside Harbor marina. A small sign quietly but firmly indicated that Point o' Woods was a private community. "Keep out" was the not very subtle message.

"The last thing they want is the crowd from Crane's spilling over here at two in the morning. You can get through to Point o' Woods closer to the ocean, like we just did, but not down here by the bay."

"Ever notice. How the nicest things. Like Point o' Woods. Are always the most. Expensive?"

She turned to him, still running, and smiled. "I've known that since I was five years old."

They ran in silence for a few minutes. Then, fearful that he'd soon be so winded he'd be unable to speak at all, he crossed his fingers and raised the issue of the murder once again. "Tracy thinks she could be. In danger. You too." They were passing the Point o' Woods Beach Club, a large gray-shingled edifice perched on the dunes by the ocean. He saw a couple, both in white pants and pastel shirts, sipping coffee on a small deck. They looked blond and happy.

Alison dismissed the thought with a wave of a hand. "That's nonsense. Tracy's paranoid."

"She said this guy. Rob something-or-other. I can't remember. His last name . . ."

"Lewis. She's nuts. He couldn't possibly be dangerous."

"Why. Not?" he panted.

"Because he's . . . he's . . . I don't know, he's educated, he's successful, he's . . . like all of us in Seaside Harbor. No way he's a killer."

Joe D., feeling like an illegal alien in Alison's rather circumscribed world, chose not to pursue the issue of Rob Lewis, educated professional. He'd at least managed to get Rob's last name, and unless they stopped immediately, further speech was out of the question. He spotted the sun, already throbbing and it wasn't even nine-thirty, looming just above the treetops.

"Let's. Turn. Around. Now," he gasped.

"You rest for a while. I'll pick you up on the way back."

Alison and Joe D. spent the rest of Saturday on the beach. A perfectly beautiful, lazy Saturday. They spread a blanket on the periphery of the crowded area and stirred themselves only to move away from the water as the tide reclaimed more and more of the beach. By the ocean's edge couples batted small hard balls back and forth between wooden mallets, adding a syncopation to the rhythm of the surf. A two-masted sailboat drifted into sight, spectral in the hot haze of early afternoon. Joe D. roused Alison to show it to her, but by the time she sat up it had already evaporated into the horizon. It was that kind of day.

She drifted in and out of sleep but Joe D. remained awake, snatches of conversation blowing over to him from the more crowded area like straggling puffs of smoke from distant, unwelcome factories.

"Read me a geography question."

"Where is Durban?"

"Where is Durban?"

"You heard me, Wendy."

"Ireland?"

"Will you do my back, Bev?"

"Hand me the stuff."

"Mmmmm. Feels good. Don't miss my neck."

"She had a boyfriend, is what I hear."

"I heard she was frigid."

"Maybe she acted frigid here in Seaside Harbor but back in New York she had a boyfriend. I met someone once who lives in her neighborhood and used to see her all the time with this same guy."

"Who was he?"

"Don't you think I'd tell the police if I knew? I can't even remember who it was I met who lived in her neighborhood."

"Shit, literature again."

"What was the pen name of Mary Ann Evans?"

"What was the pen name of Mary Ann Evans?"

"You heard me, Wendy."

"Brontë, right? I know it's Brontë. Do I have to give the first name?"

"You hear about Larry?"

"What about him?"

"Didn't make partner at Skadden, Arps."

"Larry? I don't believe it. What went wrong?"

"Beats the hell out of me. Guy busted ass for six years. Nights, weekends. And with a baby on the way."

118

"It's not like he's dead, Sam."
"Oh yeah? Ask Larry."

"He was married, they say."
"How do they know?"
"Wore a ring, plain as day. And why else the secrecy?"
"Do the cops know this?"
"About the married guy? Come on, Naomi, what difference would it make? What married guy ever killed his girlfriend? I mean, why kill the goose that lays the golden eggs?"
"Why kill a good lay, you mean."
"Yeah, exactly. Vice versa I can understand, but only a fool would kill a girl dumb enough to get involved with him when he's married."

"Which planet is closest to the sun?"
"Which planet is closest to the sun?"
"Wendy!"
"My very educated mother just served us nine pickles."
"That your answer?"
"No, dummy, it's a numeric device to remember the planets. 'My' stands for . . . oh shit, is it Mercury or Mars? That's what they never explained, how you're supposed to remember which 'm' is which."
"Just answer the question, Wendy."

"He'll find another job."
"Yeah, assistant to the assistant general counsel of some two-bit corporation. I pity the guy."
"You make it sound like the end of the world."
"If it isn't the end of the world I'd like to know what is."

"And *I'm* telling *you* there are six guys to every girl since this murder. Used to be a like a candy store here, you had your pick."

"Stan, you're exaggerating again."

"Yeah? The four girls in my house that still come back, they have this rule that we all have to stick together. Eat dinner together, walk to Crane's together, walk *back* from Crane's together."

"So what's so bad about that?"

"What's so bad is they're a bunch of bow-wows. My house is a fucking kennel this summer and now I have to act like chief vet or they get all over my case."

"What kind of mousse you using?"

"Can't remember the name. The one in the red and blue can."

"I have that one. Makes your hair look great."

"I just had it cut, maybe that's why."

"Maybe."

"My whole side aches today. They have a new machine at Health and Racquet. For obliques. It's a killer."

"What the fuck are obliques?"

"Love handles."

"So why would you want your love handles bigger?"

"Not bigger, idiot. Smaller. Tighter."

"But don't you understand? She was killed *after* the last ferry left."

"What're you telling me?"

"That it was someone from Seaside Harbor."

"But even so, he wouldn't come back, would he?"

"Of course he would, otherwise everyone would be suspicious of him."

"Great, so maybe next week I'll stay in the city and *schvitz,* thank you very much."

"I hear she was burned to a crisp, lying there dead all morning."

"And with that gorgeous complexion she had. She'd die if she knew."

"*Meredith.*"

"Sorry."

"Who is Tippecanoe in the slogan 'Tippecanoe and Tyler too?'"

"Who is Tippecanoe in the—"

"Wendy!"

"All right, all right. Tyler, of course. Am I right? Tyler, right?"

"What's a girl got to do to get a dinner invitation out of you, Joe DiGregorio?"

A familiar voice for a change. He opened his eyes and smiled lazily at Alison.

"I repeat. What's a girl got to do to get a dinner invitation out of you, Joe DiGregorio?"

Jesus, talk about hot and cold. "Well, I was going to ask you but after last night . . ."

"Fine. Pick me up at eight. I'll make a picnic for us." She kissed him lightly on the cheek and hurried off to her house. Watching her, he thought that maybe the running paid off after all: her long, tanned legs looked great in motion, sturdy and strong, but also graceful and supple.

As he put on his sneakers, he reflected that the day had been productive after all, for he'd learned one important thing, albeit by doing nothing more strenuous than lying on his back and taking in the beach gossip that floated his way. Linda Levinson was not the innocent legal secretary he'd been led to believe she was. There was a lover, a married man, and Joe D. was willing to bet this mystery man was the source of Linda's jewelry and fur coat. A week ago Joe D. had wondered if he'd ever manage to locate one suspect. Now he had three: Eric Farber, with his regularly scheduled meetings with Linda, meetings he had conveniently failed to mention; Rob Lewis, Linda's one-night stand—her last stand, perhaps; and her lover, whose identity he had yet to uncover. Linda's life was beginning, in retrospect, to look very complicated indeed.

He climbed the stairs that led up from the beach, turned, and surveyed the scene before him. The beach was half-empty now, an incomplete patchwork of blankets and towels and beach chairs and umbrellas. There's something uniquely depressing about the end of a beach day. He watched people trudge from the beach, shaking sand from their sneakers, their skin salty and tight, their energy sapped from too much sun. Only the ocean seemed unwearied by the hot summer day, pounding tirelessly against the shoreline, the first to arrive and, always, the last to leave. A twin-engine plane skimmed the shoreline trailing a banner: CRANE'S FOR FUN.

Walking back to her house, Alison made a mental list of ingredients to get in town for tonight's dinner. She hadn't felt this good, this *unburdened* in a long time. She'd shower, change, run into town for the groceries, cook up a storm . . . The important thing was to keep busy, keep her mind occupied with something other than the murder, no mean feat in itself but next to impossible in Seaside Harbor, where even the trees seemed to whisper of the murder as she hurried down the path toward her house.

Whispering. Was she imagining it, or *had* there been someone whispering? Without stopping she turned around, saw that the long straight path was empty, and continued on her way.

"Alison."

She stopped this time, spun around, then around again. The path was still deserted, but she *had* heard something.

A rustling of leaves, a squirrel, perhaps, but she quickened her pace anyway. Off the path were smaller walkways leading to the individual houses, and in between was the dense wall of brush that blanketed all of Fire Island.

"Alison, stop." That whispering again, windy, asthmatic.

She began to run, glancing over her shoulder at the still-empty path. The rustling in the bushes seemed to follow her, but she saw no one.

Too much sun, she thought . . . paranoia, and why not, after all that's happened . . . the breeze threading through these dry, crackly trees. Still she ran, as fast as her flip-flops would take her.

"Don't run, Alison."

It *was* a voice, still only a whisper, barely audible yet close by. If she stopped, she'd be able to see him, running through the brush, she was sure of it, but she couldn't bring herself to stop. Please, she thought, just let me make it to the house.

"Alison."

"Leave me *alone*," she shouted as she ran; she heard the words shrivel up and evaporate into the hot summer air. She was dizzy now with terror, felt herself not so much running as falling, falling down a long, perfectly straight chute with nothing to grab on to.

"Alison." The voice was slightly behind her now, and still off to the right. She ran as fast as she could, clutching her beach bag to her chest, her hair blowing across her face. As she turned onto the footpath leading to her house she heard it again, her name carried by the breeze, but it was now almost too faint to discern. She threw open the screen door, would have broken it down if it hadn't given right away, and found herself, panting wildly, sweat covering her face, in the middle of a crowd of people having drinks in the living room, all of whom stopped talking when she stumbled in, all of whom were staring at her now, astonishment on their faces.

"There was . . ."

They were watching her, the dead girl's friend, drinks poised midway to their mouths, eyes expectant, eager. Wondering if she were cracking up. (And who could blame her, they'd say, after what she's been through.)

She pointed outside, toward the path. "There was . . ."

Was there anything? What, after all, had she seen? Some bushes rustling? No, she'd only *heard* the bushes rustling. And her name. Or was that the breeze, conspiring with her own heightened sensitivity to alarm her? Alison's head spun with fear and confusion, and she felt hot and weak under the spotlight of attention.

She took a deep breath. Someone *had* been following her—she was sure it wasn't her imagination. And yet, what was the point of telling these people? What could she prove, and what could they do?

"I'm in a hurry, that's all," she said curtly and ran from the room.

It wasn't hard for Joe D. to find Rob Lewis. It really was a small little world these Seaside Harborites inhabited. Two people in his house knew the guy well, the rest knew *of* him.

"Real good-looking guy," said one of the girls.

"So I hear," replied Joe D.

"I'm playing hoops with him later," said one of his housemates, either Alan or David. "Want to join us?"

Just what I need, he thought, more exercise. "Sure, love to."

The court was wedged into one of the few vacant lots in Seaside Harbor. Like everything on Fire Island it was dusted with sand, which made for some impressive skids. It

turned out to be a good, fast game of basketball, and Rob

Lewis turned out to be a good if overly aggressive player. He collided with other players several times and once even hurled himself violently into the net pole. At five-thirty, halfway through the game, near collapse under a sun that showed no sign of letting up, Joe D. took a break. This was the only court in Seaside Harbor and there were plenty of replacements waiting on the sidelines. Happily, Rob Lewis joined him a few minutes later.

Joe D. never could figure out what it was that turned women on. Here was Rob Lewis, universally acknowledged to be a real looker, and all Joe D. could see was a tall guy with an oversized nose and faint traces of adolescent acne. He did radiate a kind of intensity that, Joe D. guessed, might be attractive to women. Sitting next to Rob, Joe D. could feel it: warm, physical energy held in check by a mental effort that seemed not quite up to the task. A lean but powerful torso was only partially covered by a sleeveless white T-shirt on which Lewis had enlarged the armholes by cutting away a good portion of the fabric.

"Your first summer in Seaside Harbor?" asked Lewis.

Well, thought Joe D., the guy does have a good voice—deep, resonant, a disc jockey's voice. No wonder it had been heard clear through Linda Levinson's house.

Joe D. nodded. "I'm beginning to regret it, though. What with this murder and all, the women are really tense, not easy to get to know."

"I thought I saw you in Crane's with Alison Rosen." He sounded suspicious, but he struck Joe D. as the type who was always suspicious of something or someone. There was a furtive quality to Lewis.

"You know her?"

"By sight."

"Yeah, I was with her. Still, it's tense here lately, no?"

"I know what you mean. The only way to score is to 125

volunteer for this escort service they have now. I hear there's a waiting list."

Joe D. laughed. "You knew her?"

Lewis yawned and stretched languidly, exposing a network of sinewy muscles just under his tanned skin. "Who, the murdered girl? No, not really. Knew of her. One of the girls in my house this summer, Eleanor, knows Alison, her roommate. They're cousins or something. But you must know that, since you know Alison."

Joe D. felt Lewis was prying, deliberately bringing the conversation around to Alison. "Sure, Eleanor. You seeing anyone?"

"Just playing the field this summer," answered Lewis quickly.

The game would be ending soon, and Joe D. realized he hadn't made much progress with Lewis, though he'd have been hard put to say exactly what he could have done differently. One of the problems with undercover work, he was learning, was that he couldn't just come right out and ask questions the way a uniformed cop could. And Lewis was hardly going to start talking to Joe D., whom he'd just met, about a disastrous night he'd spent with a murder victim five weeks ago. Especially if he *were* the murderer.

Joe D. thought about Monday, about telling Chief Castiglia he had nothing to report, and decided to take a chance.

"I overheard some people in Crane's talking about the dead girl—what was her name?"

"Linda Levinson."

"That's right. I couldn't believe it but they were saying that the week before she was killed she brought someone home with her and he couldn't deliver the goods in the sack." God, thought Joe D., am I really saying this?

"Yeah, so?" said Lewis offhandedly. He stretched again,

this time less comfortably.

"Well, I mean, obviously Linda must've talked about it, otherwise how would everyone know? And then bang, she's dead one week later. It just seems kind of coincidental, that's all." Joe D. made a pretense of watching the game. Actually, he was concentrating on not including Alison or any of Linda's other housemates in this conversation. If Lewis were the killer, getting these people involved could be dangerous.

After a short silence Lewis blurted: "What do you mean everyone knows?"

"You know how it is here in Seaside Harbor. You fart and they hear it three houses away. I hear this guy made quite a scene, though, apologizing one minute and then begging for a second chance."

Lewis stood up suddenly and for a moment Joe D. was afraid Lewis was going to hit him. "Who gives a shit, anyway? The whole thing gives me the creeps. He probably had too much to drink. Liquor does that to you, you know. Makes you want it bad, then you can't get it up." With this observation he rejoined the game, throwing himself into it as if fighting for his life.

Joe D. pondered Lewis's behavior as he walked home. Nothing unusual about a guy flying off the handle when he learns an entire town is aware of his sexual shortcomings. The question is, was he upset enough to punish Linda Levinson for her part in the episode? Or was there something about Linda Levinson that had inspired a violent reaction? He realized he knew only the barest facts about her—pretty, bit of a loner, sexy dresser. He'd heard all about what made her attractive to men. But what, he wondered, had made her, out of all the other attractive young women in Seaside Harbor, attractive to a killer?

He took a wrong turn and found himself lost for a while. **127**

So many of the paths in Seaside Harbor look alike, it's easy to get confused. The metallic roar of happy hour at Crane's was just audible above the ever-present boom-hiss-silence, boom-hiss-silence of the ocean. Using the two sounds to navigate, he finally found his bearings and, ten minutes later, his house.

Chapter

13

"**A**RE you sure this is legal, eating on the beach?" Joe D. asked Alison as they walked down the whitewashed stairs to the sand.

"No, but who cares? You're an accountant, remember, not a cop." Joe D.'s heart just about jumped out of his chest.

They spread a blanket at the base of a large dune, which concealed them from the houses bordering the beach. The air was warm, the sky flickered with stars, the ocean roared at them through the moonless night. As Alison emptied the picnic basket, Joe D. inserted a cassette into the portable tape recorder he'd brought along: Bach, of course, Suites 1 and 4.

Alison turned around the moment the music began. "How lovely! And how unexpected."

"You figured a Guido like me would listen to nothing but rock and roll, right?"

She smiled guiltily. "Mea culpa," she said, and handed him a glass of chilled California Chardonnay. He took a sip; the wine was so fresh and so clear that swallowing was almost unnecessary; it practically evaporated on its own. They kissed deeply, lazily, tasting the wine on their lips, in their mouths. The music, like the wine, was fresh and clear and delicate; the Atlantic slapping against the shore added a new voice to the counterpoint.

Dinner was a series of new sensations for Joe D. Alison poured soup from a thermos into two mugs. The first sip told him that this was something different. Black cherry soup, Alison told him in answer to his unasked question. "I was in a pitting frenzy all afternoon." He told her it was worth it; he loved the coolness of the soup, the unlikely interplay of sweet and tart flavors, the sleek, silky texture. Then came cold lemon chicken, a dish new to him yet so instantly and thoroughly satisfying that he felt the twenty-nine years of deprivation the moment the first forkful reached his tongue. A second bottle of wine was followed by raspberries and homemade whipped cream; he'd had raspberries a few times in his life, but they had never tasted the way they did now, dissolving in earthy sweetness in his mouth. For his birthday this year, Marie had made him an enormous but soggy lasagna and a salad of limp lettuce soaked in Kraft's Creamy Italian, followed by a strawberries-and-Cool-Whip concoction she'd made from a recipe on the side of the container. He'd been touched—she'd had to beg her parents to vacate the house for the event, and she'd worked hard—but now, on the beach with Alison, Joe D. knew he had been introduced to a whole new world, a world in which eating was not simply a way of filling up as quickly and economically and, one hoped, as pleasantly as possible, but an end in itself, an act of the imagination.

130   "Alison, I don't know what to say. That was fantastic."

She smiled broadly. "The only thing I enjoy more than cooking is watching someone eat what I make. It's the most satisfying thing."

An unexpectedly cool breeze extinguished the candle she'd lit before dinner. The sudden darkness fell on them like a heavy cloak, isolating them, drawing them closer. She snuggled up to him. "What a wonderful day," she said, her voice a bit skeptical, as if such days were new to her and thus suspect in some way.

The wine had loosened her guard a little, thought Joe D., it softened her and brightened her eyes. He refilled her glass.

"You sound surprised," said Joe D.

"Expecting the worst is a habit of mine."

"So I've noticed. At least it makes disappointment easier to take."

"You'd think so, but it doesn't."

"Is Linda's death the worst thing that ever happened to you?"

Alison waited a moment before answering. "I suppose when my parents got divorced, that was pretty hard to take. I was twelve, an only child, and I guess I figured I was the center of their universe. It wasn't until they told me they were splitting up that I realized they had a life apart from me. I also learned . . . hey, you don't want to hear this . . ."

"You mean, you don't want to say it."

Alison smiled faintly and looked down at her wineglass. "I also learned that marriages—that love—doesn't last forever."

"That's a tough lesson for a twelve-year-old."

She shrugged noncommittally. "But apart from the divorce, it's been pretty smooth sailing. I mean, no deaths in the family or scandals or anything like that. I even have four grandparents still alive—can you believe it?—each of **131** whom has pulled me aside at least once every year for the past five years to tell me they're planning on living only long enough to dance at my wedding. Maybe that's why I've never married—I like my grandparents too much, and as long as I'm single they'll refuse to die."

In the darkness, her face only dimly discernible, her voice sounded deep and hushed; he could feel her breath on his face as she spoke, warm and familiar. He wanted her to keep talking. "Tell me about your job."

Alison rolled her eyes. "Wow, this is a switch, a guy asking me about *my* job. Usually I spend the whole evening hearing about the urology practice of some doctor my mother fixed me up with. Or lawyers—they're the worst because they can't stop talking about how once upon a time they had a social conscience and went to law school to defend our rights and help the needy. Until they got an offer from Davis, Polk and Wardwell they couldn't refuse. But you're different, you don't like to talk about yourself."

"What can I say about accounting, that I became an accountant to help those less fortunate keep better books? I don't think I'd make much time with a line like that."

"Probably not, but come to think of it, you don't make sense to me. I can't put my finger on it, but something's wrong."

"How so?" he asked uneasily, sensing that she was hovering dangerously close to the truth, but intrigued at the same time by her perceptiveness.

"For starters, your living in Waterside. A single guy like you should be living in New York."

"I live in New York, remember?"

"You know what I mean, New York *City*."

"What's wrong with Waterside?"

"Nothing, nothing, but a guy like you should be in Manhattan, not the suburbs."

"Does every single person have to live in the city? What if I'm not into the singles scene?"

"If you're not into the singles scene, why Seaside Harbor?"

Now that was a tough one. "The beach, the . . ." Joe D. was at a loss.

"See what I mean, you don't add up."

"And you're not comfortable talking about yourself."

"What do you mean?" asked Alison.

"You said it felt good to be with a man who's interested in what you have to say, and then you turn the conversation around to me the first chance you get."

"Must be a habit by now, like expecting the worst."

"Nice try. The truth is *you're* not comfortable talking about yourself. I'll bet you're a real pro at leading those urologists on. 'How fascinating, you mean you can do all that through one teeny little catheter . . .'"

Alison laughed. "Not fair," she said.

"So, prove I'm wrong. Tell me about yourself."

"I told you last week, didn't I? Born in Brooklyn, raised in Scarsdale. Father in the rag trade."

"Yes, yes, but tell me about *now,* today. I don't even know what you do for a living."

"I told you. I'm a buyer. I buy better sportswear for Bloomingdale's."

"Do you enjoy it?"

Alison hesitated. "That's a question I haven't asked myself in years. It just never occurs to me. I know I'm good at what I do, and I'm paid well . . . I guess I do like it. People think being a buyer is a piece of cake, the perfect job for Jewish American Princesses who spend so much time in stores they figure they may as well start getting paid for it. Well, it's not true. It's hard work, some of it physical."

"And men?"

"You mean do I date a lot? Yeah, I date all the time. This summer I've had . . ." She counted on her fingers. ". . . six blind dates. But that's down from last summer.

I'm getting on, you see. The pool of available men is shrinking for me every year. I figure in a year or two it'll dry up completely."

"I'll bet those six guys thought you were terrific."

"Four of them did, or at least four called back for a second date." She threw him a look of mock triumph. "That's down from last summer too. Last summer all but one asked me out again."

"And?"

"And did I see them again? No. Not one of them. Truth is I'd rather stay home and watch 'Love Boat' reruns on a Saturday night than have dinner with someone who bores me to death. I keep saying to myself, 'Give them a second chance, you never know, Alison,' but in the end I usually refuse. And those awful struggles at the door. After the first date most of the men are puppy dogs, happy with a pat on the head. But they're beasts after the second date, they're really offended if you won't sleep with them, like they've earned it somehow. I also think they're genuinely surprised to be turned down, because I don't think they're used to it. I think they get their way most of the time, and when I won't let them sleep with me they think *I'm* the one with the problem. And maybe I am, who knows?"

Another deep sip from her wineglass. "So there you are. I'm thirty-two, been to every restaurant in New York at least once, and . . . it all adds up to a big zero."

Joe D. couldn't help taking this personally. "Is it all that bad?"

She smiled. "Not so bad. How about some more wine? This talking about myself sure builds a thirst."

"I was right, wasn't I? You don't like talking about yourself."

"Don't gloat. I hate men who gloat more than I hate men who talk about themselves."

134   She put down her glass and stretched out, resting her head on his lap. "It feels good being with you, Joe D. Comfortable."

Joe D. didn't respond. In his rush to get to know her, then to gain her trust and approval, at first for the sake of the case, later, he knew, for his own sake, Joe D. had never stopped to consider what learning of his deception might do to Alison. It hadn't been a problem at first, when she was so distant, so cool toward him. Then, he had sensed a toughness, a resilience that made him believe she'd survive any disappointment. But now that she had exposed a more vulnerable side, now that she genuinely seemed to like him, he wasn't so sure. He was beginning to think he'd gone too far.

He thought: all I have to do right now is tell her I've been dishonest; not the whole story, just enough of it to turn her off. Like the fact that I have a girl back in Waterside I'm practically engaged to. Alison was the one who'd started it in the first place, dragging me up to her bedroom last weekend . . .

He shook his head, derailing this train of thought. He knew there was no turning back. And as for blame—only one person in the relationship was being dishonest . . .

"Why so quiet?" she asked.

"Just thinking."

"Now, if I were my mother, I'd say 'Thinking about what?' She always does that and it drives me crazy, like I don't even own my private thoughts." She said nothing for a bit, then asked suddenly: "Have you ever been in therapy?"

"In therapy? Uh, no."

"Well I've been in therapy practically half my life. Until recently. I was on the couch for four years during college in Boston, a Freudian, he never said a word the whole four years. I swear to you sometimes I thought he was a deaf-mute. Then, after college, here in New York, I saw a **135** female social worker. I really loved her. She was like a friend who never asks for anything for herself. Except fifty bucks a visit, and my parents paid that. She taught me to like myself, to accept myself, which was great except at the time I was lonely and depressed and involved with a married man, so what was the point of accepting myself? What I really needed was to change. So I switched to a third shrink, a psychologist this time. All *he* did was bankrupt me, since by then my parents were fed up with paying my therapy bills. They said my therapists talked me out of getting married, can you imagine? We used to have the most awful fights on the subject.

"Anyway, I bring all this up because I finally quit therapy for good when I realized I didn't even own my own thoughts. Like with my mother asking me what I'm thinking. I remember I'd be jogging or something and I'd have a really satisfying fantasy about one thing or another and I'd think, 'Oh shit, now I'm going to have to tell Dr. So-and-So about this one.' Because I always felt it was my duty to be totally honest with my shrinks. I'd feel guilty if I held anything back, like *they* were paying *me* and therefore I had no right to withhold anything. After a while the lack of privacy made me crazy. Kind of ironic, isn't it? Therapy making me crazy? But it did. Now I can have my own thoughts and my own fantasies and I'm much happier. Really, much happier."

Now, Joe D. knew some people who'd been to shrinks. His cousin Alfonso came to mind. He'd been caught exposing himself to a six-year-old girl at a playground. Alfonso, however, had only seen a shrink for a couple of visits before he was pronounced cured. Alison was another case altogether. All those years in therapy! With three different shrinks! If Alison had seemed even a tiny bit crazy, he might have been disturbed by this revelation, might have thought he had a nut case on his hands. But she seemed

136

completely normal to him—a little hard to get to know, perhaps, and not the most optimistic person he'd ever met. But crazy? No way. So her three shrinks only added to her appeal, lent her a kind of fascination that Marie, for example, didn't possess at all.

"So," Alison continued. "What were you thinking?" She affected a German accent. "Don't hold back, now. I must know, what were you thinking?"

Joe D. laughed. "Actually, I was thinking about you."

"And?"

"That's all, just about you."

"How nice and uncomplicated," she said wistfully.

They removed their shoes and strolled down to the water's edge. The sand felt cool and moist underfoot. They stared out into the vast dark ocean. Joe D. was filled with a sense of limitlessness, a sense of great potential that frightened him, diminished him. He was glad he was not alone and was about to express this to Alison when a group of people passed by. Someone was singing "Follow the Yellow Brick Road." Someone else hefted a bottle of vodka overhead, took a deep swig, and passed it on. Joe D. noticed Eric Farber in the group, looking somewhat detached, as if he didn't feel he quite belonged to this rowdy bunch, and felt Alison tense up.

The group relaxed its tight formation as it passed Joe D. and Alison, absorbed the couple for a few seconds, and then closed ranks again as it continued on its merry way. "What's the matter?" he asked.

"Nothing, really. One of the guys in that group was a friend of Linda's, that's all. Not exactly a friend, more of an acquaintance. Actually, come to think of it I'm not sure *what* their relationship was, but she *did* know him. We were talking with him in Crane's the night she was killed. Seeing him just reminded me of the whole thing. Of Linda. Being with you, I actually forgot about it for a few hours." **137**

Ditto for me, Joe D. thought. "Did he leave with her, that night at Crane's?"

"No, of course not. Otherwise he'd be a suspect, right? Listen, I'm sorry I overreacted. Sometimes, though, I have the feeling that someone's watching me. Which is *stupid,* really, because *everyone's* watching me, the grieving roommate. But sometimes I sense one person watching me, someone specific. It terrifies me, Joe D., it really does."

He put his arm around her, pulled her to him. *Was* there someone watching Alison, or was she only imagining it? He'd bet there was someone, *someone specific.* Something in Linda's life, something she'd done or something she'd known or even something she'd said, had triggered her murder. Whoever killed Linda might be wondering if Alison was in on Linda's secret. Even Joe D. wondered if she knew, consciously or unconsciously, what Linda had known or done or said. If only he could ask her straight out . . .

"Why'd you come back, Alison?"

"I don't know exactly, except that there was never a doubt in my mind that coming back was the right thing to do. I promised myself that I wasn't going to let some creep ruin my summer. And I figured it was just some awful pervert who did it, not someone from Seaside Harbor, and that he'd crawled back into whatever hole he came from. Now I'm not so sure. I *feel* someone, watching me, all the time. Like earlier today, walking back from the beach, I heard someone say my name. But when I turned around, nobody was there. I started to run and then, I swear it, I heard the voice again. But when I turned around a second time—still no one. Do you think I imagined it? Am I going crazy?"

Joe D. *didn't* think she'd imagined it. "Who do you think might be following you?"

"That's just it, I can't think of anyone. That's why I figure it's probably just the atmosphere of this place. It's so goddamn ingrown, with everyone knowing everyone else's business. You know, I used to think my parents' country club was bad, the way they'd sit around the pool all summer and gossip about this divorce or that affair. But it's no different here, only murder beats the hell out of adultery in the gossip department.

"And I miss Linda, I really do. I *know* everyone here, but she was my one friend on the island. Since the murder I just never know when I'm going to get upset. Like the other day: I'm feeling perfectly okay and then, a minute later, I'm in tears, thinking about Linda . . ."

"What triggered it that time?"

She smoothed a patch of sand with her foot. "You won't believe it, it sounds so stupid. I left work early on Tuesday and I walked all the way home. I passed Linda's block and I just had to walk by her building. I don't know why, maybe to remind myself that she once really existed. Sometimes the whole thing, Linda included, feels like a bad dream I've just woken up from."

Joe D. recalled that Tuesday was the day he had gone to Linda's apartment. Thank God they hadn't run into each other.

"And that made you start to cry, walking past her building? I can understand that."

She shook her head. "No, I hadn't even passed her building yet when I saw Linda's old boss coming toward me. Jonathan something or other. I saw him once when I met Linda at her office for lunch. And I saw him a second time at my father's country club. He lives in Scarsdale too, it turns out."

"Did you speak to him?"

"No. I wanted to, to talk about Linda, but he didn't even recognize me. He seemed in a real hurry, almost running, actually. God knows what he was doing on the Upper East Side in the middle of the afternoon."

Joe D. thought he knew. "What time did you say?"

"About four, I think. Why?"

"No reason," he said quickly. "Go ahead, continue." Joe D. thought: four o'clock was just about when I was chasing someone down the emergency stairway in Linda Levinson's building.

"I just dissolved in tears after he passed me. Thinking of all the hours Linda put into that dumb job, all the nights, all the weekends. And for what? To get murdered by some creep on Fire Island. I just started to cry and I couldn't stop. Right there on Sixty-second Street."

Alison had started to cry now, too. Joe D. massaged her shoulders gently, making a mental note to pay a second visit to Jonathan Golland. He was clearly the man in Linda's apartment with him on Tuesday, and that meant he had a key to the place.

They walked silently back to the blanket. Joe D. pulled her close to him and kissed her. They sank to the sand.

"Joe, not here, please," she said, a little breathless. Scattered voices, garbled by the surf, could be heard from down the beach. Ignoring her, he continued to kiss her, his lips gently caressing her entire face, his hands exploring her warm breasts beneath her shirt.

"Joe, please, we can't. Too many. People."

He pulled away from her and saw a spot several yards back in the dunes that was almost completely hidden from the beach. He pulled Alison to her feet and grabbed the blanket. They hurried over to the spot, threw the blanket to the sand, and quickly undressed. This moment apart was almost unbearable.

"You're so beautiful," he said, his hands running over her shoulders, her breasts. "So beautiful, so beautiful." She remained standing as he knelt down and began kissing her thighs, starting at her knees and working his way up gradually. Her knees bent slightly, giving way. Finally, she

140

too collapsed to the blanket. They kissed, a deep, long, hungry kiss, before she pushed him gently onto his back and started working her way up his thighs with her mouth, pausing now and then to look at his face. When she finally took him into her mouth, he let out a short, sharp groan before catching himself. Just before it was too late, he pulled her away from him, rolled her onto her back, and entered her. When they came, together, it was as if the boundaries of their bodies had momentarily evaporated.

They washed the sand off themselves in the ocean, their bodies still warm from lovemaking. Coming out of the water, they nearly bumped into two couples walking along the beach. Joe D. and Alison, both naked, froze for an instant while the two couples stared at them. They were too stunned to try to cover themselves—until just now they'd completely forgotten that the beach didn't belong to them exclusively. Damn this place, Joe D. thought: there's nowhere to be alone. Then, suddenly, all six—the two couples and Joe D. and Alison—started to laugh. "Where'd you get your suits?" asked one of the women. "Just swim over from Europe?" asked the other. "Probably day-trippers—try the ferry next time."

Joe D. and Alison dressed hastily, hurried back to her house, undressed even more hastily, and tried once more, this time in bed, to evaporate into that single entity they'd formed on the beach.

Chapter

14

"STRICKMAN, Cohen, Allen and Golland." The voice, Joe D. thought, was classic New York receptionist: pinched, nasal, and impatient.

"Is this the receptionist?"

"Yes."

"The receptionist with the blond hair?"

"Frosted. My hair's frosted, not blond."

"Yes, well, this is Lieutenant DiGregorio from the Waterside Police. We met last Wednesday."

The voice unpinched a bit. "Of course, I remember. Do you want to speak with Mr. Golland, Lieutenant?"

"No, as a matter of fact I want to speak with you."

A pause to digest this piece of good news. "Why, certainly, go right ahead." In a hushed, conspiratorial voice: "I assume it's about the, uh, Linda Levinson affair."

Linda's affair with Golland, to be specific. Joe D. figured the best place to start was the place the two had met: forty-three stories above Park Avenue. He guessed the receptionist would be more willing to talk than one of Golland's partners. Might even know more.

"I didn't catch your name . . ."

"Lenlich, Gloria Lenlich."

"Ms. Lenlich . . ."

"Please, Gloria."

"Gloria. In investigations like this one, murder investigations, it's important that we know as much as possible about the victim. Private things, like, well for example, did the victim have a lover? Can you understand why this would be important, Gloria?"

She indicated that she could indeed.

"What I'd like to know, Gloria, is do you have any information about the, uh, private life of Linda Levinson that might be useful to the investigation?"

He heard her breathing accelerate. "I do, Lieutenant, I do," she replied.

"Good, then can we meet for coffee later? Say around eleven?"

"There's a coffee shop right here in the building."

"I'd rather we met away from the building."

"Oh my, of course, of course. No need to raise suspicions." Gloria Lenlich's voice chortled with excitement. She named a coffee shop on East Forty-sixth Street. "I won't tell a soul. You can rest assured," she practically whispered into the phone.

Gloria was already seated in a booth when Joe D. arrived. Her face was heavily made up, but the effect, doubtless unintentional, was to make her look somewhat older than she probably was, as if she were a young actress in a part that demanded that she age in the course of a play.

"Lieutenant, this is my lunch hour," she announced, lay-ing down the ground rules. "So if you don't mind, I will order lunch."

"Be my guest, Gloria. It's on me."

Here eyes widened. "Thank you," she said, and proceeded to order a bacon cheeseburger, sides of fries and cole slaw, and a chocolate shake.

"Gloria, the reason I wanted to talk with you is that when I visited Jonathan Golland the other day—"

"Wednesday at ten," she said, flexing her receptionist muscles.

"Yes, Wednesday morning. I don't think he told me everything there was to tell about Linda Levinson."

She feigned a look of innocence that didn't fool Joe D. for a second; this woman had a story to tell and keeping it to herself was causing a bad case of indigestion. She shifted uncomfortably on the vinyl bench.

"Didn't he? Well, I certainly wouldn't presume to second-guess Mr. Golland, he being our most senior partner and all . . ." As she talked her makeup erupted into a relief map of tiny lines and crevices. Joe D. guessed she was no older than forty.

"Well then, if you don't have anything to tell me, I'll just settle with the waitress . . ." Joe D. made a show of starting to get up.

"On the other hand," she interrupted, and then, for dramatic effect, paused to take a sip from her milk shake, a sip so deep her entire upper body heaved with the effort. "On the other hand, I assume the reason you went to see Mr. Golland was because of his, uh, relationship with Linda."

"Why do you assume that, Gloria?"

"Why, because . . . because, well, because everyone in the office knew about . . . *IT*." Gloria managed to verbally capitalize and italicize the word, as if 'IT' were the title of a horror movie on a Times Square marquee.

Joe D. chose to remain silent. Sure enough she jumped right in.

"It's been going on for years, you see. Since she started working at Strickman, Cohen. Almost seven years. I guess they worked late together a lot, on his mergers and things, and one thing led to another—the way it often does." She paused to let the full impact of this observation sink in. "And pretty soon they were, uh, *involved.* She never talked about it to anyone, of course. Kept completely to herself. And none of the other girls wanted anything to do with her. I mean, how could we—they—trust her, what with her fooling around with our senior partner. And she could be a bit high and mighty, with her college degree and her nice clothes and whatnot. Like she thought she was meant for better things. And maybe she was, but better things meant no more Jonathan Golland, so she just stayed on, never making friends with anyone. Except, of course, you know who."

Gloria took an enormous bite of her cheeseburger and washed it down with a swig of milk shake. "I actually think they believed no one knew about them, can you imagine? For seven years they thought they had the whole world fooled! He'd go away on a business trip and, bingo, like clockwork, a telegram would arrive, which Linda made sure we all saw: 'Client insists I provide own secretarial help. Please be at such-and-such a hotel in Paris by such-and-such a time.' I don't know who they thought they were fooling, but they were nuts about secrecy. As if there weren't plenty of other shenanigans around the office. Though I must admit none of them lasted as long as Linda's and Mr. Golland's . . . *thing.*"

She mopped up the cole slaw juice left in the saucer with a handful of fries and took a last, audible sip of her milk shake.

"Mind if I order dessert? I didn't have time for break-fast . . ."

"Please do."

"Really, she was to be pitied, poor thing. More than

145

once I'd catch her crying in the ladies' room. Just sobbing her eyes out. Before the holidays, you know. I think she actually thought he'd leave Mrs. Golland for her. But you don't divorce Dinnerman's. You just don't unless you're a little *meshugge*."

"Dinnerman's?"

She looked at him as if he had just flown in from Mars. Or worse yet, Long Island. "Dinnerman's. You know, women's clothing? Their stores are in half the shopping malls in the country."

"So what's the connection?"

"The connection is Mr. Golland is married to Sol Dinnerman's daughter. And Sol Dinnerman just happens to be the firm's biggest client. If he ever divorced her, he'd be finished in this town." She let up for a moment, pleased with this dramatic turn of phrase, and took a bite of her banana cream pie; it left an Al Jolson halo of whipped cream on her upper lip. "So you see, Linda was licked, hooked on a guy who couldn't leave his wife even if he wanted to. Which I'm not sure he did."

"Oh?"

"Well, and this is completely confidential you know, if it ever got out that I—"

"You have my word, Gloria."

"I once saw him in Saks with *another woman*." The verbal italics again.

"Mrs. Dinnerman? I mean, Mrs. Golland?"

"Nope. I know Amanda Golland. By sight, of course. And by her voice—she calls a lot. One of the partners said if we could charge for the time Mr. Golland spends on the phone with her, the firm's billings would double. No, this was a really hot-looking blond, and not his daughter, either, in case you were going to ask." She flashed him a knowing glance. "You don't fondle your own daughter the way he was fondling this broad. Anyway, he doesn't have a daughter. Or a son either."

Joe D. pondered this last piece of news.

"Say," she said suddenly, "you don't think maybe Mr. Golland is the guilty party? Like maybe Linda put it to him, either marry me or I'm going to your wife, and he just silenced her instead."

"I think you've been watching too many TV detective shows, Gloria."

She flushed with pleasure. "Oh, can you tell?" she asked. "I've always felt I had a knack for this sort of thing. You know, I almost always guess the ending on 'Murder, She Wrote.'"

"I'll bet you do," said Joe D.

"I should also tell you that Linda was not herself those last few weeks before her . . . demise. As I said, she pretty much steered clear of the rest of us girls, but in those last weeks she was real friendly, like we'd been close for years, and then all of a sudden she'd snap at one of us for no good reason, schizo-like, if you catch my drift. I think maybe our Mr. Golland gave her the old heave-ho and she was ready to snap. Or maybe she gave him the heave-ho. But one thing I know for sure, something was up between them. I've just never seen her so, so schizo, it's the only word I can think of. Up one minute, down the next. And even Mr. Golland wasn't himself."

"How so?"

"First, a cup of coffee if you don't mind."

He passed on her request to the waitress. "You were saying that Mr. Golland was not himself . . ."

She dumped three packets of sugar into her coffee and added cream. "Nothing extreme, you understand. But when you've worked in one place for as many years as I have, you get to know the habits of people, like you were married to them. Well, Mr. Golland just wasn't his usual self, that's all. He came in a little later than usual, left a little earlier, kept to his office all day, which wasn't like him, usually he'd roam around joking with all of us girls **147** like a young kid. He could really be quite charming. But not those few weeks. I'd say he was depressed about something. Or worried."

Gloria finished her coffee in silence. As they got up to leave, Joe D. cautioned her about keeping their conversation to herself.

"You have my word, Lieutenant," she promised, but he knew his lunch with Gloria Lenlich would be the talk of Strickman, Cohen, Allen & Golland within the hour.

Not for the first time Joe D. realized that being undercover had its disadvantages. How, after all, was he to interrogate Eric Farber? As a cop, no problem—he'd just telephone him, make an appointment, and ask him straight out: What was your relationship with Linda Levinson and do you know anything about her death? But as Joe Di-Gregorio, Waterside accountant, he was just another summer weekend Seaside Harbor resident, and while it was easy to get a conversation going about the murder, the quality of information was rather pathetic, a combination of speculation and nervous hysteria that amounted to very little. Seaside Harborites wavered between absolute conviction that the killer was not one of them (being a day-tripper was a crime just short of murder anyway) and suspicion of just about every male on the island. Motive never entered the picture (how could it, when there weren't any motives handy?), but opportunity did, which only heightened the speculation further, since on Fire Island everyone had an opportunity to do anything to anyone. The place was remarkably open and casual; people wandered in and out of houses all the time, parties formed spontaneously and dissolved just as easily, and finding oneself in one's living room alone with a total stranger was (until Linda Levinson) nothing to get alarmed about.

148   All of which made Joe D.'s task difficult, to say the least.

He had begun to think the whole undercover business was a waste of time. He'd even asked the Chief to send another officer to look into Farber after the Chief had informed him that a preliminary investigation of Farber had, as expected, turned up nothing.

"Out of the question," he'd replied to Joe D.'s request for assistance. "We can't spare anyone else. Besides, more police would mean more panic, and we can't have more panic over there. Orders from the mayor. And another thing. My contacts on the Island tell me you're involved with that Rosen woman. That worries me, Joe D."

Joe D. couldn't believe it. Was Castiglia turning soft on him, offering words of wisdom from one older and wiser?

"For starters, I don't want any bedside confessions to compromise the case, if you know what I mean . . ."

So much for turning soft. "Chief, I—"

"Now let me finish. I also happen to know you're practically engaged"—that phrase again!—"to Marie. So no good is going to come from this thing you're having with Miss Rosen. Get what you can from her by way of information, but stop there, you hear me?"

"Chief, you old softy," Joe D. muttered from the side of his mouth.

"What was that?"

"Nothing," he said, and left.

Alison opened the door to her apartment at six o'clock that evening wearing a long quilted bathrobe. An air-conditioned gust smacked Joe D. in the face. "You look like you're ready for bed," he said.

She smiled weakly, like a politician after a day of campaigning. "Joe, what are you doing here?"

He shivered from the cold and wondered about people like Alison and his Chief, who thrived in frigid rooms like big, sensitive computers. "I had a little business in the **149** city," he lied, "so I thought I'd stop by." He knew he should have called to say he was coming, but he hadn't wanted to take the chance that she'd tell him not to bother. With Alison that chance was all too real. "Why, are you busy?"

"No, not really, but I just never expected to see you . . ."

Now he understood. "You never thought you'd see me here, in New York, in your apartment, on your turf, is that it?"

"Something like that."

"In fact, you *hoped* you'd never see me here."

"No, Joe, I—"

"What is it with you, Alison?" he interrupted. "I thought we had a really fantastic weekend together. Two days later it's like we hardly know each other."

"We do hardly know each other."

"I think I got to know you pretty well Saturday night on the beach."

Her smile widened a bit, her resistance weakening despite a valiant struggle.

"And later, back in your room."

He could see her relenting, thawing. "My being here, on your territory, kind of makes it more real, doesn't it, Alison? Makes it a real relationship, which scares the shit out of you. This isn't some teenage beach romance, Alison. We're a little old for that sort of thing."

"God knows. All right, come in, but just for a drink. I'm really beat."

Chapter

THE radio switched on at 6:45 the next morning. Joe D. leaned over and turned it off with some difficulty, toppling a number of unidentified objects on Alison's night table. He felt blissfully happy here in Alison's bed. The sheets smelled fresh and sweet; it was nice waking up in a woman's bed, real nice. With Marie it was always his bed they woke up in on the rare occasions when she stayed the night.

Alison rolled over and nuzzled up to him. "Give me four good reasons why I shouldn't go to work today," she said drowsily.

"One, I'm here. Two, you work too hard."

"How do you know?"

"I just know. Three, Bloomingdale's will get along without you today."

"Wrong. I'm indispensable."

"Four, you don't want to."

"Right on that one."

"And five—"

"I only asked for four."

"Five, I won't let you."

"You won't?"

"No way." He grabbed her, pulled her toward him, and kept her there, using every strategy he could think of, for half an hour.

"You could become habit-forming," Alison said later, holding him.

"Would that be so bad?"

"Didn't your mother tell you habits were bad for you?"

"Only bad habits. Anyway, let's not get out of bed at all today. Or tomorrow. We'll set a record or something."

"I'd love to, I really would." She nuzzled his chest and Joe D. felt her weakening. Then, suddenly, she pushed back the covers and sprang from the bed.

"Hey, no fair. I gave you five reasons for not going to work."

"I only asked for four!" she shouted from the bathroom. "Don't you know you should never give a person more than she asks for? Makes her suspicious. Anyway, who says life is fair?"

"I do."

"Too bad you don't make the rules." She reappeared in the doorway, naked. Perfectly naked, Joe D. thought. "Or sign paychecks. But I'll make a deal with you. I'll give you a shower you'll never forget if you'll promise not to give me a hard time about going to work."

Now, this was a deal Joe D. found difficult to resist. So he didn't bother trying.

Alison was a blur of activity from the moment she stepped out of the shower. Joe D. sat in the living room of her small one-bedroom apartment, a towel wrapped around **152** his waist, and watched her with awe.

"Well, what do you think of weekday Alison?" she asked, presenting herself before him for inspection wearing a blue suit over a white silk blouse.

Joe D. was totally unprepared for Alison's corporate look. She was still beautiful—it would take more than a suit to change that—but now she was something else: sophisticated, competent, authoritative. "Very nice," he replied. "Very imposing."

Her face dropped. "You don't like it."

"No, I do, I really do. What's wrong with imposing?"

"Nothing, it's just the look I'm aiming for," she pouted. "The 'hands-off' look. The 'caution: iceberg ahead' look. Next time remind me not to ask."

"Come on, Alison. It's just that the first time I met you you were wearing a bathing suit. I guess I'll never get used to seeing you dressed."

She threw him a skeptical look. "Listen, I'm late already. You can let yourself out without a key. The door locks automatically. Make yourself a cup of coffee and help yourself to whatever you find in the fridge." Before the door shut behind her she poked her head back in. "Call me," she said gently. He felt triumphant.

The refrigerator contained three cartons of yogurt, five cans of Tab (one opened, and flat), a head of wilted lettuce, and a container of cottage cheese. Joe D. decided he wasn't hungry. He recalled the dinner she'd made for him on the beach. Apparently Alison only cooked for special occasions; a cockroach could starve in this place. He made himself a cup of coffee and called his station for messages. Marie had called several times last night, and a Mr. Levinson from Brooklyn, who'd wanted Joe D. to call him as soon as possible.

"Where the hell were you anyway?" asked the operator. She was an older woman, a forty-year police department employee, and a friend of Joe D.'s mother.

"Working on a case," he replied. The unintentional honesty of his response brought him down to earth with a painful thud. He walked across the living room with his coffee. It was a rectangular room, on the small side, and sparsely furnished: a long sofa upholstered in a brown-and-white striped pattern, an old, caned rocking chair, a wooden coffee table, a tall, narrow bookcase—these were the only furnishings of the room, which was surprisingly pleasant, even cheerful. Only the drapes seemed out of place, disproportionately heavy. He parted them with his free hand. The window looked out over First Avenue. Across the way sat a white-brick building much like Alison's. Fifteen stories down, the crowded sidewalks flowed fast in one direction: downtown, where the money's made. He could see women in suits and sneakers carrying briefcases, and men in suits and loafers carrying briefcases, and the scene depressed him with its focused energy, its hurried intensity. He psyched himself for the two calls he had to make, finished his coffee, and dialed.

"Mr. Golland, this is Joe DiGregorio. I think we should talk some more. No, Mr. Golland, you didn't tell me everything you knew. For starters, you never mentioned your affair with Linda Levinson."

There was a pause at the other end. Joe D. let it ride for a few seconds, planning his strategy. He decided he wouldn't meet Golland in his office: the man was too much in control there, seemed almost to draw strength from the place, with its view that reduced people to mites five hundred feet below. He'd meet him someplace where they'd be on equal footing. Equal footing . . . that gave him an idea.

"We'll meet just outside Central Park. Sixtieth and Fifth, at noon."

"Mr. Levinson? This is Joe DiGregorio. From the Waterside police."

Mr. Levinson whispered into the phone: "I'll call you back in a few minutes. From a pay phone. My wife . . ."

Joe D. barely managed to give him Alison's phone number before he hung up. He rang back ten minutes later.

"Lieutenant, I feel there is something I should tell you. About six months ago Linda gave me a key to a safety-deposit box. She said if anything was to happen to her . . ."

He paused to compose himself, then resumed in a voice that waivered with restrained emotion. "She said if something happened, I could open it up and keep what was inside. I asked her if something was wrong, but she said no, nothing was wrong, but you never know. I asked her what was in the box because I couldn't think what she could have so valuable she would need a safety-deposit box. She said it was just money. I said she should keep her money in a savings account but she said this money is different, this is her escape money. 'What do you need escape money for?' I asked her. 'Escape from what?' She didn't answer me. Made it clear I shouldn't ask her any more about it. And I never did."

"How much money was there in the box, Mr. Levinson?"

Joe D. heard him inhale deeply. "One hundred and fifty thousand dollars." He repeated the amount, slowly and precisely, like a chant. "I went to look in the box just yesterday, didn't have the heart for it any earlier. It was in a bank over in Manhattan, near where she lives." He started to correct himself but stopped. The inaccurate use of the present tense seemed to tilt the fragile balance between grief and composure in favor of grief for a moment. Joe D. let him work it out in silence.

"I never saw so much money in one place before," he resumed. "I tell you I was so frightened, looking at it, I put it back and ran out of that bank as fast as I could. It looked so evil, lying there in that box. I keep asking myself, what could Linda have been doing with so much money? What did she want to escape from so badly she needed a hundred and fifty thousand dollars?"

Joe D. thought this over for a moment. Jonathan Golland was what she needed to escape from, he'd bet his life on it. Well, not his life, maybe; this case was getting more complicated by the minute and he was learning the hard way not to count on anything. "Was there anything else in the box, a note or anything, other than the money?"

"Just one little piece of paper, clipped to ten thousand dollars, a hundred hundred-dollar bills. I wish I could explain to you how evil it looked—my hand shook holding it. It's shaking now, just thinking about it."

"What did it say, the note?"

"It said 'Baby Bear, ten thousand dollars.' In Linda's handwriting. Just 'Baby Bear' and then the amount, ten thousand dollars. Now what do you think it means?"

"Don't know," answered Joe D. "The words mean nothing to you?"

"Nothing."

There was a silence as they both pondered the incongruity of those two silly words connected to so much money.

"Lieutenant, this would kill my wife, to think our Linda was involved in any wrongdoing. All we have now is our memory of her. I couldn't kill that too for my wife, you understand?"

"I understand."

"One other thing, Lieutenant. About the boyfriend. Did you find him?"

"I think so, Mr. Levinson."

"So tell me, is he a good man?"

"Yes, I think so," Joe D. lied.

"And is his heart broken too?"

"Yes," Joe D. lied again. "I think so."

Chapter

16

JOE D. almost didn't recognize Golland, he looked that different. Is it possible, he wondered as they entered Central Park, that the man had shrunk since the last time they had met, in Golland's office? Of course, he only *seemed* smaller because Joe D. had something on him, knew him, now, to be less than the coldly perfect corporate lawyer he had appeared to be just a week ago.

"Linda and I were fanatics about keeping our relationship quiet," he began. "We were together seven years, and no one in the office even suspected."

Joe D. was sorely tempted to set Golland straight on this but held back, an inner voice whispering that knowledge is power, but only if it isn't shared.

"I hated myself for continuing the affair, and now, well you can imagine what I'm going through."

Actually, Joe D. had trouble imagining any such thing. Sure, Golland looked defeated, but like a defeated politician the morning after the election: self-righteous, self-pity-ing, and no doubt planning a recuperative vacation, where he'll contemplate his next move.

"You could have left your wife, married Linda," was all Joe D. said.

"Out of the question. There was never talk of any such thing. Linda understood that—I never deceived her for a minute. Well, maybe when we first started seeing each other, but not after that."

Not after it was too late, not after she was hooked, Joe D. thought, feeling suddenly indignant for Linda. "Why not leave your wife, if you really loved Linda?"

"I told you, I did love her."

"And I heard you. So why not leave your wife?"

"I told you that, as well. It was out of the question. Impossible."

"Everybody gets divorced these days, even lawyers like yourself."

"That's where you're wrong. Lawyers do get divorced, but not lawyers like myself."

"You mean, lawyers who happen to be married to daughters of very rich and powerful men."

"That's exactly what I meant," answered Golland frost-ily; Joe D. suspected Golland would rather discuss his late lover than his living wife. "Now, I'd prefer we didn't pur-sue this particular topic," he said, confirming Joe D.'s sus-picion. "It's not particularly relevant to the matter at hand, so I'm in no way obligated to discuss it further. Suffice it to say that I loved Linda very much, that I was unable to di-vorce my wife for reasons that are, frankly, none of your business, and that Linda was well aware of this almost from the start."

"Knowing all this, why did Linda stay with you so long?"

Golland flashed Joe D. a look that combined anger, con-fusion, and indignation, the look Darryl Strawberry would flash if you asked him why the Dodgers pay him so much. *Because I'm good,* his eyes seemed to say, *because I'm good.*

What his lips said was: "Linda tried breaking off, oh, I'd say every six months or so. But it was no use. She used to say her whole life was tied to me—her job, her personal life. I helped her with her rent, paid for most of her wardrobe. Before me, she dressed like a slob. She had no sense of style at all. I taught her how to dress like a woman. I showed her how to make the most of her assets, which, for your information, were considerable. She'd end it now and then, and I swear to you I would make no effort to get her back. I wouldn't call her, plead with her, nothing. I even offered to find her a new job."

Sure, you made no move, thought Joe D. You still had a rich wife and at least one other girlfriend to fall back on. What did Linda Levinson have except a crummy secretarial job and a share on Fire Island?

And a hundred and fifty thousand dollars, cash.

"But she'd always end up walking into my office at around six o'clock, looking just as beautiful as could be, and hurt too, like an injured child. 'Take me to dinner,' she'd say. It was always the same, just 'Take me to dinner,' which was her way of saying 'I'm back.' She always used to say she was addicted to me, that the only way she could leave me once and for all was to quit her job, give up her apartment, perhaps move to another city."

"Escape," Joe D. muttered.

"Yes, exactly the word she used. 'I need to find a way to escape from you,' she'd say, as if I were keeping her against her will. I suppose she finally did find her escape."

Central Park was full of people looking for noontime respite from the hot and humid city. If they found relief here, it was a miracle, for it felt even hotter in the park, almost tropical, and the crowds and the constant movement only **159** made it worse. Central Park looked worn and tired, like an abused and mangy dog left in a pen to sleep fitfully under the blazing sun. Listening to Golland describe Linda Levinson's love for him only made it seem uglier for Joe D. If a vial of crack could describe how an addict felt about it, it would sound like Golland was sounding now.

Joe D. couldn't take any more of Golland's piety and decided to change the topic. "What exactly were you doing on the night Linda was killed?"

"I think you've been watching a few too many episodes of—"

"I asked you a question," he interrupted.

"Lieutenant, I didn't kill Linda, I assure you." He affected a bored tone, but there was an anxious edge to his voice.

"I repeat: what were you doing the night Linda was killed?"

"I was with my wife at our home in Scarsdale. Watching television, I imagine."

"Will she back you up?"

"Of course she will, but you must realize that going to her with this . . . story would be devastating to her."

"To her, Mr. Golland, or to you?"

Golland stopped suddenly and turned to Joe D. "You don't like me very much, Lieutenant, do you? You think I'm an insensitive, spoiled fat cat. Isn't that true, Lieutenant?"

Joe D. said nothing, but couldn't suppress an uncomfortable smile.

"You don't believe me when I tell you I loved Linda, and you don't believe me when I tell you I couldn't, absolutely couldn't leave my wife, either. If I told you my life for the past seven years alternated between extreme happiness with Linda and the blackest, emptiest unhappiness with my . . . the rest of the time, you probably wouldn't believe me either. Would you, Lieutenant?"

"Mr. Golland, I don't think we have to . . ."

Something caught his attention, something at the outer edge of his vision. A sudden movement, out of sync with the smooth, practiced rhythm of the park's noontime flow. Distracted by Golland's lecture, Joe D. couldn't focus his attention long or hard enough to figure out what he'd seen, but he knew it was something. No, it was some*one,* someone familiar.

"You feel smug yourself, don't you, Lieutenant?" he continued, on a roll. "You feel contempt for me because I deceived my wife and kept Linda from living a normal life. But I ask you, have you never deceived anyone? Have you been totally honest and completely faithful at all times?"

Alison and Marie marched across Joe D.'s mind like leads in a morality play.

"I can see by your hesitation that you've been guilty of at least some deception. Just as I thought. Perhaps even now you're deceiving someone and you don't like being reminded of it."

True enough, Joe D. thought, feeling his control of the conversation deserting him. Sweat was soaking through his shirt like an advancing tide. They passed a junior-executive type scoring loose joints from a wiry black man. Even Golland did a double take, the transaction was so obvious. But Joe D. was again conscious of something unusual, of a presence more out of place than the dealer. Now he was positive: they were being followed.

"So you can get down off your high horse, Lieutenant. I told you I loved Linda. I had no motive for killing her, and no opportunity. If you pursue this any further you'll be wasting your time as well as mine. And furthermore, I could see to it that your future with the Bayside police—"

"Waterside."

"—Waterside police is less than brilliant, if you catch my drift, Lieutenant. I am a politically well-connected man, even in Nassau County."

"Suffolk," corrected Joe D., reasserting his authority. His concentration was split now between Golland and the person following them. He tried to keep from turning around suddenly, not wanting to scare this person off.

"There too."

Along the edge of the lake, near Fifty-ninth Street, secretaries and young executives picnicked and sunbathed, while scavengers picked through garbage bins for returnable cans. Pigeons cooed half-heartedly from the branches of ginkgoes and maples, swollen goldfish moved listlessly through the dark, still water, and all the while the sun pierced through smog and humidity to radiate a milky heat that slowed everyone, even the pigeons, it seemed, to a cautious, tentative pace.

"But you have to admit, Linda's being out of the way *is* convenient."

"In what sense? I told you I loved her."

The word love was beginning to annoy Joe D. Golland used it like an alibi and it was wearing thin. "Now you're free for . . . other interests." These last two words seemed to touch a raw nerve in Golland. "What are you talking about?" he asked with a toss of his head that was meant to look casual but came off more like an epileptic spasm.

"You know exactly what I'm talking about. Linda wasn't your only girl, even if she was your steadiest."

Joe D. felt the advantage tipping his way once more. If someone's going to be on a high horse, Joe D. thought, still waiting for an opportunity to get a look at the person following them, it might as well be me.

"Or let's say Linda finally confronted you, threatened to tell your wife everything. You'd have killed her before you'd have risked a divorce from Dinnerman's."

"She never threatened me and I didn't kill her."

"How much money did you give her, Golland?" The *mister* had vanished along with Golland's upper hand.

162   "I told you, I helped her with her rent—half of it, to be precise—and I bought her gifts. Jewelry, clothes, a fur coat, that type of thing."

"Loose joints," said a black man in a linty ski-hat as they passed, the voice automatic, tired.

"But not large amounts of cash?"

"Of course not. As you have so industriously discovered, I am married to a wealthy woman. I also make a handsome living at Strickman, Cohen, Allen and Golland. But my wife's money is her own—or her father's—so I'm hardly in a position to make large gifts of cash."

"What were you doing in Linda's apartment last Tuesday?"

He looked only mildly surprised. "I thought it might be you."

Joe D. nodded, still resisting the urge to spin around, see if someone were—no, see *who* was following them.

"Collecting some things. Nothing sinister, I assure you. A few letters I'd sent her, some photographs of the two of us, that sort of thing. She kept them in an inlaid teak jewelry box we bought together in Hong Kong on a business trip." He smiled slyly here. "It has a false bottom— nothing elaborate, but at the time it appealed to our sense of intrigue, and apparently it fooled the first round of cops who searched her place. So I didn't think I needed to risk returning there myself. But then last week I called the Levinsons to arrange to have some of Linda's personal things, things she kept in the office, sent to them. And they mentioned that you'd been to see them and that they'd given you a key to Linda's apartment. I didn't want to risk a second search by the police, so I raced over there at once. Naturally I had no idea I'd be up against a modern-day Sherlock Holmes from Bayside, Long Island."

"Waterside."

"Wherever."

A large group of children, probably a camp group, ap-

163

proached them on the path, forcing Joe D. and Golland to separate for a few moments to let them by. When the group had passed, Joe D. was a few steps ahead of Golland. Joe D. took this opportunity to turn quickly around without tipping off the person following them. He spotted nothing unusual right away; it wasn't until they were side by side again, walking, that it registered: the chiseled face, the deep-set eyes, the powerful build, visible even under the business suit. He'd vanished back into the crowd after a split second, but his image was stained on Joe D.'s memory; there could be no mistaking who he'd seen.

Eric Farber. Whose business card had indicated that he worked as a broker at Fried & Sons. All the way down on Wall Street.

Central Park is a long way to come for a picnic lunch, Joe D. thought.

"Ever heard of Fried and Sons?"

"Of course, who hasn't?"

"Do you do business with them?"

He considered this for a moment. "They're not a client, if that's what you mean. Some of our partners may have personal accounts with them, but I really couldn't say for sure."

"Know any of their brokers?"

"I just told you, I—"

"Know Eric Farber?"

Joe D. watched closely as Golland answered. "Never heard of him," he said with perfect evenness.

"How about Baby Bear?"

"I beg your pardon."

"Baby Bear. Does it mean anything to you?"

Golland shook his head.

"Not a nickname for Linda or anything?"

"It means nothing to me at all, Lieutenant. Absolutely

164 nothing."

They had made a full circle and were back where they'd started, opposite the Plaza. "Now if you don't mind, I must get back to the office. You know where to reach me if you need anything further. I sincerely hope you don't."

Joe D. wandered slowly around the park after Golland left him, hoping to draw Farber out. When, after a half hour, he hadn't spotted him, he sat on a bench and thought about the significance of Farber's being in the park that afternoon. A coincidence? No, Farber was following them, he'd sensed it all along. Following *them*? Or following one of them? And which one? Was there a connection between Golland and Farber, despite Golland's denial, or was Farber merely following Joe D.? If Farber had been tailing him, then he'd seen him leave Alison's that morning. A chill ran through him as he recalled Alison's suspicion that *she* was being watched.

There wasn't a whole lot he could do until he got to Fire Island on Friday, and this lack of any compelling reason to leave the park made it tough to get up from the bench. His conversation with Golland had depressed him, and spotting Farber had confirmed that Alison might be in danger, which frightened him. Golland denied he was the source of Linda's $150,000, but of course Golland could have been lying. It was quite possible that Linda had been blackmailing Golland for some time and that he'd finally got fed up and killed her. He could easily have hopped a late ferry that Friday night, waited outside Crane's for her, and strangled her on her way home. Then, Golland could have fled Seaside Harbor on a water taxi, though none of the taxi "drivers" remembered taking anyone back to Waterside after midnight.

There were other possibilities: Golland could have spent the night on the island, sleeping under someone's deck or even on the beach. Joe D. could more easily envision the **165** impeccably groomed Golland walking on water back to Long Island, however, than sleeping on the damp, cold ground like a derelict. Or he may have hired a boat in Waterside. Joe D. made a mental note to ask someone back in Waterside to check out the harbor to see if anyone remembered renting a boat to a middle-aged man that night. Then, too, Golland could simply have hired someone to kill Linda. Golland struck Joe D. as someone who would do anything to keep his marriage—and, with it, his career— intact. Like Linda, he was addicted, but with Golland it wasn't love he craved, it was money, his father-in-law's money and the power that went along with it, like free cocktails with a first-class plane ticket. Addicted, too, to Linda herself and God knows how many other pretty young things. But not love. In Joe D.'s experience, people who used the word *love* as often as Golland did rarely had the slightest notion of what it was. "You don't know the value of money," his mother used to scold him when he'd spend his lunch money on pinball or baseball cards. It was the same with Golland: he used the word *love* carelessly because he didn't know the value of it.

Unlike Linda, Golland wanted no escape from his addictions. On the contrary, Joe D. reflected, like the worst of addicts he'd do anything for a fix of money, power, and girls. Murder? It seemed almost beneath Golland, but then, so did walking. There was a menacing coldness about him, like a piece of steel on a freezing winter day: touch it and your skin sticks painfully to it; pull away from it and your skin rips off.

Joe D. sighed and stood up. Central Park looked like a parade had just come through. Wearing yesterday's clothes, he felt trampled, like the brown, beaten grass all around him. Even Farber's golden aura seemed sullied by his presence in the park. What was Farber doing there? Was it Golland he was following, or him? It seemed every question he asked was answered with still another question. Joe D. was tired of asking questions.

Walking back to his car, he thought of Golland's sermon on deception. He thought of the mess he was making of Alison's life, of Marie's life, of his own life. Why, he wondered, was it so much easier to get into trouble than to get out of it?

At least, he pleaded to no one but himself, let me produce a murderer for all the mess I'm making.

Chapter

IN his small apartment back in Waterside—two furnished rooms over the garage of a private home—Joe D. considered calling Alison but decided not to. With Alison it was best to hold off. He had the feeling that one premature move and she'd run like a spooked horse. Still, he hoped she was at least in her apartment, behind her three locks and out of the reach of whoever was following her.

He also resisted the urge to call Marie—with considerably less difficulty. If he called her she'd want to see him, and if he saw her he'd end up comparing her to Alison.

The phone rang around ten that night. He answered, hoping it was Alison. It was.

"You bastard," she greeted him. "You goddamn prick. I hate you. I despise you. You make me sick. You're a scumbag. You're the lowest son of a bitch I—"

Joe D. sensed she'd have no trouble continuing on this course indefinitely, but interrupting her thesaurus of abuse proved difficult.

"Alison, what the hell—?"

"You know very well what the hell. You asshole. I hate you, you hear me? I hope you drop dead tomorrow. No, tonight. You lying—"

"Alison!"

"—deceitful, selfish—"

"Alison, I don't understand . . ." But of course he did understand.

"No? How's this for starters? I called the Levinsons this evening to see how they were doing. Guess what? They said there's this really nice young lieutenant from the Waterside police force working on the case. Care to guess what his name is?"

"Alison, I—"

"DiGregorio is his name. Now, isn't that a coincidence? Joseph DiGregorio. They have a lot of confidence in you, the Levinsons do. Think the world of you in fact. But then they don't know what a schmuck you are, *Lieutenant.*" She hissed his title with such venom that everything she'd just called him now seemed like hosannas in comparison. "Lieutenant": spit from her mouth like a watermelon pit, the word sounded like evil itself.

There was a pause while Alison regrouped her attack force of one. Joe D. used the interval to plan his defense, but she didn't give him a chance.

"How could you be so awful?" she sputtered, and hung up.

He dialed her number but it was busy. A minute later he tried again: still busy. He continued dialing for some time, over and over and over again until the sound of the dial tone, the clicking of the rotary dial, and the busy signal became soothingly familiar, like Hail Marys in church. Problem was, his confessor wouldn't answer, so after a while he got in his car and drove into the city.

Forty-five minutes later, stalled in traffic on the Triborough Bridge, he concentrated on Manhattan Island, glittering off to his left across the East River. He tried to spot landmarks—it beat thinking about Alison, about his lack of any acceptable justification for what he'd done to her. The Empire State Building, the Chrysler Building, Citicorp, the World Trade Center in the hazy distance: they sparkled like distant galaxies. Manhattan looked impregnable now, as if surrounded not only by rivers but by a protective aura. Don't mess with me, it glowered, I'm bigger than you are, and stronger—and a part of him was tempted to obey.

"Alison, if you don't let me in, I'll just stand out here making a scene."

"Then I'll call the cops and have them take you away."

"I am a cop, remember?"

"How could I forget? From shitty little Waterside. If you don't leave me alone, I'll call a real cop. A New York cop."

"Come on, Alison, just give me five minutes to explain. Then you'll never have to see me again, I swear."

"What's to explain? You're a creep, period. And I hate you, period."

Five minutes more of pleading finally wore her down. She opened the door slowly, wearing a flannel nightgown (the air-conditioning was on full-blast; it was like entering a meat locker) and slammed it after him.

"Don't bother sitting down," she welcomed him.

"Alison, I wish you'd try to understand. My orders were to find Linda's killer. Part of that meant getting to know you. I had no choice."

"Oh, and did getting to know me mean fucking me?"

Joe D. winced at this vulgarization of their relationship. Their former relationship. "The relationship that developed between us had nothing to do with the case."

"Oh, so now it was a relationship, was it? You've got a lot of nerve."

170   "Yes, it *was* a relationship, Alison." He was fighting for

his life now, practically shouting. "I . . . I fell in love with you. There, now I've said it. I fell in love with you. I love you."

The way Alison flinched, it was as if he'd raised a hand to her. Even Joe D. was taken aback by his own confession, realizing for the first time that he had, in fact, fallen in love with her.

"If you hadn't been so on-again, off-again about us, I might have told you everything," he continued, afraid to stop and sensing she was beginning to weaken. "But shit, I was even afraid to ask you to dinner tonight, afraid you'd run in the opposite direction."

Alison paced the length of the living room, her arms crossed against the air-conditioning, shaking her head. "I can't believe you have the nerve to accuse *me* of anything when you lied to me and used me at a time when you knew I'd be vulnerable."

Joe D. had no defense to this.

"And what's really *killing* me," she continued, talking more to herself than to him, "is that I'm falling for it." She threw up her hands. "I'm falling for it! Why, I don't know. Maybe it's because you said you love me, not that I believe you for a second, but it's been a while—a long while— since a man other than my father said 'I love you" to me, and it feels good." She was facing the window of her living room (or, rather, the drawn drapes), not him.

"Or maybe you're in love yourself," he ventured nervously.

She turned to him. "Hah, that's a laugh. I had trouble enough with you as an Italian accountant. But an Italian cop? Forget it. That's not exactly what I had in mind."

"What exactly *did* you have in mind?"

"For starters, a cop just doesn't rate in my book of romance candidates."

"You'd prefer—"

"I'd prefer . . . well, maybe I don't know what I want, but why should I have to justify my tastes to you?"

"Anything but a lowly cop, that's what you're saying, isn't it? You'd like a professional man, a man with a law degree or medical certificate."

"Well, why not? I went to college, I've worked hard to get where I am, and now I'm supposed to fall in love with a cop? No way. I bet I make twice as much as you do." She hurled this last sentence at him like a kick below the belt. It found its target.

"Alison, you're not making sense." Even her voice was unfamiliar, higher and sharper than usual, which only confirmed for Joe D. that this wasn't Alison speaking but some hot vein of anger and defensiveness that ran inside her.

"Aren't I? Well then, let's just leave the topic of your chosen profession for a moment and move on to the little question of religion. I can just picture it. 'Mom, Dad, I have some good news and some bad news. First the good news: at long last Princess Alison is getting married. Now for the bad news: he's not Jewish, he's Italian, and, as if that weren't bad enough, he's a cop.' It'd kill them. *Kill them.*"

"No, it wouldn't. It would kill you. Because it wouldn't fit into your master plan. How did you put it? I'm not *what you had in mind.* Well, I got news for you, Alison. The master plan isn't working. You're way behind schedule. Maybe it's time to revise your precious plan." He was angry with her now and felt like continuing. But he stopped himself. What he'd done to her was unforgivable; he'd forfeited his right to lecture on honesty and trust.

They said nothing for a few moments—there really was nothing more *to* say—and stared at each other, both reluctant to make the next move. Finally he turned to leave.

"Joe," she said softly, faltering over the single syllable. **172** From the door he could barely hear her.

He turned around. Alison stood in the center of the living room, her arms still crossed, her face locked in a mask of grim resignation. "Say it again, what you said before, about what you feel about me." She said it with all the enthusiasm of a patient telling a doctor it was all right to stick the needle in now.

"I love you, Alison."

Her eyes closed for a second, then opened. She nodded: the medicine had been taken and was helping.

He turned once again and was about to open the door when she called him a second time.

"I shouldn't have attacked you the way I did. It's just that I was hurt and scared and . . ." She began to cry.

Joe D. crossed the room, took her in his arms. "I do love you, Alison. I do. God, I wanted to tell you everything, but I just didn't know how. I was afraid I'd scare you off."

She kissed him hungrily. He could feel her warm tears against his own face. "This isn't right," she said, "but I can't help it, I can't."

"Now it's your turn, Alison. Say you love me."

She smiled and kissed him.

"No, really, say it, please." She touched his lips with her fingers, deflecting his request.

"It's because I'm not what you had in mind, is that it?"

She shrugged in place of answering.

"If you're afraid of getting involved, Alison, I'll understand, just—"

"I'm not afraid," she said quickly.

But she was, he could feel it, her whole body tensing. "But you do love me, correct?"

She said nothing. He stared into her upturned face for a few moments. He thought he detected a slight nod, a tremor, as if she were responding against her will. "I guess that will have to do for now," he said, picking her up easily and carrying her into her bedroom.

173

Chapter

HE relaxed in her bed the following morning, Thursday, while she dressed for work.

"I wish you'd call in sick so we could play," he called out to her in the bathroom.

"You accountants sure don't work very hard."

He smiled.

"Besides, we've been through this before. I *have* to work, that's all there is to it. Don't you have some investigating to do today?"

"I left my magnifying glass back in Waterside."

Now it was Alison's turn to smile.

"Actually, there's not much I can do until I get to Seaside Harbor on Friday."

"Tell me about the case," she asked when she finished dressing. They had coffee at her small dining table while he related his progress.

"I can't believe it," she said after learning of Linda's

seven-year affair with Golland. "I feel so stupid. I mean, I knew there was *someone,* and I knew he was married, but her boss? Maybe it was just so obvious I never thought about it . . ."

"Alison, why didn't you tell the police that Linda had a lover?"

"I just told you, I didn't know who he was."

"But you could at least have told us that there was someone."

"You're right, of course you're right. But the strange thing is, on that awful Saturday, the day they found Linda's body and questioned me back at the house in Seaside Harbor, Linda's having a lover never occurred to me. Maybe because she kept that part of her life so separate from the rest, me included. We weren't all that close, Joe D., not confidantes, really. I don't think Linda had friends like that. But I liked her an awful lot, and I miss her, too."

Her voice had begun to waver; she paused a few moments to steady herself.

"Maybe if I'd known his name, her lover's name, I'd have told the police about him. I don't know. In any case, later that night I realized I'd forgotten to mention that Linda was involved with someone, and I thought about calling the cops and decided in the end not to. I mean, I figured it was a random thing, she was killed by a stranger, not someone she knew. It just seemed like a betrayal. You met her parents. How would they feel about learning that their daughter was fooling around with her married boss? And to be honest, calling the cops, maybe even having them come to my apartment for further questioning, just didn't appeal to me all that much. I just couldn't go through another session with them."

"You have a real thing against cops, you know."

She smiled, and then was silent for a bit.

"Summer weekends must have been hard for Linda, with

175

Golland in Scarsdale with his family. I suppose that's why she always took a share in Fire Island. You know, she was acting a little different the day she died, that Friday. Happier than usual, yet nervous, edgy. Now I remember: she said she'd made a decision, and felt good about it."

"That jibes with what the receptionist at her office said. Did she tell you what the decision was?"

Alison shook her head. "I hoped she might have decided to drop the married boyfriend, but I thought I'd let her tell me when she was ready."

"Do you think Linda was blackmailing him?"

"Absolutely not. She didn't have it in her. Not malicious enough. Not malicious at all."

"But remember the money . . ."

"Yes, all that money. Where could she have gotten it?"

They sat in silence for a few moments. "Alison, where does Eric Farber fit into all this?"

"Beats me. They weren't really friends as far as I knew, though now I'm wondering how much I really knew about Linda."

"But she did sleep with him at least once, or at any rate she was in his room, alone with him . . ."

Alison looked puzzled. "No way. Linda would have told me if anything had gone on. She always did."

"Like she told you about Golland?"

"All right, I see your point. But she always told me about all her other affairs, I'm sure of it."

"Did she have many?"

"One or two a summer. Not affairs exactly, one-nighters would be more accurate. She called them anatomical events." She smiled, but then the memory of this joke they had shared seemed to sadden her. When she resumed speaking after a short silence it was in a strained voice. "They never seemed to interest her much, these episodes. It was Golland she wanted; the anatomical events just

passed the time."

"If you're sure that Linda never had a thing going with Farber, then what was she doing in his room? And what about those appointments with her I saw marked on his calendar? I haven't heard anything about his dealing drugs."

"Linda wasn't into drugs. She did a little grass sometimes, once in a while some coke or a 'lude, but she never bought any herself and she certainly wouldn't sleep with a guy just to get high. If she liked him, that would be one thing, but not just for the drugs."

"You sound like you knew her pretty well, but don't forget she might not have been the person you thought she was."

"That seems to be par for the course lately."

Joe D. ignored the crack. "So you're sure she had no interest in Farber?"

"Positive. She never was the least bit attracted to him. I know because we discussed him, because, well, because *I* thought he was good-looking."

"What you had in mind?" Joe D. asked.

"Exactly what I had in mind, thank you."

"And then there's Rob Lewis."

"I can't believe he's mixed up in this. I mean, just because a guy can't get it up once doesn't make him a killer, does it?"

"So you think he didn't do it?"

"I don't know. He seemed awfully angry, fierce, even, the night Linda was killed. You tell me, would a guy kill a woman over such a thing?"

Joe D. thought about it. "Maybe in the heat of the moment, if she was taunting him over it and he was a little nuts to begin with. But not a week later. Unless he thought she was spreading rumors about him, humiliating him. Seaside Harbor is a small town and sex is what it's all about, it's what keeps the place going. A rumor like that could really destroy a guy."

They sipped their coffee in silence for a bit. "What's your next step, Joe D.?"

"Good question. The truth is there isn't much I can do until I get back to Fire Island. This weekend, things have really got to happen, though. My chief is putting on the pressure something fierce. I'm going to have to take a few chances."

"Such as . . ."

"Confrontations. Stir things up. But I don't want you involved, Alison. Maybe it's best we stay away from each other this weekend."

"Forget it. You couldn't keep me away from this case now if you tried."

Joe D. affected a hurt look. With his doleful, almond-shaped eyes this was not difficult. "So it's the case you're really interested in, not me," he said half-seriously.

"Oh, all right," she said, rolling her eyes. "If it will make you happy, I'll say it: you couldn't keep me away from you either, Joe DiGregorio. Honestly, you men and your needs."

Chapter

19

THEY waited several minutes for the elevator, and when it finally arrived at Alison's floor they had to squeeze in among suited men and women wearing the long, resigned faces of people about to face an ordeal. "What you had in mind?" Joe D. whispered to Alison, nodding at a tall man of about thirty wearing a blue pinstripe suit, a rich-looking red silk tie, a gold collar-pin, and tasseled loafers. "Exactly what I had in mind," she answered, smiling, "and don't press your luck, Lieutenant." They made several stops on the way down and people continued to jam into the elevator even when it seemed it could hold no more. Joe D. was beginning to wonder if he were participating in a fraternity stunt.

They filed out silently and headed in a stream toward the revolving door. "Miss Rosen!" called the doorman from his station behind a counter to the left of the door. "I have something for you." He held out a plain white envelope, sealed shut.

"It was dropped off for you an hour ago by a messenger." Alison opened the envelope and unfolded a sheet of white paper. She read it, then handed it to Joe D., looking concerned.

> Valentine's Day 1976. Madison College.
> Tell your boyfriend.

"Does this mean anything to you?" he asked, rereading the message, which was neatly typed and centered on the page.

She shook her head. "It's about the case, I assume. About Linda."

"Definitely. And what worries me is that whoever wrote it is getting you involved, Alison. I didn't want that to happen."

She put her arm through his. He could feel her trembling slightly.

"Do you remember which messenger service delivered this?" he asked the doorman, who shook his head. "Didn't notice," he said.

Turning back to Alison: "Does Madison College mean anything to you?"

She considered this for a moment. "No, not really. I know a few people who went there, but other than that . . ."

"Did anyone involved in the case go to Madison? Farber? Lewis? Linda?"

"Not Linda, that I know. Farber and Lewis I couldn't say."

"Where is Madison?"

"It's somewhere in Connecticut, a couple of hours away."

"I guess my day's pretty well set, then."

"I want to come with you."

"But you have to go to work, remember?"

"I'll call in sick. I haven't taken a sick day in three years."

"Sorry. I don't want you more involved than you already are. And try not to be alone today if you can help it. I think your suspicions about being followed were correct."

"Well, *you* be careful, too," she said, and pulled him to her. The tender side of Alison, absent so often, could make him dizzy with pleasure. He thought of it as her real self; the other, tougher self was only a protective layer. In time, he hoped, she'd shed it altogether and then only this Alison, soft and giving and vulnerable, would be left.

At least he could hope.

Joe D. had returned to Alison's apartment to call Madison College. He needed more than directions; it was August and he wanted to make sure there'd be someone on campus to talk to him. "Actually, you're rather in luck," said the Madison operator. "Many of our administrative people are back from vacation. They generally come back a few weeks before Labor Day to get things ready for the September onslaught."

Joe D. explained that he needed information on an incident that took place in February 1976. (At least he hoped it was an incident.)

"Did it involve a student?" asked the operator.

Joe D. hesitated. "Yes . . . yes, it must have involved a student."

"Then you'll want Miss Collins. She's our dean of students and has been here since the Flood. Since before we went coed, even. Shall I connect you with her?"

She did, and Joe D. made an appointment with Miss Collins for eleven that morning.

It was a beautiful, traffic-free drive through the gentle green hills of Connecticut, during which Joe D. tried to anticipate the connection between Madison College and the **181** death of Linda Levinson. Speeding along the Merritt Parkway, he couldn't help thinking that he was heading farther and farther from the center of the case as he put miles between himself and Fire Island. For the answer, he knew, was there, in Seaside Harbor, in that tight little community where a premium was placed on conformity—and where one person, on a steamy July night, had broken out of the mold and done the unthinkable. Somehow he suspected that the very insularity of the place had led to Linda's death, that whoever killed her had done so precisely because he needed to continue to fit in, to be part of that tight little group of young professionals. The question nagged at him as he drove: What had Linda done to make it impossible for someone to continue to fit in with her alive?

He parked his car in the visitors' lot on the edge of the campus and headed for the administration building. Madison College seemed on another planet altogether from Fire Island and Manhattan—how could any incident here have any bearing on the murder of Linda Levinson in Seaside Harbor? The campus was a series of small lawns crisscrossed by paths and edged by ivy-covered brick buildings. Big, ancient trees shaded the lawns, their branches sagging under the weight of dense green foliage. The place was almost entirely deserted, but still Joe D. could sense what attending college here would be like: the casual meetings with friends in front of the white-pillared library; classes in rooms with windows that looked out over the lush Connecticut countryside; parties that erupted spontaneously in dormitories; romances that bloomed easily in the intimate, self-contained atmosphere of an isolated campus. Only reluctantly did he pull open the big wooden door of the administration building, clicking off the fantasy of college life into which he had, quite unconsciously, projected himself.

Miss Collins offered her hand to Joe D., but no first

name. She stood to greet him, however, a surprisingly tall

woman of about sixty, with white hair pinned back, but just barely, behind her head. Her eyes were bright blue, with deep creases radiating from them, hinting at a suspicious nature, a vigilence.

"I'm on a murder case, Miss Collins," he began, and filled her in on the details while she faced him from across her broad desk, absolutely expressionless and still. Sunlight streamed in from a single large window in back of her, illuminating her from behind.

"Was Linda Levinson a student here?" she asked. Her weathered, healthy looks promised a kind of spunky New England charm, but Miss Collins had the gravelly voice of a smoker, possibly even a drinker.

Joe D. shook his head.

"Then what connection could this affair have with Madison?"

Joe D. explained about the note.

"I still don't understand," she said, a trace of annoyance in her voice.

Neither do I, Joe D. was tempted to confess. "Was Eric Farber a student here?" he asked instead.

"I'll have to check."

She stood and crossed the room in three long, deliberate strides to a sideboard on which were piled papers, books, magazines, and a thick computer printout. Miss Collins flipped through this last item, which looked totally out of place in her jumbled, rather old-fashioned office.

"Eric Farber is not an alumnus," she said with her back still turned, stooping slightly over the printout.

"How about Rob Lewis? Robert Lewis, I guess."

She stiffened, he was sure of it, at the mention of Lewis's name. He saw her tall, angular frame freeze for an instant, then expand slightly to take in a deep breath. She stared at the printout without flipping a page and, a minute later, **183** turned to Joe D. "Rob Lewis was a student here," she said flatly, then crossed the room to her desk.

Back in her chair, she put her hands on top of her desk, clasped them, and asked if Joe D. would like to see Lewis's academic record.

"Will there be anything unusual on it?" he asked.

"Lieutenant, we have thousands of alumni, surely you can't expect me to recall—"

"Miss Collins, I think you *do* recall something about Rob Lewis. Something that happened on Valentine's Day in 1976. Now if it's on his record, please get it. If not, then I'll hear it from you."

After a moment's pause she unclasped her hands and opened the middle drawer of her desk, a large, oak piece speckled with nicks and scratches. She took out a package of filterless Camels and lit one with a match. She inhaled deeply, as if drawing strength from the bluish smoke, and hesitated before speaking, her mouth slightly ajar. A car in need of a tune-up idled more quietly than Miss Collins.

"It started at a party, Lieutenant. A Valentine's Day party. It was Rob Lewis's senior year here at Madison. He was a good student, a model student, you might even say. The party was held in our main dining hall here, and apparently there was a lot of drinking. Mr. Lewis met a sophomore girl at the party. Her name was Janet Lynch. Apparently they danced with each other, had some drinks together, and at around midnight she told him she wanted to return to her room. She lived in one of our residence halls.

"Mr. Lewis offered to walk her to her room, and she accepted. When they reached her room, Miss Lynch invited him in for a cup of coffee. Many of our students have hot pots in their rooms, Lieutenant."

She paused to inhale on the Camel.

184   "Here the story becomes . . . fuzzy. Miss Lynch later claimed that they finished their coffees and she asked him to leave, at which point he became surly. Mr. Lewis claims she encouraged his advances and he merely took advantage of the opportunity. She made an official complaint to our campus security people, the matter was brought to my attention, and ultimately it was decided by a review board that there were insufficient grounds to take disciplinary action against Mr. Lewis."

She stubbed out her cigarette and reclasped her hands on top of her desk.

Joe D. had heard some euphemisms before, but "became surly" had to take the cake. "Miss Collins, you said Lewis 'became surly.' What does that mean exactly?"

"It's been several years, Lieutenant. Certain details are very hazy."

"You had no trouble recalling the names of the people involved, Miss Collins. The date of the incident, the time Lewis and Janet Lynch left the party."

She inserted a second Camel between her pale lips and lit it.

"Miss Lynch claimed he tried to rape her." The cigarette trembled in her hand, its smoke frozen by the sunlight in big, cottony pleats above her head.

"You said he *tried* to rape her?"

She nodded vigorously. "Yes. She never said he succeeded. Only that he made the attempt." This thought seemed to comfort her; she eased back in her chair slightly and took a deep, slow breath. "Mr. Lewis said they were already on her bed when she first protested. At that point he got up and left her."

"According to Lewis."

She smiled weakly. "Yes, according to Mr. Lewis."

"But Janet Lynch—"

"Miss Lynch said he pushed her onto the bed, covering her mouth, and began . . . and began pulling off her **185** clothes. She succeeded in disengaging herself from him and ran from the room. Most of the people on her floor were still at the party, so she ran directly to our security office, which is across the quadrangle from her dormitory. By the time she returned with a guard, Mr. Lewis was gone.

"Miss Lynch wanted to call the police, but our security people dissuaded her and called me instead. In the end I advised her that bringing in the police would be inappropriate and unwise. We'd already talked to Mr. Lewis and he denied any wrongful action. I think you'd agree that she'd have had a weak case with the police, Lieutenant. Still, Miss Lynch was quite upset and insisted on some sort of retribution. She threatened to tell the campus newspaper, our local newspaper . . . It would have been awful for the college."

"Miss Collins, nobody wants bad publicity, but I don't see how this could have been so terrible."

"Rumors of violence on an isolated campus like this one can cause panic, Lieutenant. We're very self-contained here."

Joe D. thought of Seaside Harbor, another self-contained community, and knew just what she meant.

"Plus, we have other, special concerns. Mr. Lewis was in the first coeducational class at Madison. The introduction of men to what had been an all-girls school had not been easy. There were resentments, jealousies. Many of our most generous alumnae were very much against coeducation. When men's colleges admit women, they become even more desirable, it seems. Look at Yale and Princeton. But when women's schools let in men . . . well, there seems to be some tarnishing. Not that we had any choice. Applications were down, we were struggling to maintain our standards. So you see, the last thing we needed in 1976, after four difficult years, was an attempted rape charge."

186   "So you covered it up."

She inhaled, gunning her engines. "No, we covered nothing up. The president of the college, the head of the student body, and I met with both parties the next day. We interviewed them exhaustively and concluded that . . . well, that no conclusion could be reached. It was her word against his, and we simply couldn't take disciplinary action on that basis. You know, Lieutenant, such incidents are not at all rare on college campuses."

"Such incidents?"

"There's even a name for the phenomenon: date rape." She smiled complacently, causing the Camel to dance between her lips. "Two young people have one drink too many, indulge in some kissing, perhaps they willingly take it a bit further, and at a certain point the woman says 'No further' and the man ignores her. The atmosphere on college campuses today fosters this sort of thing, Lieutenant."

"You make it sound like the girl's as much to blame as the boy."

"I don't mean to make it sound like that. But it is a fact of life on college campuses today. Perhaps colleges with a tradition of coeducation can tolerate such incidents, and I suppose larger schools can absorb them more easily. But we're a relatively small college, Lieutenant, and in 1976 we weren't all that comfortable with the presence of men."

Joe D. sensed that Miss Collins still wasn't keen on coeducation at Madison. If nothing else it had obviously complicated her job. "Was this the first complaint against Lewis?"

"Absolutely. As I said earlier, he was a model student in every way. Exceptionally well-adjusted to college life, all things considered." Her voice trailed off, triggering an alarm inside Joe D.

"All *what* things considered, Miss Collins?"

"Oh, well you know, that was the Seventies. Student unrest, that sort of thing."

"I don't believe you, Miss Collins." The thought of Lewis as a campus radical seemed ridiculous.

Her cheeks reddened, her eyes widening. "Lieutenant, I will not have you speak to me that way."

"My apologies. But I still think you know something else about Lewis that might be useful."

A long, aspirated pause. "His . . . his home life was rather unusual, that's all. You see, his mother left her husband and children to live with another man. Rob Lewis was thirteen or so at the time. I believe there was a younger sister as well. It must have been quite traumatic for him, as you can well imagine. But unfortunately the trauma didn't end there. A few years later his father was killed in a car accident and the children were forced to live with their mother and her lover. I say forced because I gather there was much bitterness between Rob and his mother. Understandably so."

Miss Collins's knowledge of Lewis's family background was impressive. Unusually impressive. "How is it you know so much about Rob Lewis's family life, Miss Collins? Somehow I doubt he included these details on his application."

He knew he'd struck something when she slowly and deliberately lit another Camel. "No, it wasn't on his application, Lieutenant. His mother, however, is an alumna of Madison, class of 'forty-seven."

"Remarkable memory, Miss Collins. Are you sure it was 'forty-seven?"

She smiled, thinly and bitterly. "She's been a generous alumna, Lieutenant. We tend to recall such things about our benefactors."

"Particularly when their sons get in trouble, am I right?"

"That had nothing to do with it," she shot back. But her voice was suddenly tired, muted. Joe D. suspected such compromises were S.O.P. for poor Miss Collins. "He did not rape her, Lieutenant. The claim was attempted rape.

He was three months from graduation, and he was told in no uncertain terms that he wasn't to lay a finger on a Madison girl under any circumstances. And he didn't, Lieutenant, we made sure of that. As to your murder case, I'm quite certain that Mr. Lewis was not involved."

Joe D. gave her a skeptical look. Nothing she'd said convicted Lewis, of course, though it did sound like he had trouble dealing with rejection. Specifically, rejection by women. Seemed to bring out the worst in him, in fact.

"I believe he's an attorney now," she said with evident satisfaction. "And doing quite well, I hear."

She escorted him to the front door of the administration building. He could sense her eagerness to be rid of him and the painful memories he'd brought with him.

"Have you had any other inquiries about Lewis?" he asked her, trying to nail down the source of the note. She held the door open for him.

"None," she said firmly.

"But I suppose there are any number of people who could have known about the Valentine's Day incident."

"There were rumors at the time, I suppose, but nothing was ever published in the papers. Miss Lynch agreed not to discuss the matter, though we had no way of controlling her. And of course Mr. Lewis was unlikely to want the incident widely known. The three members of the committee that interrogated the two people involved knew the facts, but we were quite discreet, I can assure you."

He thanked Miss Collins, who nodded in response, and was heading for his car when he had an idea. He turned and ran back to the administration building. Miss Collins was at the end of a long, windowless hallway, about to re-enter her office. He called her name, and walked quickly toward her. His steps on the marble floor echoed sharply down the deserted corridor.

"One more thing, Miss Collins. What was the name of

the student body president who served on the committee with you?" She closed her eyes momentarily, as if annoyed. "Martin Lawrence," she said tightly, then turned and entered her office, shutting the door behind her with somewhat more force than was necessary.

Joe D. didn't notice. Nor did he hear his footsteps echoing this time as he walked hurriedly out of the building. For he was rapidly running the name Martin Lawrence through his mind. He knew it from somewhere, he was sure of it.

Martin Lawrence.

Martin Lawrence.

Marty Lawrence.

Marty Lawrence! Of course. He'd been introduced to him several weeks ago on Fire Island.

In Seaside Harbor.

In Eric Farber's house.

Marty Lawrence was Eric Farber's housemate on Fire Island.

Joe D. knew right away that Lawrence himself wasn't involved. He must have been gossiping with Farber about Lewis and mentioned the Valentine's Day incident. Then Farber had typed the note and had it delivered to Alison's building.

But why? What was Farber trying to do? Lead the police *to* the guilty party? Or lead them *away* from him?

Chapter

ALISON left Bloomingdale's at six-thirty Thursday evening. The store was crowded, which was just as well since Alison was feeling edgy and the last thing she wanted was to be alone as she made her way to the Third Avenue entrance.

It was the phone calls. Four of them, spaced fifteen minutes apart, the last one just as she was changing into running shoes to walk home. Hang-ups weren't so bad, she told herself. Since moving to New York she'd periodically get a spate of annoyance calls, and once she'd even had her number changed. But this was different. She was aware of the same awful burning she'd felt in Seaside Harbor, when she'd sensed someone watching her. She'd felt exposed, even in her dark, windowless office tucked behind the Sutton sportswear department on the third floor, and knew she wouldn't feel entirely safe until she was triple-locked in her apartment. She wished she had made plans for the evening. **191**

She was frightened and tired and, threading her way along the crowded sidewalk, felt isolated and alone.

It was one of those rare summer evenings that can happen only in New York, the air warm and dry and charged with the prospect of limitless choices and untold entertainments, the sky purply blue as the setting sun dissolved to the west. She walked quickly up Third, the Reeboks adding a spring to her step. She thought of the unanswered memos waiting on top of her desk, the unread reports growing obsolete in her in-box, and felt she'd deserted them.

Crossing Sixty-second she became aware of someone walking next to her. She recognized him and immediately turned away. Bad memories from the past few weeks, bad memories from Fire Island, circled menacingly overhead; she picked up her pace and tried to blend into the uptown flow. He must have seen her, however, for he, too, accelerated, leaving her with no alternative but to acknowledge him.

"Rob Lewis!" she said, as if noticing him for the first time.

"Alison," he said, smiling faintly, as if they ran into each other often. "Headed uptown?"

They slid effortlessly into a conversation as they walked. She talked a little about Bloomingdale's, he about his law firm. He has the most wonderful voice, she thought, not merely deep but three-dimensional, as if each word he spoke could be captured and held, turned in one's hand and viewed from an infinite number of angles. She felt the voice deep inside her, a vibration that alarmed her, though not unpleasantly. Her initial uneasiness at seeing him evaporated as they walked. She was relieved to be with someone familiar, felt less isolated now. She glanced at him a few times. He stooped slightly from the shoulders, looking down as if fearful of tripping. He was handsome, she decided, in a funny kind of way, because none of his features, least of all his oversized nose, was particularly pleasing. But he gave off something, an intensity, a purposefulness, that appealed to her. He seemed angry and confused, always squinting slightly as if the truth were just beyond his range of vision, yet also completely in control, and this combination of energies resulted in a tension that attracted her, like a rubber band that one is tempted to keep pulling on to see how far it will stretch. She recalled his failure with Linda, recalled too his fierceness the night she was killed, and knew that while she'd been wrong to suspect him of foul play (he was charming, really, charming in a . . . well, in an *intense* way) she would probably be wise to turn him down if, as she expected, he asked her out.

"Here's where I get off," she said at Seventy-third Street. "Guess I'll see you in Crane's Friday night."

"How about a drink right now?"

He took her elbow before she had a chance to respond and gently led her across Third. They were in McMullen's before she managed to analyze why she hadn't said no to him.

The bar was three-deep with the happy-hour crowd— good-looking men and women in good-looking suits, the men drinking beer, the women white wine. McMullen's had a polished preppiness that never failed to reassure her.

"Let's get a table where we can talk, at least," Rob suggested.

"But I think we have to order dinner to sit."

"After a drink or two we'll be hungry," he said with irrefutable logic, and thus it was she found herself having dinner with Rob Lewis.

Alison ordered a seafood salad and Rob, who hadn't looked at the menu, ordered the same. He did most of the talking, his voice distracting her so that occasionally she missed what he was saying, heard only the words, not their message. And there was a remoteness about him that inter- **193** ested her. She felt there was something else going on inside Rob Lewis, a thought process that had little to do with their conversation but paralleled it, following its twists and turns without ever making actual contact, like a concealed access road alongside a highway. It was as if there were a third person with them, whom only Rob could see, and part of Rob was with this other person, the other part with Alison. It had to do with the amazing control she sensed in him, the tautness, this ability (or was she only imagining it?) to navigate two thought patterns, two energies, into contiguous but separate channels.

Of course, she avoided the subject of Linda, though her thoughts drifted often to her friend as she tried to imagine the unsatisfying night the two of them, Rob and Linda, had spent together. The hours they'd spent together, more likely. Funny, they were two of the most controlled, compartmentalized people she knew; perhaps when two such people meet they're bound to let each other down . . .

Tell me about that night, she wanted to ask him. *Tell me what went wrong.*

"Tell me about your family," she asked instead, during a lull.

"There's not much to tell," he answered. His eyes were pale blue and very small. His mouth undulated a bit as he talked, shaping each word with lathe-like precision.

"Oh, when I hear that, I figure there must be a Peyton Place of things to tell," she said, leaning toward him, sipping her wine, her second and, she promised herself, her last.

"My father's dead, I have a sister and mother, that what you want to know?"

A glimmer of the fierceness she'd spotted in Crane's was evident now, the monumental control showing some stress.

"Not exactly juicy stuff, but I gather this is something you'd rather not go into."

He smiled broadly, his tanned face metamorphosing into something just short of beautiful, she thought, the undistinguished parts achieving a near-perfect harmony not evident before. "Very perceptive, Alison. Very perceptive."

He walked her back to her building, despite her protests. He didn't argue with her, but rather seemed deaf to every excuse she offered; it was as if he'd already programmed his mind as to how the evening would end and simply couldn't process the notion that things might turn out differently.

Under her building's canopy she thanked him for dinner and said she'd see him that weekend on Fire Island. Once again Rob seemed not to hear her, however, for he followed Alison into her building.

She told him she was tired, and even yawned once, but when the elevator arrived he was still standing there.

The elevator door opened.

She looked at him and something in his eyes, a determination, a *frightening* determination, told her that there was no polite way to get rid of him. There was also no way she would let him in the elevator with her, let alone inside her apartment. She allowed the doors to close two-thirds of the way and then just managed to slip into the elevator before they shut. When the door closed between them she felt a surge of relief, for she had caught a glimpse of Rob at the moment he realized that she'd tricked him; he looked furious rather than hurt, as if he'd been assaulted, not merely rejected. She reached to push the button for her floor and realized that her hand was shaking.

Chapter

21

BEFORE heading for Fire Island on Friday, Joe D. made a lunch date with Marie. Having come clean with Alison (or rather, having been scrubbed clean *by* her), Joe D. now wanted to come clean with Marie. It just wasn't fair to keep her hanging.

"But we were practically engaged," Marie complained over lunch in a crowded Roy Rogers on the Sunrise Highway. Joe D. took some comfort in knowing that he'd never again hear the dreaded *practically engaged* used in reference to him and Marie. Otherwise he was miserably uncomfortable.

"You're so young, Marie," he said blandly. "I bet there are lots of guys who'd want to go out with you."

"What's her name?" She pouted. She was wearing a pastel-striped dress and, on her head, a white ribbon tied into a bow. He'd never seen the dress before and figured she'd bought it specially for their lunch together.

"Alison."

"Alison," she repeated, nodding her head as if it explained everything. "I just don't know what I'm going to say to my parents." Tears started to form around the edges of her eyes like morning dew; Joe D. found himself concentrating on them, waiting for them to fall with an altogether irrational sense of foreboding.

"I *said,* I don't know what I'll say to my parents. They'll be so disappointed."

"Tell them Joe D. turned out to be a shit."

"I can't use language like that with them. You know that, Joe D."

He smiled in spite of himself and felt a pang for Marie. A few minutes of awkward silence elapsed. Marie coughed, and Joe D. almost jumped, he was so tense.

"Joe, say something," she pleaded.

"What more can I say? I'm sorry, Marie, real sorry."

The tears finally began rolling down her cheeks and Joe D. felt oddly relieved. One rogue tear fell onto the bun of her untouched hamburger, which repelled it as if Scotchguarded, sending it sliding onto the plastic plate. Joe D. watched this with rapt attention.

"I knew something was going on," she said. "I knew you had changed." She wiped away the tears with a napkin. "It wasn't just that I never saw you anymore. You have your career to worry about and I always respected that."

Joe D. thought: I'm in love with the wrong girl. Alison thinks being a cop is the bottom of the barrel; Marie thinks it's a career.

"It was just that when I did see you you were so cool toward me, like you were somewheres else."

She had stopped crying: the satisfaction of being proven right about Joe D.'s change of heart seemed to have assuaged her pain. She turned her attention to her hamburger, quickly catching up with Joe D., who had wolfed **197** his down in the first few minutes that followed his confession. Now it churned in his stomach like laundry in the rinse cycle.

"Like I said, Marie, there'll be other guys." They were walking to his car. The day was hot but not sunny, and humid, and still. Cars and trucks whizzed purposefully by on the Sunrise Highway. Joe D. felt like shit.

"I guess so," Marie said glumly. Her white pumps clicked on the asphalt as she took two steps for each one of his.

"You'll be all right, Marie. I'm sure of it." Which was the truth. Marie was the opposite of Alison. She had slipped easily into their relationship, expecting only the best from him. Alison fought relationships, expecting the worst, expecting to be hurt. The irony was that for all her defensiveness, Alison was the one more likely to suffer in the long run, for Marie, though wounded now, would recover in time and ease into a new relationship, while Alison would continue to fan the flames of her protective fire with each new disappointment, with each new hurt.

She wasn't cunning or calculating, Marie, she just had a primitive but effective survival instinct, and she instinctively knew she needed a boyfriend—no, she needed to be *practically engaged*—to survive. Alison's instinct, it seemed, was toward self-destruction, and he was beginning to wonder if perhaps he wasn't similarly afflicted, for wasn't he abandoning a woman devoted to him for one devoted only to keeping him at a safe distance?

Joe D. drove Marie back to the Grumman plant, and as she joined a crowd of employees heading back inside, he felt all alone, as if he were standing still but the whole world was moving away from him like the horizon in a video arcade car-racing game.

Chapter

JOE D. took an early evening ferry to Seaside Harbor. As the town came into focus he saw the large water tower that presided over it, then the single church that held its ground with quiet dignity among pricey houses at the center of the island. He spotted Crane's jutting out into the Great South Bay, the adjacent harbor percolating with boats bobbing arhythmically on the choppy water. As the ferry cut its engines on entering the harbor, he could hear the clanging of metal hardware against metal masts, the thumping and groaning of boats nuzzling each other in the crowded marina, the angry shrieks of a lone gull. Then he saw Castiglia.

Joe D. could tell instantly that Castiglia was not in a buoyant mood—he looked about as buoyant as an anchor. Standing on the ferry dock, his face was the color of an overripe peach, a blotchy melange of red, orange, and sickly brown. It was the color he turned when enraged. **199**

"Where the hell have you been?" Castiglia asked him, as if they'd had an appointment.

Since leaving Marie, Joe D. had spent the day trying to figure things out—like, what was the connection between Farber and Linda? The connection (or lack of one) between Lewis and Linda he already knew. He knew one other thing: the solution to Linda Levinson's murder was on Fire Island, not Connecticut, not Manhattan, not anywhere else.

"Chief, there wasn't much I could do until I got here, and since this place is empty until Friday night I—"

"What you're telling me is you haven't done a thing, diddlyshit, am I right?"

Concentrate on his wiggling nose, Joe D. told himself—how can you take a person seriously whose nose does the twist when he's excited?

"I'm getting closer, Chief, I really am. I told you I have three suspects. I know it's one of them. I'm positive." Farber, Lewis, and Golland. The trio sounded more like another law firm than like three suspects. Still, he knew it was one of them, though his conviction was not shatterproof.

"We're one week away from Labor Day weekend, DiGregorio. Do you know what that means?"

Joe D. shrugged. "I get Monday off?"

"Smart ass. You'll get three hundred and sixty-five days a year off if you don't watch it. What Labor Day means, in case you're interested, is the end of summer. Our killer disappears back into the city after Labor Day, DiGregorio. Disappears for good."

"Chief, I'll find him, I'll—"

"Labor Day is also when people start thinking about renewing their leases for next summer. Only they're not renewing them like they should be on account of this murder business. It kind of puts a damper on things when you have to be escorted back and forth to your house just because you're afraid you'll get knocked off on route. Why the hell should you pay all this money to live in fear when you can just stay put in New York City and live in fear for no extra charge?"

"Look, Chief," Joe D. said, angry now. "I've been doing my best. If that isn't good enough for you, fine. Find someone else. I told you I'll get this guy, and in the meantime there haven't been any more murders since I've been on the case, so please . . ." He caught his breath, unaccustomed to talking to his chief this way. "Please, lay off, okay?"

"You're a regular guardian angel, DiGregorio. A guardian angel."

Joe D. smiled weakly.

"And as for your suspects, I don't want you messing with that lawyer fellow."

Two-thirds of his suspects—and half of Fire Island— were lawyers, but Joe D. knew which one Castiglia meant. "Golland?"

"Golland. He's a big shot and if you're wrong about him, which you are, we could all be in big trouble."

So, thought Joe D., Golland wasn't kidding about having influence in Suffolk County. Apparently he'd already gotten to Castiglia.

"How do you know I'm wrong about Golland?"

"You are, that's all," the Chief replied in a voice that declared: Challenge me at your own risk. Joe D. declined the challenge.

"I haven't made any accusations yet—"

"And you won't," he exploded. "Just find the killer." Joe D. felt the dock beneath them tremble. "This weekend. I'll give you through the weekend and then you're off the case. Understand?"

No reply was called for and none was offered.

He watched Castiglia lumber down the pier, a one-man stampede. He circled over to where a Coast Guard launch stood waiting. The dock rose a good ten inches once Castiglia managed to hoist himself onto the boat.

Joe D. had often lamented that weekends were only two days long, but never with as much urgency as on this evening.

Friday was turning out to be a day of confrontations for Joe D. Confrontation number one was with Castiglia. Numbers two and three were with Rob Lewis and Eric Farber, respectively. Confrontations were not Joe D.'s style, but he had no choice: he had little time, two days to be exact, in which to produce a murderer.

Castiglia's ultimatum—*Just find the killer. This weekend*—echoed painfully in his head, and the worst part was, he knew Castiglia was right. The killer was here in Seaside Harbor, where the murder had taken place, and once the community disbanded after Labor Day the chances of finding him would be virtually nil. Walking to his house, he looked deeply into each face that passed, studied the houses bunched together along the interlocking paths; it's here, the key to Linda's death, it's here on Fire Island and someone—Lewis or Farber or maybe, without realizing it, Alison—knows what it is. Seaside Harbor is such a small community, really, as close-knit and insular as a rural town. And with everyone living on top of each other, six, eight, ten or more to a house, surely a killer couldn't hide for long. Surely he has to do something to give himself away.

But time was running out. If it weren't, he could wait the killer out, wait for him to slip up in this community where slip-ups are all too obvious and none too tolerated. But with only a week left, waiting was a luxury only the killer could afford. He'd have to lure him into making a move, force his hand. And he'd have to do it this weekend.

Joe D. had another motive for wanting the case wrapped up this weekend. He hoped to go away with Alison over Labor Day weekend, which he certainly couldn't do with the killer still at large. He hadn't mentioned it to her yet, but he was sure she'd go along with the idea. Joe D. hadn't spent much time in Seaside Harbor, but he had spent enough time there to conclude that he didn't like it very much. There was something too competitive about the place, with everyone constantly looking each other over, and looking themselves over, to see how they stacked up against the competition. He felt everyone in Seaside Harbor had a checklist and that he just didn't rate on anyone's list. Oh, he did okay in certain categories—his physical appearance, for example, passed muster. But while sex on Fire Island is casual, nothing else is, and so he flunked in the categories that counted most: profession, salary, place of residence. Alison had a checklist of her own, but Joe D. believed he had just about convinced her to discard it. Continued exposure to the peculiar values of Seaside Harbor, however, might induce her to begin comparing him again to What She Had In Mind, so he thought it best to try to avoid the place for the one remaining summer weekend. To do this, however, he had to find Linda Levinson's killer, and he had to find him this weekend.

It was a hot, sticky Friday. The sky hung low and gray and heavy. The afternoon breeze had petered out with the approach of evening; even the ocean sounded unenthusiastic, unwilling to exert itself in the heat. At the very center of the island, a few yards from his house, Joe D. paused for a moment and looked behind him. What a thin, flattened-out place Fire Island was, and how fragile; the ocean is in control here, never mind the architects and masons and carpenters who had transformed this forty-mile sandbar into choice real estate; the ocean's ever-present **203** thundering declared who was boss here, made it quite clear that it could reclaim the island with one giant heave.

He got to his house at six and was surprised to find most of his housemates already there, early evacuees from the urban inferno.

Joe D. hung around with them for a while. He felt bad that he hadn't bothered to get to know any of his housemates very well. Joe D. knew that this regret was absurd: he was on assignment and his very presence in the house was a deception. The less well he knew them the less he'd have to explain when the whole thing was over. Which, with luck, would be soon. Still, Joe D. liked to be liked, and he felt a certain resentment toward him hanging over the household like a faint but unpleasant odor, resentment that he'd been invited into the house late in the season and then had essentially snubbed them all. It was worth an hour or two of his time to undo this impression.

One of his housemates had mixed a large pitcher of margaritas. She poured each of them a glass and then raised hers. "To the poor schnooks stuck in the city this weekend," she said. "God bless 'em."

"T.G.I.F.," said someone else.

"Yeah, T.G. I think it's worth the risk of getting murdered to be out here in this heat."

"Only murderers and rapists are left in the city on a weekend like this anyway, so we may as well take our chances here. At least there's the beach."

They sat in the large, un–air-conditioned living room, careful to maintain distance between themselves, as small pools of sweat formed where bodies made contact. They were temporarily drained from five days in the hot city and also from the difficult trek out to Fire Island. Conversation ignited occasionally, only to suffocate in the malaise that hung thick and heavy over the room. "I feel wiped out, like I just escaped from someplace," said Stacy, and she spoke **204** for all of them.

He spent nearly two hours with his housemates, during which he managed to accomplish three things: he resuscitated his reputation among them, he polished off three margaritas, and he found out where Rob Lewis lived. Pulling himself up out of that room was like starting a car with a weak battery, however; it wasn't that he was enjoying himself so much as he felt enervated by the margaritas and the heat and the choking lethargy. Later, he knew, they'd all perk up, start the weekend party that continued straight through to the LIRR, Sunday night. But for the moment they were content just to recuperate, and he couldn't blame them.

Walking to Rob Lewis's house as the glowering sun sank reluctantly to the west, Joe D. tried to reassure himself that what he was about to do was both wise and necessary. If Rob Lewis were Linda Levinson's killer, proving it would be difficult, because Lewis's only possible motive was psychological, and how do you prove psychological motivation? What evidence do you look for? That he'd attacked a girl during his senior year at college? *Allegedly* attacked her? That his mother had walked out on him almost twenty years ago and now he flies off the handle every time he feels rejected by a woman?

Joe D.'s only recourse was to confront Lewis directly and hope for some sort of reaction that would nail him. A confession, for example, would be most welcome. Worried that the reaction might be violent instead, Joe D. had brought along a pistol, which was strapped under a cotton shirt and windbreaker. The windbreaker was making him unbearably hot, but the reassuring press of the gun against his side was ample compensation.

Lewis's place was somewhat nicer than the typical Seaside Harbor house. For starters, it was directly on the Bay. And it was newer, larger, less worn down by summer after summer of indifferent sharers. Like all Seaside Harbor **205** houses, Lewis's was full of people. Some of them were weekend residents, others just visiting. Most of them were relaxing on a large wooden deck that looked out over the water. Entering the house, Joe D. felt the momentary heat of attention as all heads turned his way, sized him up, and turned away. There's more privacy in Sing Sing, he thought.

Lewis was in the kitchen mixing piña coladas in a blender. Joe D. stood in the doorway and watched him for a few moments before Lewis became aware of his presence. He was struck by the guy's intensity, evident even as he mixed the drinks with pharmacological deliberation. Still, Lewis seemed so *normal,* he fit in too well. Could he really have attacked—and killed—Linda Levinson?

When, at length, Lewis spotted Joe D., he did not look pleased. He had one of those faces on which a scowl grows easily, and it grew quickly as Joe D. walked across the kitchen to greet him.

"Listen, Rob," he began casually, assuming a friendly tone from which Lewis noticeably recoiled. "I've got to talk to you."

Lewis stared at him for an uncomfortably long time, his cold eyes moving slowly, intently up and down, as if searching for defects on Joe D.'s body. Finally, without a word, he led him up to his bedroom, correctly sensing that whatever Joe D. had to say was best said in private. Like most bedrooms in Seaside Harbor rentals, this one contained two twin beds separated by a nightstand, a chest of drawers, a small closet, a single painting that made motel art look good, and nothing else. It smelled oddly antiseptic, of cedar and mothballs. They each sat on a bed, facing each other.

"I know we're not friends, Rob, but I thought you should know something."

Still, Rob said nothing, just nodded his head to indicate that Joe D. had his blessing to continue.

"I'm from Waterside, and I know a couple of the guys on the police force there."

A second nod, but still no words.

He swallowed, took a breath, and let him have it. "So they think you killed Linda Levinson."

Lewis stood and took a step toward him. For a second Joe D. thought Lewis was going to slug him. Perhaps that was his intention, but he gained control of himself quickly; Joe D. could see this happening, so deliberate was Lewis's effort to keep his emotions in check. Long, purple veins appeared like restraining cords just beneath the surface of his neck and arms. He swallowed uncomfortably, his Adam's apple bobbing mechanically.

"Why would they think that?" he asked, his words slurring slightly, as if fear or shock or both had weakened his jaw.

"I think you know, Rob."

Lewis sat back down, collapsed, really, a marionette whose strings had been severed by one sweep of a blade. His elbows rested on his legs, his head hung limply between them.

"I wish I were dead," he said softly but convincingly.

Joe D. readied himself to hear a confession. This filled him with a curious mixture of hope and dread: hope that he could wrap the case up right now, dread at having to witness the unraveling of another man's life.

But he needn't have worried.

"So everyone knows that Rob Lewis couldn't get it up, is that what you're telling me?"

"Not everyone, Rob, but—"

"Fucking women. They lay these goddamn demands on you and then they fucking humiliate you if you don't perform up to their standards. It sucks."

"Did Linda humiliate you?"

Lewis's head jerked up and Joe D. recognized in his eyes a new look: determination.

207

"I didn't kill her, if that's what you're getting at. I can't say I give a hoot that she's dead, but I didn't kill her. I'll tell you one thing, though. You breathe one fucking word of this to *anyone,* including your girlfriend, and you'll regret it."

This reference to Alison was unexpected and chilling. "Is that what really bothers you, that other people found out about it?"

"Other people didn't *find out* about it. She fucking told half the universe."

"But she can't tell anyone else, right, Rob? Not anymore."

"Damn straight she . . . hey, wait a minute. I know what you're trying to pull. I didn't kill her to shut her up. I didn't kill her, period. Get that through your thick wop head now, you hear me?" He turned to leave the room.

"What does Baby Bear mean to you?" It was Joe D.'s last hope, offered with little expectation of a return.

Lewis paused and looked at Joe D. It was obvious he hadn't the slightest idea what Baby Bear meant. "You're fucked up, you know that, DiGregorio?" he said in a voice churning with arrogance and disdain. With that diagnosis he left the room.

Leaving the house, Joe D. spotted Lewis back in the kitchen mixing piña coladas again and making small talk with a few of his guests. He looked like the perfect host—charming, confident, without a care in the world. But Joe D. had seen a different Lewis upstairs, had glimpsed the anger that was always just under the surface like a benign tumor waiting for the signal to turn malignant.

Chapter

23

ALISON was wearing an off-white jumpsuit when Joe D. picked her up later that evening. It was loose-fitting but managed to make her look fuller, sexier. One thing he liked about Alison, she never looked exactly the same twice. Prettier faces he imagined he'd grow tired of over time, like too rich food. Alison had a face he knew he'd never get used to and so never get bored with. She could look conventionally pretty, pretty in what was called a "different" way, handsome, womanly, girlish, sophisticated, even kind of goofy in a way that made Joe D.'s heart ache with pleasure. When she smiled she looked entirely different than when she frowned, not merely modified by a new expression but transformed by it.

That her feelings for him could also fluctuate was something he chose to ignore as much as possible given the intensity and regularity of her emotional swings.

"Do we have to go to Crane's tonight?" she asked as she

put on her makeup before a small travel mirror she'd placed on top of a dresser. He had never paid much attention to her makeup and was enjoying the sight of her applying it, the way she squeezed and stretched and crunched her face as she dabbed and brushed and poked with miniature brushes and delicate little pencils. "What's the point of having a boyfriend if I still have to subject myself to that meat market?"

"Oh, so I'm your boyfriend, am I? I consider that a triumph." Joe D. grinned, but in fact he appreciated this first acknowledgment from Alison that he played a more than casual role in her life.

"I'm going to try to find Eric Farber in Crane's tonight," he said by way of explanation. "Try something out on him."

"So you don't think it was Rob Lewis?"

"Don't know, but he didn't exactly confess earlier this evening. He did scare me, though, when he mentioned you."

Alison shivered. "There's something I have to tell you, something that happened to me this week."

"Since I saw you Thursday morning?"

"It happened Thursday night. I was walking home from the store and . . ."

"And?"

"Well, you see, there were these hang-ups at the office, and I was feeling kind of creepy all day, and I was crossing the street . . ." She hesitated.

"So you were crossing the street . . ."

Her voice turned reflective. "Joe D., have you ever felt yourself lose control of a situation? I mean, you know something's happening to you and you want to stop it but you don't because you can't because, well, because there are conflicting things going on inside you and—"

"Alison, what does this have to do with your crossing the street?"

"Well, I . . ." She shook her head. "Oh, it's really very boring. I'll tell you some other time."

"You're sure?"

"Sure. Anyway, you were saying that you don't think it was Lewis . . ."

"I was saying I'm not sure. But in any case, tonight I'll work on Farber. And I'm afraid you'll have to stick by me for a while. Police orders, you understand."

"An order's an order. But God, I hope you figure it all out this weekend."

"Me too, Alison. Me too."

They could hear the music several hundred yards away from Crane's. Fifty yards away they could *feel* it in the ground.

Crane's was as crowded as the IRT at rush hour, only noisier. It took Joe D. close to half an hour to find Farber. He was standing on the edge of the dance floor, alone, watching the dancers. Farber was wearing a light blue cotton shirt with more buttons opened than closed, khaki pants without a belt, Topsiders without socks. The gold chain around his neck was one shade lighter than his richly tanned chest. He was drinking a beer.

Joe D. reckoned Farber scored well on just about every Seaside Harbor checklist—he was handsome, charming in an aggressive manner that did him no harm, and very successful on Wall Street, which was still, even after the crash (*particularly* after the crash, for the elite few who weren't laid off), the ultimate credential in this credential-happy town. Yet he looked oddly pathetic standing at the edge of the dance floor, as if his golden quality, his chiseled intensity, held him back, prevented him from jumping into the action. His very withdrawal imbued him with the detached, unworldly beauty of an eyeless Greek statue.

Joe D. reached into his pocket and took out a small piece **211** of paper on which he had already written the two words he knew were at the center of the whole affair.

Baby Bear. At first it had seemed so silly, these two fairy-tale words buried in a safety-deposit box with all that grown-up money. A mistake of some sort, obviously. Perhaps Linda had clipped the wrong piece of paper to that wad of hundred-dollar bills. But Joe D. knew you didn't make mistakes when that much money was involved. You just didn't.

Now all he had to do was slip the note to Farber without his knowing where it came from. It hadn't seemed like such a big deal earlier, when he'd devised this plan, but now it seemed nearly impossible. If Farber looked detached from the external world, he quite obviously was in touch with his own perfectly developed body. He carried it like a possession; it seemed not a part of him but a piece of property he owned and inhabited—an expensive car he'd purchased rather than a body he'd been born with. And like all owners of expensive cars, Farber would be wary of people who maneuvered too close. How then was Joe D. to slip this piece of paper to Farber anonymously?

He decided, reluctantly, to enlist Alison's aid. She was talking to some friends out on the terrace.

"Everybody," Alison said, "this is Joe D. Joe D., this is Michelle."

"Hi Michelle."

"And Melissa."

"Hi Melissa."

"And Sheldon."

"Hi Sheldon."

"And Stu."

"Hi Stu."

"Melissa and Michelle were in a house with Linda . . . with Linda and me last summer." Melissa and Michelle smiled uneasily. (He'd already forgotten which was which:

both were wearing short dresses that revealed legs that were best kept under wraps.)

"What business are you in, Joe?" asked Sheldon or Stu.

"I'm an accountant," he replied, thinking this was a sure-fire conversation-ender. He was wrong.

"A man after my own heart," said SheldonorStu. "I'm a bean counter too. My specialty is s-corps. You?"

He looked at Alison, who was grinning. "Oh, general stuff, you know . . ."

"You don't have a specialty?" he exclaimed in a voice that implied that a specialty was only slightly less critical than an immune system. Joe D. searched frantically for a way to douse this conversation.

"Joe D. does investigative accounting," volunteered Alison. "Don't you, Joe?"

"What the hell's investigative accounting?" asked SheldonorStu with a touch of annoyance.

Joe D. tried without success to restrain a smile, but SheldonorStu didn't appear to notice. In fact, he had migrated to a neighboring conversation, this one a lively debate over the next target of Kohlberg, Kravis. One of the distinctions of conversation in a place like Crane's, Joe D. was fast learning, is that paying attention to what the other person is saying is strictly optional. In a place where the next president of Citibank is a hotter topic than the next President of the United States, where leveraged buyouts are very much to the point while Eastern Europe is but a tedious abstraction, being undercover is a piece of cake, Joe D. realized, because in the end no one really cares about anything but himself, his career, his image, and, of course, his sex life. He knew he could pose as a man from Mars and no one would look askance as long as he was dressed right.

"How about a dance, Alison?" he asked suddenly. Be- **213**

fore she could answer, he took her hand and quickly led her off the terrace.

"Gee, I never expected a dance invitation from the world's greatest Bach lover," she said as they headed for the dance floor. "Or is this a minuet?"

"Don't tell me you know how to minuet."

"What do you take me for, anyway? I grew up in Scarsdale, don't forget. In Scarsdale they never gave up the minuet."

"Well, actually, I'd love to dance, but not right now. I have a favor to ask you. I hate to get you involved, but I don't have a choice."

"What is it?" she said with unconcealed eagerness.

"You said you knew Eric Farber?"

"Vaguely."

"Well, would you ask him to dance?"

"Sure, but I don't see how that will help anything."

"Trust me, Alison, it will."

"And what if he refuses?"

"He won't," Joe D. replied with less conviction than hope.

Luckily, Farber said yes. In fact his face lit up, as if he were genuinely, unexpectedly flattered. For all his good looks, Farber struck Joe D. as a guy without much confidence in himself. He danced fluidly but in step to the rhythm. Still, he exuded a desperate self-consciousness that made him appear painfully uncomfortable, as if he were dancing not for enjoyment but to make a favorable impression on an unsympathetic jury. Joe D. recalled Rachel Garvin and her teenage crush on Farber that had never completely worn off, and he wished he could tell her that fifteen years later Eric K. Farber was no happier than she was, despite his wealth and his charm and those blue, blue eyes to die for.

214   More importantly, Farber did what Joe D. expected he'd do: he put his bottle of beer down on an empty table before dancing. While Farber was on the crowded dance floor with his back to him, Joe D. stuffed the small piece of paper into the neck of the bottle so that most of it stuck out the top where it couldn't be overlooked.

Ten minutes later Alison was still dancing, and Joe D. realized she was waiting for a signal from him to stop. The next time she looked his way he nodded. She shouted a few words in Farber's ear over the din of the music and left the dance floor with him. They talked a few seconds before he reached for his beer. He picked up the bottle without looking at it and almost gagged on the note. He opened it with little apparent interest, assuming, no doubt, that some inconsiderate soul had disposed of a scrap of paper in this unpleasant manner, glanced at it, and dropped his bottle. It shattered on the hardwood floor messily but silently, the sound of the crash obliterated by the deafening music. No one seemed to notice but Alison.

And Joe D. He was concealed behind a column about ten feet from the dance floor where he could watch Farber without being seen.

Farber's reaction confirmed at least one thing: Farber had a direct connection to Linda Levinson and that connection was money. $150,000, to be precise. The source of that money was still a mystery, but it had something to do with Baby Bear and it had something to do with Eric Farber.

Farber stood in one place as if rooted to it, but glanced around the bar with quick, furtive turns of the head.

"Eric, what's the matter?" asked Alison, who had only just managed to read the two words on the slip of paper before Eric crumpled it in his fist.

"Like you don't know?" he asked venomously, his eyebrows forming sinister arches.

"No, I don't know," she lied with forced indignation.

He looked at her intently for a few seconds, deciding whether or not to believe her, then quickly walked across the bar and out of Crane's.

Chapter

FARBER had exited Crane's so fast Joe D. almost lost him. He signaled to Alison to stay put and ran after him.

Joe D. looked both ways on Main Street, but Farber seemed to have disappeared into the misty end-of-summer evening. Most of Seaside Harbor lay to the west of Crane's, so Joe D. turned right and walked briskly in that direction, toward the ferry landing and the center of town.

A few hundred yards from Crane's he spotted him. Farber was in a phone booth talking animatedly, his free hand gesturing wildly, liked a crazed puppet. Joe D. got as close to the booth as he could without being noticed but still couldn't hear what Farber was saying.

Farber hung up abruptly and hurried to the ferry landing a short distance away. In the darkness it was difficult for Joe D. to keep track of him but easy to remain concealed. Farber read the ferry schedule posted on a community bulletin board. Joe D. heard him curse from the other end of the dock.

Farber stood for a minute, the effort of making a decision visible on his face and body even from twenty-five yards away, then rushed over to the docks where the smaller private boats were kept. Most of them were empty; they bobbed noisily on the water as if possessed of invisible spirits, reprimanding the choppy water occasionally with peevish little slaps. The air was humid and heavy; Farber moved like a specter through it, dissolving one moment into the late evening haze, reappearing moments later, gauzy and incomplete. Joe D. watched Farber approach a man on the dock and talk to him. Both arms now gestured excitedly, as if he were talking to a foreigner who spoke no English. From across the harbor, unable to hear a word of the exchange, it looked to Joe D. like a manic game of charades. Farber was obviously extremely agitated, had been since finding Baby Bear stuffed into his beer bottle.

Farber flung both arms heavenward, apparently rebuffed, and approached a second man, to whom he repeated the pantomime (the southerly breeze quashed any chance of hearing even a single word spoken across the dock). Frustrated a second time in his quest, he tried a third man.

This conversation lasted somewhat longer than the first two. Joe D. inched farther down the dock, hiding behind mooring poles. He almost stumbled over a couple sitting on the dock, smoking a joint that glowed in the warm, murky night air. They eyed him suspiciously, then got up and left, the joint sizzling for a split second where they had tossed it into the water. Joe D. watched Farber remove his watch, then hand it over along with his wallet to the third man. He jumped into the nearest boat, a small outboard, started it up while the man loosened the ropes, and sped away from the dock.

The boat veered drunkenly as it sped between aisles of boats in the crowded little marina—either Farber was not an experienced skipper or he had more important things on

217

his mind than navigating a straight line. In any case, the man who was the boat's likely owner shouted something to Farber, probably a warning. Farber didn't turn around to respond, but by the time he left the marina, he seemed to have gained control of the boat, which disappeared into the still night a few seconds before the sound of its engine.

Joe D. raced over to the dock and approached the third man Farber had spoken to, the one who had let him have the boat. "He wanted a boat. Offered me two hundred dollars' cash to borrow it. I said no dice. Boat's worth more than that. He gave me this as collateral." The man reached into a pocket and extracted Farber's wallet and a watch.

"Mind if I take a look?"

The man handed him the items. The watch was a Rolex, worth, Joe D. calculated, at least as much as the boat, a small, peeling affair not nearly up to snuff with its ship-shape neighbors. The wallet contained two hundred dollars in cash as well as a deck of credit cards and a driver's license.

"Did he say where he was going?"

"Over to Waterside. Said he'd be back in an hour or two. I said I'd wait right here for him. Shit, even if he sinks the boat I'll come out ahead on the deal, am I right?" The man seemed pleased with himself but also anxious to have his business acumen confirmed.

"You made a good deal," Joe D. obliged.

With forty dollars and a Texaco credit card in his wallet, and a beat-up Timex on his wrist, Joe D. didn't think much of his chances of convincing any of the other boat owners to lend him a boat. Reluctantly, he flashed his badge at a man at the very end of the dock. The man resisted, but Joe D. ignored him and jumped into the small speedboat. He was starting the twin engines when he felt someone else step into the boat.

"Sorry, Alison," he said, shaking his head. "I'll meet you back at your house later."

"No way. I'm coming with you. Remember, police orders." She sat down in the seat farthest from him and crossed her arms in front of her. He didn't have time to argue—Farber was probably halfway to Waterside by now—and he didn't think it would do any good anyway. Instead he called for the owner to loosen the ropes and cast them off.

"Still don't see why I have to let you do this!" the owner shouted over the gurgling of the engines, but he untied the ropes anyway, with excruciating slowness, and pushed them off.

It was a soupy night, the air dense with fog and a sharp, fishy odor. Joe D. easily guided the small boat out of the marina. Growing up on Long Island, he'd been on motorboats often as a boy, and he had no problem with this one. He pointed the boat toward Waterside and opened up the engines. The front of the boat heaved from the water, throwing a spray of saltwater over the entire boat. Alison, grasping the side of the boat, made her way to the back and sat down next to Joe D.

The Great South Bay appeared completely deserted, though with visibility limited to just a few feet it was hard to tell. The boat's bow light seemed to hit a solid wall just a short distance ahead of them; Joe D. navigated by a compass attached to the boat's tiller. Waterside, he knew, was practically due north of Seaside Harbor. Even so, he was pleased to see a ferry emerge from the fog thirty yards off to the left, coming from Ocean Beach to the west, confirming that he was headed in the right direction.

The note had triggered Farber into action, Joe D. thought as they sliced through the mist. Was he leaving Fire Island because he felt someone there was on to him, or was he meeting someone, perhaps the person he'd called from Seaside Harbor? Joe D. was counting on the second possibility. He was also counting on Farber not knowing Waterside Harbor as well as he did. This might buy a few **219** minutes for Joe D. to catch up. His own car was parked in a lot at the ferry landing, so he'd be able to follow Farber if he took off after docking.

The fog had become almost impenetrable, a swirling black curtain that imprisoned them in darkness. Even the compass was hard to read. The moon was just a curved sliver, darting in and out of clouds illuminated by its own reflected glow. Reluctantly, Joe D. cut the engines.

"I don't want to get off-course even for a second," he told Alison. "Otherwise we could end up drifting in circles." He guessed that Farber had already arrived in Waterside, while he and Alison were only halfway there. It had been an hour since Farber made the phone call from the booth near the ferry landing in Seaside Harbor, forty-five minutes since he'd managed to secure a boat. It occurred to Joe D. to give up, turn around and head back to Seaside Harbor, but he figured there was at least a chance that Farber was meeting someone in Waterside, that he'd still be there when he and Alison arrived, so he decided to persevere.

He guided them through the night, the boat slapping on-coming waves with a slow, steady rhythm. His eyes strained through the haze to spot a light on the other side, some confirmation that they were making progress.

"You want my jacket?" he asked Alison; he could feel her shivering next to him, soaked with saltwater.

"I'm okay. How much farther?"

"Fifteen, twenty minutes, but I'm only guessing. It could be . . ."

He stopped, listening.

"Joe, what is it?"

"Hear it? An engine."

She listened for a moment. "I hear it."

"It's coming toward us, a boat."

"I don't understand . . . what's the big deal about a boat coming. . ?"

"It could be Farber, that's what. How many other boats do you see out here tonight?"

He turned off the engines and cut the bow light. The darkness swallowed them instantly. The hum of an approaching engine was the only sound they could hear other than the now gentle lapping of the water against the side of the boat.

"Why would Farber be coming back?" asked Alison, whispering unnecessarily; the darkness was so absolute it seemed to conceal countless spirits all around them, listening.

Joe D. shook his head. Farber might have picked someone up in Waterside, or he might have simply changed his mind. Or it might not be Farber at all . . .

Suddenly the boat broke into view for a mere second before the mist reclaimed it. "It's out of control," Joe D. said, for unless he was hallucinating, the small boat had just made a drunken U-turn in the middle of the bay.

"Was it Farber?" asked Alison.

"Couldn't tell, but I think I saw two people, not one."

The boat was still nearby—they could hear its engine sputtering only a few yards away. Occasionally they would spot a faint ray of light and the boat would be partially illuminated, only to fade instantly. "This is so strange," said Alison, still whispering. Joe D. agreed: it was like being in a fun house and not knowing what was going to pop out of the darkness next.

Every few seconds they could hear a muffled shout, but it was impossible to make out what was being said. The boat seemed to be circling them; it would drift away occasionally, the engine inaudible for a brief while, but just as they were despairing of seeing it again it would drift back into range, appear for a moment, then evaporate into the night.

Joe D. was sure there were two figures in the boat, but still couldn't make out who they were. He guessed they were arguing—perhaps fighting—and had left the steering of the boat to the whims of the tide and the choppy water.

A minute later the boat wandered back into view, offering Joe D. and Alison a grisly spectacle. One figure lifted his hand, which held a metallic object of some sort—it caught the faint light from the slivered moon and glinted sporadically through the fog—and brought it down onto the head of the other figure. Joe D. was about to cry out, hoping to stop what was clearly an assault taking place, when the boat made a sharp, unbalanced lunge to the right and disappeared. It reappeared a second later, however. Now one figure was no longer in view, but it looked as if this unseen figure were being pummeled from above by the other, visible figure. The entire scene was like a shadow play, with only the faintest outlines visible, though the action was occurring only ten yards or so away. Even through the shifting haze, even without the aid of sound, what they were witnessing was a hideous sight.

Joe D. shouted through the darkness, but could hear his words swallowed by the thick haze. He started the engines, which coughed a few times before turning over. At the sound of the motor the standing figure, just barely visible now, took control of his own boat and opened up the engines. Joe D. expected him to head back to Waterside; instead he sped off to the south, toward Fire Island.

Farber's boat (for Joe D. was sure now that this was the boat Farber had borrowed in Seaside Harbor) had a thirty-yard head start, and quickly vanished from sight. Joe D. was forced to follow it by sound only. For five minutes he sped into the murky haze, but the noise from his own engine made it almost impossible to pinpoint the other boat. He decided to head directly for Seaside Harbor instead, hoping to catch up with Farber (or his companion—Joe D. had no idea which of the two had been the victim of the metallic object) back on Fire Island.

It took them a full half hour to reach Seaside Harbor, during which Joe D.'s mind spun with theories and conjectures and, most of all, questions. Their progress was frustratingly slow, for Joe D. did not want to risk missing Seaside Harbor and ending up in a neighboring town. Finally a light appeared through the mist, then still other lights, and minutes later the familiar profile of Seaside Harbor was faintly visible. He sped into the marina, surveying the area as he guided them to the dock.

Farber's boat was nowhere to be seen.

Back at Alison's house Joe D. called his station and had them post an alert with the Coast Guard. Alison changed into dry clothes, and on the way back into town they stopped at Joe D.'s house so he could change as well.

Joe D. felt too keyed up to eat, but Alison was hungry, so they had a late dinner at a small restaurant with a view of the marina. From their windowside table Joe D. could keep an eye out for Farber.

"Not that I'm sure Farber is still alive," said Joe D. "He could have been the victim."

They pondered the events of the evening in silence for a while. Thanks to the haze the whole episode had taken on an abstract, dreamlike quality—actually, nightmarish would be more accurate, he thought, picturing that metallic object rising and falling on the unseen victim in the small, borrowed speedboat.

"If only we knew what the connection between Farber and Linda was." He had ordered bluefish, but it might as we have been fillet of Styrofoam, for all he tasted it.

"I can't imagine what the connection could be. The whole thing still seems so unreal. At first, just Linda's being murdered was impossible to deal with. But now there's the money, and Farber and Golland and Lewis. I feel like a stranger was murdered, not one of my friends. I **223** suppose I knew she was leading a double life, but I never guessed the complexity of it."

"Triple life, really," added Joe D.

"How so?"

"There was the Linda you knew, the pretty secretary with not much of a social life and no ambition to speak of. There was the Linda Golland knew. And then there was the Linda who managed to make herself a pile of money in a way that somehow involved Eric Farber."

They thought about this for a few minutes. Joe D. picked at his fish and glanced out the window. The marina was quiet.

"So you see," Alison said, "she's died twice for me. Once that Saturday when I found out she'd been killed. And a second time earlier this week when you told me about her other life. Or lives."

"I guess people with more than one life die more than once."

"I hope so, because then you'll be safe for a while."

He smiled. "Believe me, Alison, nobody wants to see Joseph DiGregorio the accountant dead more than I do."

"You know, these past few days I've been feeling kind of guilty about Linda. There was so much about her I never really understood, and I just never made an effort to break through. Maybe if I had, things would have turned out differently for her."

"You couldn't have saved her, Alison. She was involved in something very deep, and she deliberately kept you in the dark about it."

"This morning on the way to work I told myself it was time to stop mourning her. As you said, she deliberately kept me in the dark about at least two-thirds of her life, and I was thinking that that amounts to a kind of betrayal. We weren't all that tight, but still she owed me some honesty, don't you think? But this afternoon I started to feel guilty about thinking about Linda in that way. I mean, maybe she betrayed me, but she paid with her life, so who am I to criticize . . . hey, what's so funny?"

Joe D. was smiling. "Nothing," he said. Actually he found Alison rather fascinating. This kind of intense self-examination was new to him. He certainly never put a microscope to his emotions the way she did. Nor, for that matter, did anyone else he knew. Marie had been about as complicated as tic-tac-toe; she would have thought Alison was off the wall.

"No, really, what's so funny?"

"I don't know. Why can't you just relax and go with it instead of always examining everything so closely?"

"I don't examine everything so closely," she protested.

"Yes, you do. If you're angry at Linda for hiding so much from you, okay. What's the big deal? Why worry about it so much?"

Alison stared at him as if she found his laissez-faire policy as curious as he found her psychoanalytic outlook. Or inlook. "You really believe it's possible to just stop worrying on command, to simply turn off your emotions like a television set?" It was more of an observation than a question.

"I didn't say you should turn off your emotions. I said to stop trying to decide if your emotions are good or bad. There's no such thing as a good or bad emotion. It's just what you feel."

"Twenty thousand dollars of analysis and this is what it all boils down to: stop worrying so much. Is that it? Well, thanks a lot, Sigmund Freud, but not all of us have that kind of self-control."

She stared down at her empty plate, radiating hurt and anger. He could see her straining to hold back tears.

Joe D. took her hand. "It isn't always so easy for me either, Alison."

225

She looked up. "Really?" she said, wanting it to be true.

He nodded. "I have doubts too, I really do. And I examine my emotions all the time." This was true enough, though next to Alison he was an unexplored planet.

"Oh, I'm glad, I really am. I can't stand chronically happy people. Being with them when you're depressed is like eating meat in front of a vegetarian. You feel so guilty . . . oops, sorry."

"Let's go back," he said, meaning to her house. It was twelve-thirty and there was still no sign of Farber.

They found Tracy looking very glum on the living room couch. She pointed to her room. "I've been evicted. Again. I'm beginning to feel like a welfare case or something."

"Don't let it get you down," said Alison. "I've been exiled to the couch myself a number of times and it isn't all that bad."

Tracy nodded but didn't look any less miserable with her situation. The roots of her unhappiness obviously went beyond having to sleep on the couch: being Miss Congeniality's younger, plainer sister takes its toll.

Chapter

JOE D. awoke early Saturday morning, rolled over expecting to find Alison in bed with him, and didn't. He recalled their first morning together and thought: the queen of hot and cold strikes again.

He rolled over the other way and found her on her back on the floor. This gave him a momentary fright until he noticed a tremor in her legs. Slowly, so slowly that at first he hadn't noticed any movement at all, she lifted her legs an inch or two off the ground, held them like this for a few seconds, then let them down, slowly, deliberately. He saw no evidence of strain on her face, just intense concentration. He counted thirty leg raises and wondered how many she'd done before he woke up.

Unaware that she was being observed, Alison next performed a masochistic variety of sit-ups that Joe D. could feel in his own gut. Finally, she executed a series of contortive stretching exercises that Joe D. would until now have thought anatomically impossible. All the while her face was frozen in a pose of angry determination that proclaimed: this is not fun, this is *work*.

She sprang to her feet and noticed he was awake. "Want to run with me?" she asked energetically.

"Not a chance," he answered, recalling the workout she'd subjected him to the last time they ran together. "Besides, it's only seven-thirty."

"Best time to run, before the sun is too strong." She bent forward at the waist and touched the floor with her palms. Her hair was in a loose ponytail that flopped over her head.

"You remind me of a gym teacher, all sweaty and gung ho," he said.

She frowned. "I don't have heavy calves, do I?" She lifted one leg in front of her and inspected it critically, rotating her foot at the ankle. "All my gym teachers had heavy calves."

"Your calves are perfect. Come over here and let me admire them close up."

"Forget it. I never get in bed with men who compare me to gym teachers. Anyway, got to run. Ha ha."

"Running's no fun," he whined. "Come back to bed."

"Lazybones. Besides, who said it was fun?"

"Then why do it?" he asked, comfortable in the bed, which smelled sweetly of Alison. But she had already left the room.

He was fast asleep when she returned from running but wide awake by the time she finished showering. Her hair was wrapped, turban-style, in a large white towel. Another towel covered her torso, just barely. Her skin glowed, still dotted with droplets of water. Her tanned legs looked long and smooth and strong; he wanted very much to touch them, to run his hands along them and feel their smoothness and strength.

228

"Aren't you going to ask me how many miles I did?"

"How many miles did you do?" he obeyed.

"You don't really care, you're just asking me because I told you to."

"No, really, how far did you run?"

"Thanks for asking. Five miles."

He was impressed and said so. "Now, how about some more exercise right here?" He stretched his arms to her from the bed. She hesitated: he looked like an ad for something sexy, lying naked on his stomach on the bed, the sheet bunched around his ankles.

"Sorry, but I just showered."

"So what? We'll take another shower later. Together."

"And I want to get down to the beach as soon as possible. It's a gorgeous day."

"But it's only eight-thirty," he complained, glancing at the clock by the bed.

"Exactly. The prime tanning hours are about to begin and I look like Hellmann's mayonnaise. Now get your unexercised body out of bed and I'll make you some coffee. I've got half an hour to get to the beach."

"No dice. Remember, I'm on a case." And I've got a deadline, he thought, that's starting to look awfully close.

"But what can you do today?"

A question he'd already asked himself. "For starters, I've got to find Farber." Joe D. had left Alison's number when he'd called his station the night before, but so far had heard nothing.

"But he may not even be alive, let alone on Fire Island," she protested. "And anyway, I want to spend the day with you."

This rare admission of affection was not lost on Joe D. She must have seen it in his expression: "I mean, this case has me hooked. I don't want to miss a thing."

Joe D. smiled at her and shook his head. She shrugged guiltily, as if caught doing something naughty.

"I've got to find Farber dead or alive," he said. "I'm going to start down at the marina, see if the powerboat turned up. Though if Farber *wasn't* the victim last night, I don't know why he'd come back here knowing someone in Seaside Harbor knew all about Baby Bear."

"That isn't really true, is it? I mean, we don't know the first thing about Baby Bear, do we?"

"No, but Farber may think we do. Anyway, we do know it links Farber to Linda through the money in the safety-deposit box. And he's smart enough to know that spells trouble for him. Don't forget, he was already worried that we were on to something. That's why he tried to distract me with that note about Lewis and Madison College."

"You're sure it was Farber who left the note?"

"Who else could it be? Farber knew about Lewis from his housemate, Marty Lawrence. And he wanted to deflect suspicion from himself. Lewis was an easy target."

They had coffee and toast with Alison's housemates, all of them lured from their beds by the beautiful weather. Joe D. was not the only outsider at the big Formica kitchen table; Ronnie was sitting across from a bleary-eyed hang-over case who she introduced as Harry, or Henry—"whatever," she'd said when he finally identified himself, with little enthusiasm, as Herbert. He had, Joe D. thought, probably been handsome the night before, but now he looked merely defeated, with the pea-soup complexion and hangdog look of someone about to throw up; they all gave him wide berth.

The boys, as Alison had begun to refer to them, looked a little battered themselves. "Jesus, what a night," said Jason, staring down into a mug of untouched coffee. **230** "Yeah, incredible," said Larry, looking around the table for some encouragement to continue; when none was offered he too sought consolation in his coffee mug, the steam forming a gray beard under his chin.

To Joe D. the group felt about as cohesive as an S-line at a bank on payday, but perhaps it was only that they had spent the past weeks avoiding the one topic on all their minds—the murder of one of their housemates—and were left circling on tiptoe around a conversational black hole.

"I'm off to the beach," announced Ronnie to no one in particular. "Come on, Tracy, let's get a good spot." The sisters, wearing identical bikinis, Ronnie's filled to overflowing, Tracy's a bit limp in places, left the room, leaving Harry or Henry—whatever—looking even more hangdog than before.

"Emily Post she's not," said Alison in an effort to console him, but a moment later he shoved his chair away from the table, excused himself in a voice full of marbles, and ran from the room.

Joe D. decided to walk to town to see if Farber's boat had been returned. He also wanted to call his station from a booth—there was only one phone in Alison's house and it was in the kitchen, where he'd have no privacy. He told her he'd be back in twenty minutes.

The sidewalks were nearly deserted at nine o'clock; the air was dry and warm. It was a beach day all right, Joe D. thought, glancing up at the cloudless blue sky. He was surprised at how quickly Fire Island changed in response to the weather. Last night, the air hot and humid, the whole island had felt damp and spongy. This morning the island seemed crisp, almost arid. The bushes on either side of him crackled softly in the gentle breeze.

A hundred yards from Alison's house, he heard footsteps behind him, the crunching sound of feet on the sandy path. A vision of Linda Levinson on her way to meet her killer flashed through his mind.

231

A moment later he heard the footsteps again, closer this time. The brush on either side of him was high and dense, impenetrable as a wall; the sidewalk cut through it like a tunnel running straight to the bay side of the island. It could be anyone, he told himself, a jogger or someone out on an early bagel run, but he decided to check it out anyway. He started to turn when he felt something heavy hit him on the side of his head. In the split second remaining before he crumpled onto the sidewalk he felt hot pain spread to every part of his body the way a sudden flash of intense light suffuses a dark room.

Lying face down on the ground, nearly unconscious, Joe D. felt a second blow, to the back of his head this time. He tried to get up to defend himself, but felt his energy draining from him in a torrent. Instead he instinctively curled up into a tight protective ball and prepared his short-circuiting mind for the blows he correctly sensed would follow.

He awoke with the suspicion that his head had tripled in size. It throbbed wildly with pain: he could envision it swelling and contracting like a blowfish on speed. He was aware of other people and tried unsuccessfully to lift his head, which only confirmed his suspicion that it had grown to a size heretofore known only in science fiction.

"Joe, it's me, Harrison. Can you hear me?" Harrison was leaning over him. He looked to Joe D. like a grotesquely large, winking clown.

It took him a minute or two, but he finally understood the winking. He winked back at Harrison, a feat that caused some pain, and brought his index finger to his lips in a silencing gesture. He didn't know who else was in the room and didn't want Harrison to identify him as a fellow cop. Amazing, he thought, what the mind is capable of even when pureed into spaghetti sauce. That his fingers had found his lips he took to be a positive sign.

232

"What happened?" he asked in a mumbled voice he barely recognized. Another good sign, though: he could speak.

"Two joggers found you on Tupelo Road a hundred yards from here. You were in a heap, pretty badly beat up. They heard someone running off through the bushes. They must have come on you just as the assailant was working you over."

"Good thing they did, too," said a man's voice, not Harrison's. "You couldn't have taken much more."

"This is Doctor Kaplan, Joe D.," explained Harrison. "You're lucky you were hit outside this particular house, 'cause there's two doctors in it."

"What luck? In Seaside Harbor there's a doctor in every house," said Kaplan.

"No kidding?" said Harrison, who was deaf to sarcasm.

"Seriously, though, you've got some bad bruises, some cuts, possibly a concussion. I'm going to find you a stretcher and get you to a hospital on Long Island for some X rays. You're very lucky, Joe. That guy, whoever he was, was out to kill you."

Joe D. nodded, a big mistake: it felt as if two steel balls as sensitive as testicles were rolling freely inside his head.

"Doctor, if you don't mind I'd like to be alone for a few minutes with him," said Harrison, his voice practically choking with reverence.

"Alison?" Joe D. said drowsily, remembering through the pain that she might be in danger. He felt some strength returning to both his mind and body.

"I'm here," she said. Joe D. smiled; his lips felt badly parched. "When you didn't come back I went out looking for you. There was a small crowd outside this house. It's about six houses down from mine."

"Okay now, miss, please step outside for a few minutes," said Harrison in his best policeman's voice.

"She can stay," said Joe D. firmly.

Harrison looked at her suspiciously for a moment, then shrugged. "Does she know?" he whispered.

Joe D. nodded, with less pain this time.

"Okay by me, then."

Kaplan left the room with the injunction that the patient not be left alone for even a moment.

"Did you get a look at the guy who did it, DiGregorio?" whispered Harrison conspiratorially as soon as the door was closed.

"Didn't see him." Joe D. tried hoisting himself on his arms but made only slight progress. "Shit," he said, summarizing his feelings about the entire morning. "Shit, shit, shit." He lifted himself some more and was almost sitting up now.

"Take it easy, Joe D.," cautioned Harrison.

"I guess you'll be calling Castiglia about this."

Harrison nodded.

"Ought to make his day. Now they'll really be panic around here."

"You stay put until we can get a stretcher and take you across for X rays. I'll ask the Chief to send a Coast Guard boat."

"Never mind the boat, Harrison. I'm fine." He started to swing his legs over the side of the bed. A migraine-like pain coursed through his head. Oddly enough, his whole body ached.

"Stay put," ordered Harrison. "I'll be back in a short while." He looked at Alison. "Take care of him."

As soon as Harrison left the room, Joe D. stood up and fell right back down onto the bed, as if a powerful gust of wind had blown him over. He tried again, despite protests from Alison, and this time managed to stay upright.

"Since when does Fire Island rock back and forth?" he asked her.

"Joe, please do what Doctor Kaplan says and stay in bed until they can take X rays."

"Doctor Kaplan," he said. "What does he know? The guy's younger than I am." He walked to a mirror that rested on top of a bureau. He didn't look too bad, he thought, all things considered, sort of like a boxer after a particularly brutal match. A match he'd lost.

"Doctor Kaplan said you're lucky your hair is so thick, there were no deep cuts."

"What was it that hit me?"

"A log, believe it or not. A small log. They found it next to you."

Joe D. practiced walking around the room.

"If someone wanted to kill you, why would they use a log?"

"Good question. A gun would have been more effective but too noisy, would've woken up the whole island. Assuming, of course, my would-be killer had a gun in the first place. Don't forget, we're not dealing with a professional killer here. Linda wasn't shot, she was strangled. Anyway, you heard Kaplan. One more blow and I *would* have been dead, so I guess a log's as good as anything if you have the chance to use it."

Alison shuddered. "Joe, please, you really should sit down."

"The one thing that bothers me," he continued, ignoring her advice, "is that anyone can get hold of a plain old kitchen knife, and a knife is so much quicker, so much cleaner than beating someone to death with a log. Unless . . ."

He paused to run an idea through his head.

"Unless what?"

"Unless the attacker doesn't have a house in Seaside Harbor. If he didn't, he wouldn't be able to get himself even a kitchen knife."

"But we're pretty sure it's Farber or Lewis, right?"

"I don't know. Besides, anyone *not* from Seaside Harbor who came here for the purpose of killing me would probably have come prepared with a weapon, wouldn't you think?"

"Unless he came here for another purpose and *then,* once here, decided to kill you."

"Unless, unless, unless. The deeper into this mess we get the less we know for sure." He was silent for a moment, then asked her what time it was.

It was two o'clock.

"You're kidding, right?" Alison shook her head. "I can't believe I was out that long. Come on, the first thing I have to do is finish the errand I set out to do this morning."

"You mean see if Farber returned the boat?"

"If *someone* returned the boat. Remember, Farber may be dead for all we know. Castiglia only gave me until Monday to solve this thing, so let's hurry."

"Joe, I wish you'd stay in bed like Doctor Kaplan told you to."

"You had your chance this morning to spend the day in bed with me and you blew it, Alison."

"No second chances?"

"No second chances."

Chapter

WALKING into town for Joe D. was like walking through a spinning tunnel in an amusement park: remaining upright took all his concentration. The web of paved footpaths, normally a perfect grid, now undulated like some pop art optical illusion; there were no straight lines left anywhere, no right angles, no clean corners. He wondered if this was a symptom of brain damage and if maybe he should have gone to Long Island for tests.

Might as well quit his job while he was at it, because if he didn't wrap up this case by Monday he'd be fired anyway. Alison tried to help him but he refused, thinking the only way he was going to regain his sense of balance was to use it, and by the time they neared the marina he was indeed feeling much steadier.

"We're in luck," he said as they walked onto the dock. "There's the guy whose boat Farber took last night."

He picked up his pace slightly and then became so dizzy he had to lean against a mooring pole to regain his balance. **237**

"Easy, Joe," said Alison. "I don't want to have to fish you out of the bay."

The boat owner recognized Joe D. and introduced himself as Hugh McAlee. He lived in Babylon, he told them, on Long Island, and had come over the night before just for the hell of it. Joe D. guessed he was about forty, with an unkempt beard and breath so densely fragrant with liquor he could have powered his boat with it. Assuming it had been returned.

"You get your boat back?" asked Joe D.

"Nope. I was stranded here all night. But I had myself a swell old time anyway. Went over to Crane's and partied with some of the money I made on the deal. You wouldn't believe some of the chicks they got over here."

He winked at Joe D. With a little encouragement he would happily have filled them in on the details of his exploits of the night before, but no such encouragement was forthcoming.

"I had some good news this morning, though. The boat turned up earlier today in Seaview, one town over from here. I'm heading there now."

"In Seaview?"

"That's right. The harbor patrol people, they saw it tied up at the end of a dock there. There was an alert out for it, so they called the harbormaster in Waterside this morning to say that it had turned up. I called Waterside myself this morning to report my boat was missing, and that's when I found out it wasn't missing at all but was tied up in Seaview and just waiting for me to claim it."

"Do they have any idea who brought it to Seaview?" asked Joe D., more confused than ever.

"Nope. Just appeared there. No sign of the guy who took it last night, but I still got his cash and his watch. He'll probably show up for his watch. But I'll keep the two hundred bucks. Plus, I get my boat back as soon as I go and claim it. I guess it was a pretty good deal any way you look at it, plus what a time I had last night. These Seaside Harbor girls, they . . ." From behind rheumy eyes he practically pleaded for the opportunity to continue on this track.

Joe D. turned to Alison. "It's what, a twenty-minute walk from here to Seaview?"

Alison nodded.

"Say, you must be the guy got beat up," McAlee interjected. "I heard all about it this morning."

"News travels like lightning around here."

"Tell me about it. I watched three ferries leave so far today and all of them was full, like that one there." He pointed to a ferry about fifty yards from the dock, both decks jammed with passengers. "Just like those boat people leaving Vietnam."

"People must really be panicking," Alison said, "to be leaving in the middle of a gorgeous weekend like this." She sounded almost wistful.

"They sure are," continued McAlee. "And I don't blame 'em one minute. First a murder, now this. I can't think of a worse place for this to happen than here on Fire Island. People here are sittin' ducks. Now, where I live in Babylon, we'd just run out to our cars, lock the doors, and drive to wherever we had to go. Safe and sound. But here? Like I said, you're all sittin' ducks. Not to mention the chicks here in these skimpy little dresses and shorts. Last night, I was—"

Joe D. interrupted him. "What are people saying about all this, about who the killer might be?"

"I don't live here so I'm no expert. But this morning nobody's talking about nothing else. They're saying it's a maniac who just attacks for no reason. Makes sense to me, else why would he go for someone like that chick he knocked off last month and then go after you? He's got to

239

be a maniac. When it was just the girl you figured it had to be an ex-boyfriend or something. But now, after this morning, there's no telling what could happen next. Say, why were you so interested in that guy who took my boat?"

"He's a friend, that's all."

"Well, when you see him, tell him he can get his credit cards from the harbormaster here. I just dropped them off. I think I'll keep the watch, though. Let him come and get it if he wants it bad enough." With that Hugh McAlee started off for Seaview to reclaim his boat, a happy man.

Joe D. glanced around the marina. Half of the berths were empty, like toothless gums, and the thought of all these boats out for a pleasurable day of cruising made him feel curiously detached from the real world, hollow. He felt a million miles from that sort of day, a day of self-indulgence under an unobstructed sun beaming high in the sky solely for the benefit, or so it seemed, of these weekend sailors and their fortunate guests.

"Shit," said Joe D.

"What's the matter?"

He considered describing the hollow feeling to her, then thought better of it. "I just don't think we're getting any closer, Alison. Who hit me this morning? Farber? But we don't even know if he's alive. And if he's dead, then there's someone else . . ."

He was quiet for a few moments. "Whoever it was, he knew I was the one who slipped Farber the Baby Bear note."

"Farber could have guessed, and then told the person he called. I was dancing with him at the time, and he knows I'm . . . we're . . . you know, together. So it wouldn't have been hard for him to add it up. He knew as soon as he saw that note that you were onto him."

"But you're forgetting one thing."

240   "What's that?"

His voice turned bitter. "We don't have the slightest fucking idea what the hell Baby Bear is."

They were heading back to Alison's to get a bite to eat (neither had eaten since breakfast) when they were overtaken by Lieutenant Harrison.

"You're supposed to be in Waterside getting X-rayed," he said, but it was obvious from his whole manner—his faster than normal breathing, his expectant eyes—that he had important news and couldn't care less about Joe D.'s health.

"What's up?" asked Joe D. impatiently.

"You're not going to believe this."

"Try me."

"A body washed up a couple of hours ago on a little private beach in Waterside. Guess whose body it is?"

Joe D. shook his head, unwilling to play along.

"Come on, guess."

"Harrison."

"Farber! Eric Farber!"

Joe D. and Alison looked at each other but said nothing. This confirmed what they'd been thinking all morning, but assessing the implications of this latest bit of news would require some concentrated thought.

Their silence apparently unnerved Harrison. "Well, isn't Farber one of the names you mentioned before? Isn't he one of the suspects?" Harrison looked like a schoolboy who'd just been named hall monitor. "Well, is he or isn't he?"

"He *was* one of the suspects," Joe D. replied sullenly. "How did he die?"

"The autopsy isn't until later, but his head's pretty well bashed in. They found blood all over a boat tied up in Seaview this morning, too. Kinda fits, don't it?"

Joe D. recalled the shiny object pumping up and down **241** last night through the mist. Now he knew its target. And there was no need to wait for forensics to confirm that Farber hadn't hit his head falling off the boat. "At least we now know one thing," he told Alison. "It wasn't Farber who decked me this morning."

Harrison gave Joe D. what he must have thought was a penetrating look. "So this about wraps it up, eh? This morning you said you had two suspects, now one of them's dead, so it's got to be the other one, right?"

"Wrong, Harrison, the two suspects had nothing to do with each other," said Joe D.

"For that matter," added Alison, "do we even know that Lewis knew Farber was a suspect?"

Joe D. looked at Alison. "Do you think it's possible," he asked with a sinking feeling, "that we had the wrong suspects in the first place?"

Chapter

27

JOE D. napped back at Alison's house while she watched over him for signs of a concussion (doctor's orders). By early evening he felt, surprisingly, okay. Not great, but better, like he'd live. They decided to head for—where else?—Crane's. Joe D. thought he might be able to learn something there: what, he couldn't say, but he certainly wasn't going to learn anything hanging around Alison's. His sense of urgency about the case was far greater than the pain he was feeling. Failure loomed big and ugly.

He knew people in Crane's were staring at him. Even if word of his mugging hadn't spread through Seaside Harbor, his appearance would have done the trick. His forehead sported a protrusion the size and shape of an egg, colored purple as if for Easter. The top of his head sprouted hornlike lumps ill-concealed by his thick, curly black hair. Both eyes were bloodshot. He was not a pretty sight and he knew it.

Crane's was unusually empty tonight, even for the tail end of happy hour. It looked like a different place altogether; its big rooms were meant to be filled, to accommodate flows of people, large migrations of amorphous groups. Its atmosphere derived entirely from its patrons and their energy; half-empty and tinged by an off-season mustiness, it was as anonymous as an American Legion Hall. Nothing like a murder and a follow-up assault to keep people in their homes or off the island entirely. Joe D. wondered if news of Farber's demise had reached Seaside Harbor. That ought to clear out the town completely.

He bought Alison a gin and tonic. "Time to face the music," he said, then left Crane's and carried his beer to a bank of pay phones near the ferry landing, passing up the phones in Crane's, which offered no privacy and no protection from the blaring music. He called Chief Castiglia at home.

"I guess you heard, Chief."

Joe D.'s only hope was that his injuries would arouse Castiglia's concern. The Chief inhaled deeply before speaking. Joe D. heard a bull getting ready to charge and began preparing his defense.

"Oh, I heard all right. DiGregorio, your ass is in the fire this time. The mayor called me three times today. First he calls me at eight A.M. and asks how come we don't have any progress to report. I tell him we'll have progress any minute. Then he calls me at noon to say I was right, we have progress: some guy is attacked leaving his girlfriend's house. He doesn't know it was you and good thing, too. So I say I have confidence in my man and he says he wishes he could say the same about me. That was before the third phone call, when he wants to know about this body washing up in Waterside."

He paused here for maximum effect.

244   "I have just one question for you, DiGregorio. How many more murders before you get this guy? One? Two? A baker's dozen? I don't need an exact number, but I would like a rough estimate."

"Chief—"

"How many, DiGregorio? More than two? Four?"

"Hopefully none, Chief."

"Hopefully none," he mimicked in his sweet, calm-before-the-storm voice. "You bet your sweet ass, none," he exploded, "because there won't be anyone left in Seaside Harbor pretty soon to *be* murdered. I went down to the harbor to watch them coming off the ferries. Thousands of them, it was a fucking stampede, DiGregorio. On a Saturday afternoon. Tell me, is there anyone left there to kill except you and that girlfriend of yours?"

"Chief—"

"Don't say nothing, DiGregorio. Nothing. Unless you're going to tell me you know who the killer is. Is that what you're going to tell me?"

His silence was his answer.

"I hear you, DiGregorio. I've already sent two more guys from the force to patrol over there. They'll pretend not to know you unless you tell them otherwise. I don't want anyone else to get killed over there, hear me? I want our killer locked up by Monday so Labor Day weekend will be just as crowded as ever over there and I won't get wake-up calls from our esteemed mayor. Monday, DiGregorio."

"I'll do my best, Chief."

"No you won't, you'll do better than that."

"I got to go now, Chief. I'll call you tomorrow."

"Yeah, do that."

"So long, Chief."

"By the way, I hear you got hit pretty bad. You okay, Joe D.?"

"Yeah, okay, Chief."

Walking back to Crane's, Joe D. recognized someone **245**

he'd met at Farber's house. It seemed like an age ago but in fact it was just a couple of weeks. The recognition was mutual.

"Hey, you lived with Eric Farber, right?"

He nodded solemnly. "I'm Steve. You were the guy who thought he found Eric's ring, right?"

"That was me. Name's Joe D. I was sorry to hear about your friend."

"He wasn't much of a friend. Kept to himself mostly. Still, it's pretty creepy, knowing a guy who's been murdered. Most of my house has gone back to the city. Doubt many of them will be here next weekend. Kind of blows the summer." Steve had tight curly hair and a friendly face that in profile was almost a perfect arc, beginning with his short forehead, tapering out along a gently convex nose, receding at the mouth, and trailing off where his chin should have been.

"I heard the cops think it was murder. Can't figure who'd want to kill the guy. And what the hell was he doing on a boat in the middle of the night?"

They had entered Crane's, where Joe D. bought Steve a drink.

"When something like this happens it really makes you think, doesn't it?"

"How so?"

"Farber was a very successful guy. On Wall Street. A big producer, one of the biggest, and not yet thirty. We all envied him, but look at him now. I mean, it makes you ask what's the point of it all."

Joe D. shrugged: *he* certainly didn't have the answer. Alison joined them and greeted Steve by name. Everyone knows everyone else here, Joe D. thought, not for the first time. No wonder the murder had set off a stampede for the mainland; even if the murderer isn't a friend, chances are he's an acquaintance.

"Thing is," Steve continued, "I'm a broker too and I bust ass to make half of what Farber made. And you know something, I don't know if I'm going to hustle as hard anymore. I hate to admit it, but maybe it takes something like this to put your values in the right perspective, know what I mean?"

Joe D. nodded with appropriate solemnity.

"You say you're a stockbroker?" Joe D. asked.

"Not in Farber's league, but yeah, I'm a broker."

"Let me ask you something. This may sound dumb, but what does Baby Bear mean to you?"

"You mean like from the Goldilocks story?"

Joe D. nodded.

"I guess I read it as a kid." He looked at Joe D. like he might be deranged. "Why?"

"No reason, just curious." Joe D. felt a little stupid and hoped Steve would quickly forget the question. He didn't.

"The only other Baby Bear I ever heard of was Fluck and Johnson."

A spark of hope ignited deep inside. "Fluck and Johnson?" he said, almost whispering.

"Sure, you know. The Philadelphia department store."

"What's a department store got to do with Baby Bear?"

He smiled indulgently. "I can see you don't play the market. F and J was acquired earlier this summer." He paused and looked at Joe D. for some sign of recognition. "What are you, a hermit or something? This was one of the biggest deals of the year."

Joe D. ignored what was no doubt intended as a putdown. "Where does Baby Bear come in?"

"In these takeovers the investment bankers and lawyers always use code names for the parties involved to ensure secrecy. If you know about these deals in advance you can make a bundle, which is illegal, so they always use these cute nicknames. Like in one deal I read about they called the acquiring company Jaws and the target company Charlie the Tuna. Cute, right?"

"And Fluck and Johnson was Baby Bear, correct?" interjected Alison.

"Right. And the acquiring company was Papa Bear."

Joe D. felt tantalizingly close to a breakthrough, although the contours of that breakthrough were still vague. "Tell me something, Steve, was Farber's firm involved in this deal?"

He shook his head. "As investment bankers, maybe. But Farber was a retail broker. He wouldn't be involved in this sort of thing."

He felt the breakthrough slipping away from him like a greased watermelon.

"Except," said Steve, "that some of their clients may have bought or sold some F and J using Fried as a broker."

"But a broker at Fried and Sons wouldn't necessarily have had inside knowledge of the deal," said Alison glumly.

"No, an investment banker would have, but not a broker. Hey, now I remember something. Farber bragged a few weeks ago that he had put his clients into F and J at around twenty dollars a share. It was eventually sold for thirty-four or thirty-five, so I guess he was involved indirectly after all. I only wish I had done the same for my customers. Say, does this have anything to do with Eric's murder?"

"No," Joe D. assured him, "of course not."

"The F and J deal was basically a friendly merger," Steve continued.

"Friendly?" asked Joe D.

"You know, no bidding war or anything. The two companies agree to merge, and all that remains is for their lawyers and investment bankers to get together to iron out the details."

248   "Lawyers?" The spark had reignited.

"Sure. Lawyers always get involved in these deals."

"Would a lawyer know about the deal before it was announced? I mean, could a lawyer profit the way, say, Farber's clients did?"

"No way. That's trading on insider knowledge and it's against the law."

"But the lawyers *do* have knowledge of the deal before the general public, correct?" asked Alison.

"Correct. But profiting on that knowledge is illegal."

"Any idea who the lawyers were for F and J?" asked Joe D.

Steve thought about this for a minute. "Couldn't tell you, but it's usually one of two firms."

"Which two?"

"Newman and Walters is the most active in the takeover field, but they usually represent the acquiring company . . ."

"And the other one?

"Strickman, Cohen is the other one that comes to mind. They usually represent the target. If I had to guess F and J's lawyers, I'd say it was probably Strickman, Cohen."

Alison and Joe D. looked at each other, then back at Steve. "But you don't know for sure?" asked Alison.

"No, but I know how to find out real quick. Hey, Mike!" he shouted down the bar.

They were joined by a short, porcine man wearing a pink alligator-shirt and shorts that, on him at least, were Bermudas.

"Mike here is with Newman and Walters," said Steve by way of introduction. "I've been trying to get a few insider tips out of him for years but he's always refused."

"An ethical lawyer," said Alison. "How refreshing."

"Ethical schmethical," said Mike. "He never offered to split his profits with me."

249

"Tell me something," asked Steve. "Were you the firm for F and J on the buyout this year?"

"We missed that one. Say, did you believe the market yesterday? Jesus, talk about a rally."

"No shit. At least my clients won't be calling me this weekend with their usual bellyaching. Last month I had a guy wake me up at nine in the morning here in Seaside Harbor—"

"Uh, Mike," interrupted Joe D. "Who did you say was the law firm for F and J?"

"If it wasn't us it could only be one other firm," he said. What is this, twenty questions? "And that firm is?"

"Strickman, Cohen," said Mike, then turned back to Steve. "And the over-the-counter index, I couldn't fucking believe it."

Joe D. wanted to raise a fist and shout. He knew he was close to a solution to the whole mess. Not there 100 percent, but getting closer. He glanced at Alison: her eyes were lit with excitement.

Steve and Mike continued to reminisce about Friday's stock market with all the fervor of two Yankee fans discussing a play-off game. Joe D. and Alison had no trouble slipping away.

"I hate to say it," said Joe D. to Alison when they were finally alone on the terrace. "But it looks like your friend Linda was selling stock tips to Eric Farber."

"No," said Alison firmly. "I can't believe she would do that kind of thing."

"There was a lot you didn't know about Linda."

She said nothing for a few moments. "You're right, I suppose. That would explain the 'LL' notations in Farber's book."

"They must have used Fire Island to trade the secrets or to exchange the cash, probably both. In the summer only, of course. In the winter they must have had another rendezvous spot."

"So the last ten thousand, which was clipped together with the Baby Bear note, that was the payoff for the Fluck and Johnson tip."

Joe D. nodded, then started to think it through out loud. "If she had invested in the stocks herself she would have been caught. So she somehow found Farber—"

"She met him here, in Seaside Harbor."

"—and used him to profit from her inside knowledge. The beauty of it was he didn't even have to buy the stock himself, he had his clients buy it. That way it was twice removed from the source of the tip."

"And when investors are happy, the broker is happy because his commissions keep going up. Still, it just doesn't fit. I simply can't imagine Linda putting this kind of scheme together."

"You might be right. My guess is that Linda wasn't the mastermind behind the whole setup."

"Then who was?" asked Alison. "Farber?"

"Could be, but he's dead and someone murdered him. Which means that someone is still alive who was involved. That someone is the brains behind this whole scheme. I'd put my money on Golland."

"Golland! I'd almost forgotten about him."

Joe D. continued: "I'm positive he's at the center of this whole thing. He gave the info to Linda, she passed it along to Farber, he passed it along to his clients. Who could ever trace it back to the source, to Golland, with all those layers in between?"

"Poor Linda," said Alison softly, the excitement of discovery momentarily absent from her voice. "When I think that she was involved in all this . . . She loved Golland so much she even broke the law for him. I don't think she would have done it otherwise. I might not have known her very well, but I knew her well enough to know that she wasn't a criminal."

"Not a criminal? Come on, Alison, you didn't think

Farber the criminal type, remember? And don't forget that Linda called this her escape money. I think she knew she'd need a lot of money to get away from Golland when she finally found it in her to make the break. New apartment, new job, and no one left to buy her those expensive presents."

"I told you before, I think she was finally getting ready to escape that weekend she was killed. She seemed nervous. One minute happy, the next depressed. I think she was finally making the break from Golland, I really do."

"But someone wouldn't let her escape, either Farber or Golland. She was a link in the chain, and she knew enough to put them both in jail. Maybe she threatened one of them."

Alison looked puzzled. "You mean by going to the police or the SEC or whoever?"

"Or blackmailing them."

They were both silent for a few minutes, thinking it all over. A small sailboat under motor pulled into the marina, its sails wrapped neatly around the boom. They watched it approach its slot, heard the engine cut, then watched as it glided silently in. It was Alison who broke the silence:

"My money's on Farber. He was here on the island the night she was murdered. Remember, I saw him in Crane's just before she left. Plus, he didn't have any romantic involvement with her the way Golland did."

"I think I agree with you about Farber killing Linda, but don't put too much stock in Golland's feelings for Linda. From what I know, and I don't know everything yet, he spread his feelings around pretty liberally. And I think he'd kill in a second just to keep his wife from knowing about Linda."

Another thoughtful silence, this one broken by Joe D. "The thing is, if Farber killed Linda, who killed Farber? And who, by the way, came after me with a log?"

"Golland, of course," said Alison.

"Why 'of course'?"

"Who's left? We know Lewis had nothing to do with this whole mess, and Farber's dead. That leaves only Golland."

"Care to explain *why* he'd want to kill Farber?"

Alison thought about this for a bit. "I pass," she said at length. "But you do agree, about Rob Lewis not being involved."

"Like I said, he had nothing to do with either Farber or Golland, and we know *they're* involved. True, Farber tried to implicate Lewis, but that was just to throw us off the track."

"I'm glad to hear you say that because I ran into Rob in the city last week and . . ." She looked suddenly uncomfortable.

"And?"

"And he scared me, that's all."

"Scared you how?"

"Just by the way he is."

"But you must have spent some time with him for him to have made this kind of impression."

"I ran into him on Third Avenue and something about him frightened me. But I like him, too, in a funny, sad kind of way. I guess I feel sorry for him and I'm glad he's not a suspect anymore. So what's next?"

He sensed there was more to this than she was saying, but with Lewis no longer involved there seemed little point—and much risk—in going into it deeper. "I pay a visit tonight to our friend Jonathan Golland, that's what."

Alison shook her head. "Not tonight, Joe. It's already nine o'clock and you need rest. Let's have a quick dinner and then call it a day. You've been through hell today and I'm worried about your head."

"I promised Castiglia I'd present him with a murderer by Monday, Alison. I don't want to waste any more time." **253**

"So dinner with me is a waste of time, is it?" She took his head gently in her hands and kissed him lightly on the lips. He inhaled deeply.

"Doctor's orders are doctor's orders, Joe. You've had too much activity today as it is."

"You mean I can't have any more activity tonight? None?"

She grinned and put her arms around him. "Leave the activity to me tonight. You just lie there and take it easy."

Easier said than done, thought Joe D.

Chapter

IT'S fifty minutes from Waterside to Scarsdale when there's no traffic, which is almost never the case. There wasn't much traffic Sunday morning, however, as Joe D. and Alison drove to Golland's house in Joe's ebony Trans Am.

Joe D. loved his car. It was his one true luxury (he was still paying it off), but it embarrassed him a little, too, because, well, you had to be a *certain kind of guy* to pull off a car like a Trans Am, and sometimes, as he left a parking lot and people stared at the gleaming black car, so sleek and stealthy it almost looked sinister, Joe D. felt an urge to roll down his window and shout, "Hey, this isn't really my kind of car, I'm not the kind of guy you probably think I am!" But of course he never shouted any such thing. And he had, after all, bought the car. No one had forced him.

"Wow," said Alison on seeing the car for the first time Sunday morning in the parking lot at the Waterside ferry dock. Her tone was more incredulous than admiring. She circled the vehicle warily.

"It's not me, really," said Joe D. with a defensiveness he immediately regretted.

"I hope not," Alison said with exaggerated relief. "I'm not sure I even want to get in. What's your survival rate?"

"Aw, come on. I'm really a cautious driver."

"You may be cautious, but I don't think this car is." She got in, however, looking for all the world like she was settling into a dentist's chair for root canal. Without novocaine.

Ten minutes later she was still noticeably tense, her knuckles white from gripping the sides of her seat. There was something else going on too, Joe D. felt; a murky but highly charged cloud had settled between them.

"Lighten up, Alison," he said with trepidation, sensing that anything he said could trigger a storm.

"I'm sorry. It's just that living in the city, I'm not used to cars in general and especially not . . . this *kind* of car. It seems so . . . powerful."

"You're embarrassed to be seen in it, is that it?" They were approaching the Southern State Parkway.

"I'm not even going to respond to that," responded Alison, turning away from him.

Joe D. floored the Trans Am as he merged onto the parkway, throwing Alison back into her seat. "Very funny," she said and then said nothing for a while.

He put on a tape: Bach's Concerto for Flute, Violin, and Harpsichord in A Minor. Its intricate serenity, and about fifteen minutes without talking, helped ease the tension.

"You're really something," said Alison, shaking her head and smiling. "Bach in a Trans Am. That's got to be a first."

It was only eight o'clock but already the sun had burned a widening blue aperture through the morning haze.

"Are you nervous, Joe D.?" Alison asked as they **256** crossed the Throgs Neck Bridge into the Bronx.

"Yeah, a little bit."

"Me too."

"No reason for you to be nervous. Like I said before, I'm dropping you off at your mother's house on the way."

"But I want to come with you."

"I understand that. But it could be dangerous. I doubt it, but it could be. I'll pick you up when I'm done with Golland."

"Anyway, I don't feel like seeing my mother. She'd know something was wrong if I showed up on a beautiful day like this when I'm supposed to be at the beach. Especially," she added unnecessarily, turning toward the window and mumbling just loud enough for him to hear, "if I showed up in this." Alison closed her eyes, wondering why she had been unable to resist this sudden burst of hostility.

"You mean with some dago cop from Long Island."

"That's not what I said, Joe," she protested—too quickly and much too emphatically.

They were quiet again for a while, uncomfortably so. Then Alison spoke, her voice muted:

"I have to face facts, Joe. My mother has this fantasy for me. For herself, really. One day her princess is going to arrive in a beautiful new Cadillac or better still in a big new Mercedes—but not a black Trans Am. Behind the wheel is my prince, a lawyer or a doctor or even a Seventh Avenue prince—she's less choosy now that Princess Alison is past thirty."

Joe D. laughed in spite of himself. "How old will you have to be before she'll settle for an Italian cop?"

"At least sixty, because by then she'll be dead."

She laughed at her own joke but Joe D. had turned serious. "You really wouldn't cross your parents, would you? I mean, my parents wouldn't exactly jump for joy if I brought home a Jewish girl, but they'd get over it. And what the hell, it's my life, not theirs. But you'd stay single your whole life, or until you're sixty and your parents are dead, before you'd disappoint them. Wouldn't you, Alison?"

"Do we have to discuss this now?"

"I think so, yes. Anyway, you brought it up."

"Well, if you must know, it's not just my parents. For one thing, I was raised in the Jewish faith and it means a lot to me."

"I was raised in the Catholic faith and it means a lot to me, so what's the big deal?"

"That doesn't make sense, and slow down or we'll have an accident." They were speeding through Westchester County on the Hutchinson Parkway. Along the side of the highway trees drooped dispiritedly, made limp and brown by August's dry heat. The roads were still almost deserted, adding a lonely, eerie quality to the morning.

"Yes, it does. Religion is important, but so is love. There's room in my life for both, why not in yours?"

"But that's just it, Joe. The way I was raised, religion and love aren't two different things. They're tied together along with everything else. I just can't compartmentalize everything the way you can. I mean, I suppose you can just go to confession and tell your priest everything bad you've done, including all about your Jewish girlfriend, and then leave feeling like a million bucks. Well, it's not that easy for me."

"It's not that easy for me, either. For one thing, I haven't been to confession in ten years."

"Okay, so forget religion for a moment. Then there's the question of our life-styles."

Joe D. groaned.

"Make fun of me, I don't care, but I went to college for four years—"

"All expenses paid."

"I went to college for four years because I wanted certain things out of life. A career, a circle of intelligent, educated friends who read books, go to the theater—"

258

"So what am I, illiterate?"

"Of course not, but we live in two completely different worlds, don't you see?"

"You may live in a different world, but I don't."

"That makes no sense."

The conversation was going nowhere. "You were right, Alison. What's the point of discussing it now? We leave Fire Island and you're a different person." He opened his window slightly to let out some of the hostility that was making the car unbearably close.

They said nothing further until the Weaver Street exit, at which point she began giving him directions to her mother's house, curt little orders like "right at the light" or "next left." Another Bach concerto was playing now, but this one sounded angry, furiously fast and insinuating, its interwoven voices competing noisily for attention. He switched it off.

Alison stole a glance at Joe D., then quickly turned away. She wanted very badly to apologize, but something inside wouldn't let her, something stubborn and guarded and mean. I'm going to lose him, she thought, and end up with someone like Rob Lewis, someone whose only virtue is his familiarity. I'm going to lose him and I'll have no one to blame but myself.

At length they arrived at a large, white, pillared house only slightly smaller, Joe D. thought, than his elementary school. Alison wished him luck without looking at him and left the car. He watched her walk up the long slate path to the front door, watched her ring the doorbell and throw her arms around the elderly black woman in a maid's uniform who answered, and thought perhaps she was right after all: they did inhabit different worlds.

259

Joe D. had found Alison's mother's house impressive,
which was precisely the response it had been designed to
elicit. Golland's house had been designed to elicit *awe*. It
was a castle-like structure made of stone, with three tur-
rets—a large one at the center and two smaller ones off to
the sides. The house stood, brazenly, concealed by neither
trees nor hedges, a hundred yards from the road. In front
of it lay the greenest, smoothest, thickest lawn Joe D. had
ever seen—it looked as if it had been rolled out only an
hour ago. An underground sprinkler system caressed this
emerald carpet with a diaphanous spray. Tiny rainbows
glistened here and there, as if they too had been
painstakingly planted and nurtured. To Joe D. the whole
effect was unreal, even surreal, and eerily unappealing, a
pointless victory of man and his technology over nature.

You have to be a certain type of guy to carry off a house
like this, thought Joe D. Just like you have to be a certain
type to drive a Trans Am.

Golland's door, like Alison's mother's, was answered by
a black woman, also wearing a maid's uniform. She seemed
dwarfed by the house, as if she, or perhaps the house itself,
were an optical illusion, a special effect.

"May I help you?" she asked.

Joe D. stepped around her and walked in. "I'm here to
see Mr. Golland. Joe DiGregorio, from the Waterside police."

She smiled and nodded in one smooth movement,
turned, and started up a wide wooden staircase. Her slow,
deliberate steps were silent; Joe D. could hear only the
swish of her nylon uniform as she headed upstairs, and the
assertive ticking of a clock from somewhere deep in the
house.

A few minutes later Golland appeared, wearing a yellow
260 alligator-shirt, green pants, red belt, and white moccasins.

Joe D. found the sight of Golland in carnival-colored mufti reassuring. His arms were unexpectedly thin, his middle unexpectedly broad.

"We have to talk, Golland," he greeted him, sensing the importance of speaking first.

"We don't have to do anything of the kind, DiGregorio." He spoke in a loud whisper.

"I know all about Baby Bear now. And all the other animals in your zoo." Joe D. was feeling real tough. The residue of hostility from his spat with Alison was coming in handy. "I also have you to thank for this." He pointed to the egg under his forehead; this morning it was the color of purple cabbage.

"Follow me," said Golland suddenly. "I don't want my wife involved."

"I'll bet you don't," said Joe D. loudly.

Chapter

GOLLAND led Joe D. across a large front hallway, down a short flight of stairs, through another wooden door heavy enough to withstand siege, and onto a surprisingly small but very pleasant screened porch. Two minutes in Golland's massive but oppressively dark house and Joe D. had almost forgotten that the sun was shining. In contrast, the porch was sunny, sparsely furnished with wrought iron chairs and tables, and brightened further by hanging pots of extravagantly lush and colorful impatiens. In the distance he saw a diving board poking above a row of carefully clipped shrubs.

"I'll get to the point. What were you doing last night and this morning on Fire Island?"

"Oh, come now, Lieutenant. Be serious. I was nowhere near Fire Island." Golland smiled indulgently.

"Murder's no joke," Joe D. said, determined to block Golland's attempt at gaining the upper hand through patrician nonchalance.

"No, you're right: murder's no joke."

"Linda Levinson's murder, for example. And Eric Farber's. You're under investigation, Golland. *Serious* investigation."

This seemed to have a sobering effect on him. "I told you before," he said, slowly and precisely, as if he were speaking to a foreigner (which, Joe D. thought, is probably what he thinks I am). "I loved Linda. I would never have harmed her in any way, let alone kill her."

"But you love your wife, too, correct? Or her money and all this." Joe D. waved his arms to indicate all of Castle Golland.

"I'm a senior partner at a major law firm. I don't need Amanda's money or anyone else's for that matter." Aha, thought Joe D., detecting a new, less confident tone in Golland's voice; I have him on the defensive.

"I'll bet your father-in-law could make life very difficult for you with just one word from his daughter, couldn't he?" Golland said nothing but raised his head a bit in what was obviously meant to be a gesture of defiance.

"I'll bet he could destroy you with one wave of his left arm, couldn't he, Golland?" Joe D. was guessing now; he really had no notion of how one person could "destroy" another except by killing him. Still, it seemed to work. Golland had come down a notch or two from his lord-of-the-manor posture, though he was by no means defeated.

"There's a wide gap between accusing me of infidelity—without proof, I might add—and accusing me of murder. If you want to ruin my marriage and my career, as you think you can, so be it. I can't stop you, though I will make your life as miserable as possible if you do. There are people who would side with me, not my father-in-law, in any kind of altercation."

This last statement was delivered in an unbecoming tone of childish one-upmanship, as if his father-in-law were actually present.

"But as for murder," he continued, "you have no proof, you've identified no motive, and you're treading on very dangerous ground. Very dangerous. Now if you'll forgive me, I have a golf date. You may let yourself out through the porch door."

He pirouetted regally on one foot and headed toward the house. Joe D. knew he had to try something drastic, for Golland was right; he had no proof, though he had identified a motive.

"We found almost a hundred and fifty thousand dollars in Linda's safety-deposit box. You and Linda and Farber had this real sweet thing going. You gave Linda tips on mergers you were working on. She passed the tips on to Farber, which was a way of washing them so they couldn't be traced back to you. Baby Bear was Fluck and Johnson, right? For that bit of laundering, Linda got ten thousand dollars, not bad money for delivering a message at the beach. I figure at ten thou a crack that's at least fifteen counts of fraud. I have a feeling the FTC would be very interested in every one of those counts, don't you?"

"I doubt it," Golland said in that air-conditioned voice of his that Joe D. found so intimidating. "The FTC has nothing to do with securities transactions. You mean the SEC, I believe." He smiled thinly, indulgently, as if he were dealing with a pesky child.

"I mean you're in hot water no matter how you look at it."

"You're still missing something, Lieutenant. Motive. As you can see I hardly need the money. Do you honestly think I'd risk all this for a few thousand dollars?"

"Linda's share, one hundred and fifty thousand, isn't a 'few'."

"Several, then. And tell me something else, who paid me? Linda? Farber? Or did I simply buy the stocks myself? If I did that there'd have been no reason to 'wash' the tips, as you put it, through Linda and Farber, would there?"

Golland had a point. "We have evidence that Linda fed tips to Farber, who fed them to his clients." *Evidence* is a pretty strong word for what he had, thought Joe D., but what the hell.

"I don't doubt you do, Lieutenant. But I'm hardly going to jail on account of someone else's transgressions."

"Just knowing what she and Farber were up to and not doing anything about it is enough to put you behind bars." He was guessing, but his hunch was apparently correct; Golland looked sincerely taken aback:

"But I didn't know until after she was dead."

As soon as he said this he froze, and for the first time Joe D. saw a glimmer of defeat in his eyes, for Golland had just admitted he knew about Linda and Farber, though he still hadn't owned up to any direct involvement. Nevertheless, the home court advantage had been forfeited.

"How did you find out?"

Golland's head dropped a few inches. His voice dropped along with it, taking on a bitter cast. "Goddamn her, I was so fucking generous. I practically paid her rent. I bought her jewelry, furs, trips. Why the hell did she have to betray me?"

"You're a fine one to talk about betrayal."

Golland ignored this bit of self-righteousness. "It's the thing I can't understand. If you had known her, so sweet, almost guileless. Why?"

"To escape."

"Escape from what?"

"From you. Her life. She figured leaving you meant leaving her job, giving up her apartment, which she couldn't afford without you. It wouldn't surprise me if she wanted to leave town completely, get as far away from you as possible and start over somewhere new. All that takes money, Golland. Lots of money. And I think, I really think deep down a part of her hated you, hated you for having this hold over her and not letting go. I think she just wanted to get back

265

at you, betray you the way you betrayed her and all the other women in your life."

"But I loved her . . ." Golland said plaintively, almost wistfully.

Joe D. was unmoved. "Who told you she was selling stock tips?"

Golland looked hesitant, deciding whether or not to answer, whether he *had* to answer.

"You're in trouble no matter how you look at it, Golland, so you might as well start telling the truth," Joe D. warned. "You may find it a refreshing change."

Golland took a deep breath. "The day after she died I got a call from Farber. I'd never heard of him but he said I had to meet him or I was in big trouble with the SEC." The voice was somber, almost robotic. "I had no idea what he was talking about but he did just what you did, he mentioned 'Baby Bear' and a few other code names I was familiar with. Needless to say, I met with him as soon as I could. He told me he and Linda had had this arrangement for almost five years. Said they had met on Fire Island, and when he found out she worked for me, he proposed this little scheme wherein all she had to do was give him the name of the company being acquired in a takeover deal and he'd give her a big reward. I believe ten thousand dollars was her usual fee—all for one little name. Farber said Linda resisted for a while but finally went for it. He said *she* sought *him* out a few weeks after he'd first proposed the idea to her. Farber named all the tips she'd given him and I knew he was telling the truth. They were my biggest deals, my best clients."

Golland shuddered, as if this tarnishing of his professional reputation were the most unpleasant aspect of the whole affair. More distasteful, even, than the two murders that had ensued.

266   "Farber said he saw no reason why Linda's death should change anything. For him. He said I was to continue in Linda's place, passing him insider information in return for which he wouldn't tell my wife about Linda, or the SEC about what had been going on."

"He knew about Linda and you?"

Golland nodded. "Linda must've let it slip at some point, or perhaps he followed her, I don't know."

"But if you had nothing to do with their arrangement, why worry about his going to the SEC?"

Golland chuckled bitterly. "Farber knew my reputation would be ruined even if I could prove it was all Linda's doing. Which I'm not sure I could have. At any rate, Farber had me by the short hairs and he knew it. I agreed to pass along to him the next bit of insider information I was privy to. We agreed that I'd do this only once, but I could tell just by looking at Farber that he was a hungry bastard and wouldn't settle for just one deal. Since our conversation that day I haven't been directly involved in any significant mergers or takeovers, so I haven't had the opportunity to assist Mr. Farber in his get-rich-quick schemes.

"The Tuesday before she died," he continued, "Linda gave me one month's notice. Said she was leaving her job and leaving me as well. I protested, of course, but I couldn't very well protest too much, you understand. I don't believe she told anyone else at the office. Unfortunately, she did tell Farber. That Friday night on Fire Island at some bar in Seaside Harbor."

That explains the tension Alison had sensed that night between Farber and Linda, Joe D. thought. "Did Farber tell you this, about Linda quitting her job?"

Golland nodded. "Well, of course, for Farber this was like finding out that the goose that lays the golden eggs has reached menopause. Apparently he put some pressure on her not to quit. I asked him if he had threatened her and of course he denied doing any such thing, but he struck me as such a . . . such an intense, hungry individual, one of those people who are so completely absorbed by money they'll do anything to get it."

"We all know one of those, don't we? Did Farber admit to killing Linda?"

"Of course Farber killed her. It was that or jail. You see, Linda told him she was going to the SEC to confess everything. It seems she was getting cold feet. Some of the insider cases were making headlines and she didn't want to find herself on the front page of the *Wall Street Journal*. Let alone the *Post*. She told Farber she'd been to a lawyer who advised her that if she turned in Farber, and if they got his clients as well as Farber, she'd be granted immunity."

"Do you think Linda was serious about going to the SEC?"

Golland considered this for a while in silence. "I don't know. She might have been. I find it hard to believe she'd betray me in that way—maybe she was bluffing. If she could have helped the Feds nail Farber and his clients, she would probably have gone free herself. The SEC is quite zealous about prosecuting insider cases—overzealous, in the minds of many of my colleagues. I think they would have been willing to make a deal. But the important point is not whether she was seriously considering going to the SEC or not. It's that Farber *believed* she was."

"Believed her enough to kill her to keep her quiet," Joe D. said. "And you killed him."

Golland froze, hesitated, then swiveled around with somewhat less panache than he had shown earlier. "You're bluffing," he said. "You have no proof of that."

With no honorable alternatives springing to mind, Joe decided to lie.

"Who do you think was on that little speedboat Friday night, Golland? The one you ran into in the middle of the bay off Fire Island? Give up? It was me. And I saw everything."

Too late, Joe D. saw Golland's right hand slide into his pants pocket, slowly, deliberately. It hadn't occurred to him that Golland would have a gun on him, not in his own house. Damn, he thought, reaching into his jacket to pull out his own gun. Golland beat him to it. By only a second, but that was all it took.

"Stop right there, Lieutenant."

Joe D. eased his hand out of his jacket.

"Did you really think I'd let you walk away from here?"

"You tried to kill me once already, didn't you? Yesterday morning."

Golland nodded, a hint of smugness in his expression.

"When Farber called you Friday night, it was to tell you I was on to him, right?"

"He called me to say I had to meet him at the dock in Waterside. Right away. I resisted, naturally, but it was no use. Farber acted as if I were as involved in this whole mess as he was. You can imagine the time I had explaining to Amanda why I had to run out all of a sudden Friday night.

"I drove to Waterside and met Farber at the end of a dock, as he had instructed. He was sure we were being watched, that I had been followed. So he insisted I get in this small boat he had managed to procure. Then he pushed off, into the bay."

"'We're both fucked,' he said to me. I swear to you, those were his exact words. 'We're both fucked. This guy DiGregorio knows everything.' Farber had followed us that day in Central Park, you see, so he knew you were circling around him. When I left you in the park, he came after me. Needless to say, he was surprised to learn you were a cop. And I, of course, had no idea you were masquerading as a swinging single. Farber even tried to throw you off the track by putting you on the scent of someone else. Somebody named Lewis, I believe."

"How did you know where I'd be Friday night?"

"He told me where to find you. He said we had to 'take

care of you.' I believe that's the expression he used. He said you would probably be at your girlfriend's house on Tupelo Road. He even told me which house."

"So you hid outside Alison's . . . outside my girlfriend's house all night—"

"I would have preferred to 'take care of you' that night, but you didn't return until much later, and then with Miss Rosen. I had to spend the night like some sort of fugitive. I passed a few hours productively, looking for a suitable blunt instrument, if you'll forgive the cliché. I found a log and spent the time hidden behind some bushes peeling off the bark. You very cooperatively emerged bright and early the next morning, yesterday morning. If it hadn't been for a couple of joggers you'd be a dead man, and I—" His eyes widened here, almost wistfully. "I'd be playing golf, even as we speak." He was silent a moment, and then the hard look returned to his face. "So I have to do it now."

"Put the gun down, Golland. You can claim self-defense with Farber, but not with me." Joe D. was arguing for his life now, but Golland had the fixed, almost serene expression of one who's already decided exactly what he's going to do.

"We're going outside now, Lieutenant. We're going to get into my car and we're going for a ride." He indicated the screen door with his gun, a small, boxy affair that had been invisible in his ample trousers. "Now, *move.*"

Joe D. started to turn, his mind searching for a way out of this mess.

"Stop there, Lieutenant."

It was a woman's voice.

Joe D. whirled around. Standing at the door that connected the house and the porch was a woman whose expression was so fierce, so full of rage, that she would have been frightening with or without a gun in her hand. In this
270 case, with.

"Drop the gun, Jonathan," said the woman.

Golland looked at her blankly but held onto his gun.

"I said, drop it."

"This has nothing to do with you." Golland was pleading.

Casually, as if tossing a tennis ball to an eager puppy, she fired a shot in her husband's direction. It missed him, just barely, but it did the trick: he let his gun fall to the slate floor.

"Now it's your turn, Lieutenant." She waved her gun in his direction. Joe D. knew there would be no point in arguing, so he reached inside his jacket, brought out his gun, and dropped it to the floor.

Chapter

30

IF Golland had looked defeated confessing to Joe D., now, facing his wife, he looked like a prisoner awaiting the executioner's ax. "Amanda, what are you doing?" he whispered hoarsely.

"Mrs. Golland?" said Joe D. He had almost forgotten that such a person existed, and was rapidly calculating the odds that Amanda Golland would use her gun a second time. His conclusion: she might enjoy a bloodbath, if her appearance was any indication.

It wasn't so much her features that created this impression—she was plain, Joe D. guessed, though it was impossible to tell with certainty since she had disguised her face behind a layer of thickly applied makeup. Mrs. Golland's looks were quite obviously the result of a painstaking, deliberate *process;* there was nothing even remotely natural about her. Even her hair was unreal, neither white nor yellow but some chemical color in between, yanked back tightly from her face only to balloon out in a gravity-defying bouffant. No, it wasn't her features but her expression that sent a chill through Joe D. Her eyes were widened in a look of astonished revulsion. Her lips puckered, revealing a fierce determination. The color in her cheeks seemed to be intensifying by the moment, like mercury rising in a thermometer.

Golland took a step toward his wife, who extended her arm to thrust the gun closer to her husband.

"Stop there, Jonathan," she said in a muted trumpet of a voice; it seemed to originate deep in her throat, as if it had already traveled a long, weary journey before escaping through her brightly painted lips.

Golland gave vent to a nervous titter, as if dismissing the notion that his wife would use the gun on him.

"I'm serious, Jonathan. Move any closer and I'll shoot you."

The simplicity of this warning seemed to frighten Golland further. He recoiled into the corner of the porch as ordered. Joe D. remained motionless, afraid to make the slightest move.

"Did you really think I was fooled all these years, Jonathan?" she asked blankly.

He cocked his head, not understanding.

"I believe you really did think you had me fooled. It's an indication of the size of your ego that you imagined you were capable of deceiving me simply by telling me you had a late meeting or had to leave town on business unexpectedly. You couldn't imagine my doubting you for a moment. Really, Jonathan, your ego was like a giant pair of blinders . . . blinders lined with mirrors so all you could see was yourself, yourself, and yourself."

Joe D. turned to Golland, half-expecting to see the blinders.

"You were actually quite inept," she continued. "I really **273** wasn't interested in the details of your love life, or sex life, as it were, but little bits of evidence just kept popping up everywhere I looked, like daffodils in the spring." She smiled, pleased with the simile. "And you were so pathetically obsessed with secrecy. You might have spared poor Miss Levinson *et al.* a great deal of humiliation if you'd just given in and spent the night now and then. Believe me, you wouldn't have been missed. But you showed up here every night. Oh, sometimes it was three in the morning, but you always came home."

She turned to Joe D. "We didn't even share a bedroom, yet he came home every night. Now, I ask you, why would he do that?" She turned back to her husband. "I asked myself that very question every time you came home late and made a big ruckus in your room to make sure I'd hear you, but I never came up with an answer that stuck. Until a few years ago, when I got bored with asking and stopped."

"You knew," uttered Golland incredulously. "I just can't believe you knew. How?"

"Oh, Jonathan, don't be stupid. There are thousands of people in New York who want a favor from my father, or want him to invest in some new project, or simply want to get to know him in the hope that some of his power and influence will rub off. And they all think they can get to him through me. So they ask me to lunch and start dropping hints, and when I don't respond they become less subtle, and then still less subtle, until they finally just come out and say it: 'Your husband is having an affair.' I suppose they expect me to be grateful for the news, expect me to return the favor."

"But who would do such—"

"*Everyone,* darling. Some of your closest friends took me to lunch. And their wives. Everyone wants a hook into my father. You even married me to get one."

"You know that's not true," Golland ventured weakly, but his wife shot him a dismissive glance that effectively silenced him.

"Why did you put up with it all these years?" asked Joe D.

"I suppose because I never really felt I had the capacity for anything better," replied Amanda Golland. "For *real* love. And also because he . . ." She turned to Golland, searching for the right word. ". . . he fit. That's right, he fit."

"I don't understand," said Joe D. There was something compelling about this whole story. Oddly compelling, given the circumstances. But not nearly as compelling as the elegant little pistol in her right hand.

"I was an only child, Lieutenant . . ."

"DiGregorio."

"DiGregorio. My father and I are very close but I was not a son and he wanted a son very badly. Unfortunately, my mother died soon after I was born and . . . things just never worked out for him after that in the marriage department. In every other department, things worked out very well indeed.

"So along comes Jonathan Golland. Handsome, a Harvard Law graduate. He was from a poor family from Brooklyn, but he wanted to be rich so desperately he transformed himself into a rich man in every way—clothes, grooming, demeanor, even his voice was rich. By the time I met him, he had already made himself over into a rich man in every way except one: he had no money. That's where I came in.

"Father adored him, still does, and I adored my father. So that when he introduced Jonathan to me, I really didn't see that I had a choice: Jonathan fit perfectly, so that was that. We married shortly after my twenty-first birthday. Father was disappointed Jonathan didn't join him in Dinnerman's, but I think he secretly admired him for it too, thought it showed backbone. But of course backbone had nothing at all to do with it. My father threw enough business Jonathan's way to ensure he was made a partner very soon after we were married, and kept throwing business his way until his name was on the door at Strickman, Cohen. I suppose Jonathan figured there was no need to work for his father-in-law when he'd get his money eventually. Isn't that right, Jonathan?"

He said nothing, just stared at her as if seeing her for the first time.

"My father's one disappointment was our not having any children. I think he believes it's my fault. All I ever said to him was that we can't. I didn't specify, didn't offer any explanation. In point of fact, it's Jonathan who—"

"Amanda!" he shouted.

"In point of fact it's Jonathan who can't have children."

"Amanda, please."

"Honestly, Jonathan, you'd think after all that's gone on this would be the least of your embarrassments! I mean, he knows you're a murderer; finding out you're sterile as well is hardly going to shock him." She turned back to Joe D. "At any rate, my husband is a biological rarity. You see, only one man in a million produces no sperm. Many men have *low* sperm counts, but not Jonathan. He has none whatsoever!"

She spoke as if she found this clinically fascinating but of no personal or emotional relevance. "You, Lieutenant, I assume can, and do, manufacture millions of tiny sperm all the time without giving it the least thought. But not poor Jonathan here. I often wondered if he told his girlfriends not to bother with the diaphragm or whatever. Did you, Jonathan? Did you tell them not to bother?"

"Amanda," he whimpered, "this is not necessary—"

276   "I asked you a question, dear. Did you tell them not to bother with contraceptives? Or did you insist on some sort of device each time? I know! You used a condom. I can just picture you making a big scene about putting it on. Safe sex and all that." She heaved a deep, guttural laugh and Joe D. glimpsed the depths of the hatred and the anger that simmered within her. She was breathing heavily, the gun trembling in her hand. She wore a white tennis shirt, white tennis skirt, and white sneakers, but she was so translucently pale it was difficult to tell where her skin stopped and the fabric began. The overall effect was eerily one-dimensional, as if she could disappear—*poof!*—simply by turning sideways.

She paused for a moment to compose herself, then continued: "Running around was one thing, Jonathan. After all, I at least have the comfort, however slight, of knowing you haven't left a trail of little bastards in your wake. But murder and scandal I won't tolerate. I simply can't . . ." She faltered here, emotion welling up at last. "I couldn't bear to see my father hurt, to suffer the humiliation."

"If your father's so powerful, a son-in-law in jail wouldn't be too damaging," Joe D. offered, trying to placate her. "Lots of millionaires are in jail nowadays."

"Oh, but you don't understand."

"Understand what?"

"Baby Bear," she answered bitterly, shuddering as the two words escaped her lips.

These were the last two words Joe D. expected to hear from Amanda Golland's pallid lips. "What does Baby Bear have to do with your father?" he asked.

"Everything. My father *bought* Baby Bear."

Joe D. looked at Golland. "You mean . . ." He paused, trying to recall the companies involved. "You mean Dinnerman's bought, what was it? Fluck and Johnson?"

"Exactly what I mean. And thanks to Linda Levinson, my father paid a dear premium for it."

"But I had nothing to do with that," Golland protested meekly from his corner.

"But you didn't turn her in when you found out, did you, Jonathan? You could have averted the scandal by going to the SEC—or even to my father—but you didn't."

Joe D. turned to Golland, expecting a response. A defense. Instead, Golland just stood there, panting as if from physical exertion.

"I could tolerate what you did to me, Jonathan, with your *women.*" She spat out this last word, her grip tightening on the revolver, which was still aimed at her husband. "But betraying my father—"

Golland interrupted her. "Amanda, there's only one way to avoid a scandal." He looked briefly at Joe D., then back at his wife. "Kill him," he whispered at her. "Shoot him."

"Please, Jonathan, you don't have to whisper. He can hear you perfectly well anyway." She sounded less grief-stricken than annoyed now.

"I can get rid of the body," he continued, still whispering.

His wife looked at him as if he were a talking dog, her expression a combination of curiosity and revulsion.

"We'll never have to deal with this whole mess again. Ever. I only killed Farber because he was blackmailing me into doing something that was totally against my professional ethics."

A curious thing had happened to Golland's voice: its rich, unaccented veneer had fallen away, revealing the unmistakable intonations of a place that seemed light years away, though in fact it was just fifteen miles or so due south: Brooklyn.

"And Linda Levinson?" she asked, *her* voice still as calm and expressionless as a newscaster's.

"I swear to you, I didn't kill her. I loved . . ." He stammered, wisely avoiding a knee-jerk recitation of his "I loved her too much to hurt her" routine.

"You loved her? Is that what you were going to say? Don't make me laugh." But she laughed anyway, deeply and bitterly.

"Farber killed her, he practically admitted it to me. So you see, all I did was kill a murderer, a blackmailing murderer. He deserved exactly what he got."

"Please, Mrs. Golland," broke in Joe D. "Give me the gun. Your husband will stand trial, your father will survive . . ."

Just then Golland began to move toward her, arthritically slow and with a wary eye trained on the gun.

"Darling," he began gently. "We could start all over again. I'll be more attentive. We'll travel, we'll go to the theater more . . ." Sweat was forming like hoarfrost on his forehead, and his right eye began to twitch, neither of which helped his case any. "I love you, Amanda, I always have."

Joe D. sensed immediately that Jonathan Golland had uttered the wrong line, the line that got him thrown out of court for good.

"Love me?" she shrieked, raising her voice for the first time. "Love me? You really are a despicable man, Jonathan. You don't love me now and you never did, and that was the one thing about you I could always stomach. You never lied, you never pretended I was anything more than a means to an end. And now you have the gall to say you love me? You don't even know what love is." Joe D. saw the gun shaking in her hand. "You've tarnished the honor of this family. *My* family. And you talk about love." Joe D. saw her finger quiver around the trigger.

"Mrs. Golland, *don't.*"

The finger jerked and a bullet sailed into Golland's gut.

Joe D. lunged at her and they both fell against the screen, but she managed to get off a second shot before the gun tumbled from her hand. This one hit Golland in his chest, propelling him against the screen door. He looked at **279** his wife, his face questioning, still not comprehending how this could have happened, then looked at Joe D. He collapsed with a dull thud onto the hard slate floor.

"If only he hadn't gotten my father involved," Amanda Golland said, still on the floor. Tears had begun to roll down her painted cheeks, slowly, one at a time, like the first drops of rain on a parched desert. She turned back to her husband, also on the floor, his yellow shirt now a deep, murky red. "We both had only one love," she continued, addressing the body of her husband. "Yours was money, Jonathan. You never loved Linda Levinson, or any of the others. They were attracted to your money and your power and *that* attracted you. To be loved for your wealth and influence—most people would call that pathetic, but to you it was the ultimate acceptance, the ultimate success."

She looked at Joe D. "And my one love was my father. I don't think I ever thought about love as anything other than what I felt for him. If only Jonathan had turned her in . . . If he'd acted with honor . . ."

"I'm going to call the Scarsdale police, Mrs. Golland. Why don't you come inside with me?"

He took her arm and was startled by how cold it felt.

"If he hadn't involved my father," she said softly, looking at Joe D. as if anxious to explain everything to him, to justify herself. "If he hadn't done that . . ."

Chapter

JOE D. and Alison had found a secluded spot on the beach, but only after fifteen minutes of walking on scorching hot sand through an obstacle course of sunbathers. Seaside Harbor on Labor Day Weekend had much in common with Coney Island. After an hour, even their oasis was engulfed by the crowd.

Alison dozed while Joe D. let the sun sweat out unpleasant memories of the past week. Voices drifted in and out of his consciousness, voices almost familiar to him now, though still strangers' voices.

"I can't believe it's Labor Day Weekend and I'm still not on baby oil."

"You weren't here at all in August. What d'you expect?"

"If they hadn't found the killer I wouldn't be here even now."

"They didn't find the killer. He's dead."

"Same difference."

"To you maybe, but not to him."

"When he asked her she threw up. Swear to God, she ran to the bathroom and puked her guts out."

"Romantic, huh?"

"Well, they'd lived together five years. She'd given up, I think, and when he finally asked her, ring and all, one and a half carats, I hear, she was overwhelmed."

"She always throws up when she gets emotional. Like when Lennon was shot . . ."

"Eric Farber a killer—it's still hard to believe."

"And that insider deal with the Levinson girl blew my mind."

"How come I was in a house with him all last summer, he never tried to sign me up as a client?"

"Tough break. He made his clients a fucking fortune."

"She has on this cute cover-up at breakfast last week. Then she and Stu go to the beach and she's got on a red one-piece. In the afternoon she puts on a second suit to sit out on the deck, then she showers and puts on a pair of gorgeous white pants with a turquoise cotton sweater. Just before dinner she runs upstairs and puts on this shift-type thing, stunning, and a pair of shoes I never saw before either. We have dinner, and afterwards Stu says to her, 'Marsha, get dressed and I'll buy you a drink in town.' I counted five changes of clothing, all brand new like every weekend, and he tells her to get dressed."

"And they're not even married."

"I don't care if I look like a prune in five years, I'm switching to baby oil."

"Shari, you'll fry."
"I'll risk it, I'll risk it."

"The Waterside cops figured it all out, including the Golland connection."
"That's Golland as in Strickman, Cohen?"
"The same."
"I knew there was something unsavory about them."
"Christ, Henry, they're the third biggest firm in New York, what're you talking about?"
"So a pig can weigh a ton, doesn't make it kosher."

"She and Ralph went to Spain for a week."
"I was in Spain during my junior year abroad."
"You went to Spain for junior year abroad?"
"Paris, but we took a side trip to Madrid."
"Ralph and Alissa aren't going to Madrid, just Ibiza."

"The Scarsdale cops arrested Golland's wife, but her father came through with the bail."
"I read she's pleading justifiable homicide."
"I'd kill my husband if he was sleeping with his secretary, I swear I would."
"Yeah, but did you see the wife's picture in the *Times*? Maybe it was justifiable adultery."
"Lenny, that's disgusting."

"What'ja reading?"
"*Trump: Surviving at the Top.*"
"Good?"
"Yeah, I guess. Can't get past the first paragraph with this racket."

"Are my shoulders burnt?"
"They look fine, Michelle."

"How can you tell without touching them? Touch my shoulder and tell me if it turns white. And hand me the atomizer, I need a spritz. Lord it's hot."

"It sure is noisy here today."

Now *this* voice he recognized. Joe D. sat up and looked at Alison, whose eyes were still closed against the sun. "*Now* don't you wish we had gone somewhere else?" he asked pointlessly.

"I *like* the beach and this may be the last weekend of the last summer I'll ever spend here. I didn't want to miss it."

"Why the last summer?"

"I think I'm getting a little old for this place." She was on her back, shimmering under a layer of liberally applied baby oil. "Haven't you noticed I look a little . . . *used* next to the younger things in Crane's?"

"You look dynamite compared to all of them. Besides, why do you have to have all these rules? This age. That profession. This religion. It just makes you crazy."

She shook her head. This was evidently a discussion she didn't want to have. Joe D. leaned over and kissed her. "Next summer we'll rent a place upstate, in the country."

"What's Fire Island?"

"A lot of things, but it isn't the country. It's as frantic and pressured and crowded as the city. I don't know how anyone relaxes here."

"People don't come here to relax."

"I rest my case. Next summer, the real country."

"Joe, *this* summer isn't even over yet. Why don't you try and enjoy what's left of it?"

He kissed her again. "I love you, Alison."

She opened her eyes and smiled languidly. "You're **284** blocking my sun."

                    *   *   *

High noon found them waist-high in the Atlantic Ocean.
The water was finally comfortable to swim in, giving back
some of warmth it had been absorbing over the past three
months.

"Anyway," said Alison out of the blue, "this would
probably be my last weekend in Seaside Harbor even if I
weren't over the hill."

"Why's that?"

"Too many awful memories. When Linda was killed I
came back because I felt somehow that *not* coming back
would be a surrender, like giving in to the person who
killed her. And, to be honest, Friday rolled around and the
thought of spending the weekend in the city depressed the
hell out of me."

"Of course, my being here had absolutely nothing to do
with it."

She smiled and dunked herself underwater. "All week I
kept thinking about Eric Farber," she said, brushing wet
hair back from her face. "I don't understand how money
could mean so much to him he'd kill someone like Linda
for it. This past week I thought a lot about how when I was
a teenager, and even in college, my friends and I, we all
scorned material things. We criticized our fathers for working so hard just to make lots of money, and we criticized
our mothers for devoting their lives to spending it. We
wore nothing but faded blue jeans with patches, and we
swore that when we grew up we would devote our lives to
meaningful things, like making the world a better place to
live in. So what happened to us all? How did we get from
there to here, where we don't just *work* for money, we
steal and kill for it?"

"You rejected material things because you *had* them.
You can't reject what you don't have. I grew up in a two-
family house—we weren't poor, but we weren't in your **285**

league by a long shot. So there was no way I looked down my nose at big houses and big cars and all the other things money could buy. Don't forget, Farber once had all those things and then lost them when his father killed himself. He couldn't afford the luxury of scorning money."

"I guess you're right, but I still feel we've lost something along the way. I'm as guilty as the next guy—I mean, Bloomingdale's isn't exactly the Peace Corps—but at least I do sometimes question it. I still ask myself once in a while if it's all worth it, the long hours I put in and the inevitable compromises I make for the sake of getting ahead. What's sad is that I ask myself less and less frequently. I guess people like Farber just stopped asking altogether."

"His father killed himself because his business failed," Joe D. reminded her. "I think he learned the wrong lesson from that experience. What he *should* have learned was that the worship of money can destroy you if you don't put it in perspective. Instead he learned early on that life was the price you paid for money, and death was the punishment you got for not making it. I don't think he ever really questioned that."

"In the end he paid with his own life, didn't he?"

They dried off, lay down on their blanket, and held hands as they drifted in and out of sleep. But their peace was interrupted by still another voice, this one familiar to both of them, deep and reverberating. It was the very last voice Joe D. wanted to hear.

"Well, if it isn't the two lovebirds of Seaside Harbor."

"Rob." Joe D. sat up, dizzy from the sun. Alison propped herself on her elbows, squinting.

"Must have really disappointed you two to find out I wasn't a murderer after all. Must have really blown your day."

"Hey, Rob, really, I'm sorry," said Joe D. halfheartedly. "I was only trying to warn you—"

"Don't apologize, DiGregorio. I'm a sport. No hard feelings, right? Let bygones be bygones."

Rob was standing between Joe D. and the sun, his features indistinct, though the gestures that accompanied his words were exaggerated, puppet-like.

"I mean, here's this Farber guy running loose all summer, organizing a stock fraud, murdering poor old Linda Levinson, ripping up her clothes and getting his rocks off on her after she's already dead . . . I mean, compared to that, what've I got to be ashamed of, right?"

At a loss for words, Joe D. and Alison were silent. He stared down at them for a bit, then shrugged as if disgusted. They watched him walk down to the water, his stride long, almost military. Without hesitating, he dove right into a large wave.

"My fantasy," announced Alison cheerfully, still on the beach at four that afternoon, "is that a waiter in a crisp white uniform will emerge from the dunes carrying a tray of daiquiris in all sorts of different flavors. Wouldn't that be wonderful?"

The sun was still blazing hot. She leaned over Joe D. and played with the hair on his chest.

"You're blocking my sun," he said with his eyes still closed.

"You don't need it. You're a dark-skinned Latin, remember?"

"And you're a dark-skinned Jew, remember?"

"How could I forget?" She began massaging his chest and shoulders. "I always forget how hard your body is. I suppose because you're such a soft person."

"Thanks a lot."

"No, I meant that as a compliment. Really muscular men, the ones that look armor-plated, are kind of frightening. I like your body because it's cozy and inviting but still

287

hard underneath. I just seem to remember only the cozy part and forget the hardness."

"I could make a bad joke of that."

"But you won't because you're nothing if not a gentleman."

He pulled her down onto him, his eyes still closed. "You're kind of cozy yourself," he said, nuzzling her neck and shoulders.

It was six-thirty before they finally left the beach, as thoroughly and pleasantly exhausted as if they had exercised strenuously. They walked slowly back to Alison's, dragging their feet along the sandy path. The foliage alongside them was brown-edged and crisp, the sun already fading low in the sky as if impatient for its winter rest. At Alison's house only Al and Fran were in, the rest having made the season's last pilgrimage to Crane's for Saturday happy hour.

"There you are!" exclaimed Fran with her usual cheer. "We were wondering when you'd show up. We're having a house dinner tonight in town after happy hour. We made a reservation for you and Joe D." Fran, like everyone else in Seaside Harbor, still didn't know Joe D. was a cop. He'd asked Castiglia to play down his role in the whole affair. An easy request, as it turned out: Castiglia was only too happy to take all the credit.

The only people who knew who he really was were dead. Except for Amanda Golland and Alison, of course. This thought occurred to him frequently, and never failed to depress him.

"So," asked Fran, "are you coming with us or aren't you?"

Joe D. and Alison exchanged noncommittal glances, both deferring to the other. Finally Alison took the initiative:

288   "I wish we had known about this earlier, Fran. We've been on the beach all day and we're really beat—I think we'll just take a nap and eat in."

"Suit yourself," said Al. "Your loss."

"And ours," added Fran hastily, ever polite.

Alison and Joe D. took a luxuriously long shower together in the outdoor stall behind the house. By the time they finished, Al and Fran had left.

"Alone at last," Alison said brightly.

"How about a nap?" he proposed, to which she readily agreed. They made love slowly and easily, exhaustion only heightening their pleasure in each other. Afterward they lay for a few hours in that delicious, utterly relaxing limbo between slumber and consciousness, accessible only during naps.

Later, Alison surveyed the kitchen to see what was available for dinner. "I'll make a deal," she said. "I'll cook you the best fettucini Alfredo you've ever had if you'll run into town for some heavy cream and Parmesan cheese. Otherwise I have all the ingredients."

"Fair enough."

"And some wine, too."

"Okay, but I hope you're up to this. I'm Italian and used to good pasta."

"I'll bet Mama DiGregorio never made a white sauce in her life."

"You really are a smartass, you know that?" he said, thinking, as he left, that as usual, she was right.

Alison put a Springsteen album on the stereo, turned the volume up, and set about making a salad.

A feeling of contentment, as unfamiliar as it was pleasurable, enveloped her like a warm breeze. She still had to struggle not to reflect on the last few weeks—but less and less as time passed. The real struggle was against her ten- **289** dency to look forward. There, in the future, she could list any number of reasons why this contentment, so obviously the product of her relationship with Joe D., was all wrong. When she was apart from him she would focus only on his faults—or, rather, on the reasons he was not right for her; they were only "faults" in her eyes, and then only when he wasn't present. When he was with her nothing seemed important except the man himself: honest, intelligent, undeniably handsome, and—maybe this is what scared her most of all—deeply in love with her. Why, she wondered, did she always run in the opposite direction of the very thing she—

Alison looked up from the pepper she was chopping by the sink. There had been a noise in the living room, just barely audible over the music. It sounded like the high-pitched whine of the screen door when it was opened or closed.

"Joe D., is that you? Did you forget something?" she called from the kitchen, which like all the first-floor rooms opened directly onto the living room. She received no reply, shrugged, and returned to her chopping. It had grown dark outside; there was the faintest aroma of autumn in the air. With the stereo blasting it was impossible to isolate any sound with certainty.

A moment later, however, Alison knew she was not alone in the house. *How* she knew was unclear, but she sensed another presence with absolute certainty. And she knew it wasn't Joe D.

Had the events of the past month not occurred, she might not have been disturbed by this sudden awareness of someone else's presence. This, after all, was a communal house in Seaside Harbor, one of the freest, most open towns in the world. People came and went constantly, and without announcing themselves. Yet the past month had altered the contours of her mind like a coat of fresh paint still not completely dry. She was terrified.

"Who's there?" she called out weakly.

No response. Stay calm, she told herself. True, there had been some violence lately, a lot of violence, but the guilty parties were all . . . dead. They can't do any further harm to anyone.

Suddenly the music died. She heard the needle dragged roughly across the record, a harsh, throat-clearing sound that made her jump.

"Who's *there*?" she shouted in the direction of the living room, still unwilling to venture out of the kitchen, her back to the counter, a serrated kitchen knife clutched in her hand.

The kitchen was lit by a fluorescent ceiling fixture, but no living room lights had been turned on. From the brightness where she stood, the living room looked cold and sinister, like a cave. If the kitchen had a door to the outside of the house, she'd have used it without hesitation.

Alison quickly calculated that Joe D. had been gone for at most seven or eight minutes. He wouldn't even be in town yet, and he was going to stop at the liquor store as well as the deli. She heard someone walk slowly across the uncarpeted living room floor, from the far end where the stereo was to the kitchen entrance. It was not a large room but the visitor's journey from one end of it to the other seemed to last forever.

She was staring at the empty black doorway when a figure suddenly appeared in it.

A man's figure.

"Rob," she gasped, almost whispering. She didn't know whether to be relieved or frightened, but when he didn't say anything, just stood there in the doorway glaring at her menacingly, she knew fright, not relief, was the appropriate response.

A minute later he still hadn't said anything. The silence lingered between them like a poisonous gas that seemed only to affect her, for while she was trembling and felt her **291** heart racing, Rob Lewis was motionless, framed in the doorway. She began to babble just to break the silence.

"Rob, you scared me to death. You shouldn't just barge into people's houses like that. And why did you turn off the record? I heard you do it and you scratched it badly. It's—"

"Shut up," he said with such force she instantly obeyed. The sound of his voice, cruel, totally serious—dead serious—frightened her more than the silence she had found so intolerable only a moment before. Still poised in the doorway, wearing a sleeveless T-shirt and blue jeans, he seemed very large and very strong. Veins ran the length of his thick arms; in Alison's terrified eyes they appeared to be throbbing wildly, grotesque, pulsating manifestations of rage.

"Rob, if you're here because of two weeks ago—"

"First you and your friend humiliate me because of one lousy night. Then you don't give me a chance to prove myself to you, after I followed you up Third Avenue, bought you dinner and—"

"You *followed* me up—"

"I knew you couldn't keep your mouth shut," he said in an acid but strangely calm voice.

"How can I be silent when—"

"*I said shut up!*" he screamed. "You don't know how to keep your mouth shut, do you? Like your friend Linda. Like all fucking women."

This outburst had transformed him from a threatening but still human figure into a monster, his face now a hideous mass of vascular, throbbing rage.

"If your friend had been a real woman, I wouldn't have had a problem, but it's always the man's fault. All the girl has to do is lie there while the man does all the work. And then she goes and blabs about it all over the fucking place. **292** As if it wasn't her fault to begin with.

"She was like a fucking sack of potatoes, your friend Linda. I would have had more fun with a goddamn blowup doll. And she had the fucking nerve to throw *me* out! I asked for a second chance but she said she was tired. *Tired?* She was a fucking zombie."

"Rob, Linda didn't tell anyone, I swear."

"She told you, didn't she?"

"We were friends—"

"Fucking dykes, I'll bet. How many other close friends did she have, huh? Five? Six? That wop boyfriend of yours, he a close friend too?"

"No, you don't understand, I—"

"With her dead I figured I could have some peace. But no, you had to open your fucking mouth all over the place, including to the cops. And you taunted me . . . in Crane's. You taunted me and pointed at me and you wouldn't give me a second chance. Like your friend. She threw me out when I was *naked*. Right there in the bedroom she decided I wasn't *good* enough for her. Not *man* enough for her. Well, maybe now you'll know what kind of man I am . . ."

He was sounding less angry and more hurt, his voice breaking occasionally. Alison took this to be a positive sign. "I wasn't taunting you, Rob, I was—"

"Shut up, bitch."

The anger was back.

"You don't know how hard it is being a man. How could you? Fucking chicks put pressures and demands on you all the time. Like you can't even take a girl out for dinner without her wanting you to screw her the first night. So what if I can't deliver every time? That makes me a fucking faggot? Maybe I had too much to drink, or maybe I'm just tired. What the fuck's the difference? I'll tell you the difference. You buy a girl a nice meal, you take her dancing maybe, and then, whammo, you fizzle out in the sack and you're dirt, a piece of shit, a fag. Don't bother staying the night, don't bother calling. Oh no, just scram, get lost."

He was quiet for a moment, but his chest continued to heave and his burning gaze never left her. She found the silence painful.

"Rob . . ." she began.

"How many other people did you tell about me and Linda, huh? One? Ten? A goddamn thousand?"

"None, I swear!"

"You're a lying cunt, you know that? Like Linda. She threw me out in the middle of the night, like I was garbage. And you wouldn't even let me up to your apartment. Did you think I'd fizzle out on you like I did with Linda? Let's see if I fizzle out now . . ."

He took a step forward, and as he did, her grip on the knife tightened visibly.

"You going to stab me with it?" he said mockingly. "You going to stab me?" He took another step.

"I will if you come any closer," she replied, but her voice betrayed a lack of conviction that he detected with the heightened sensitivity of a prowling animal.

"I don't think so," he said, grinning. "You're good with your mouth. And your cunt too, I bet. But not with a knife. Just hand it over, Alison, hand it to me. Then I'll show you what Rob Lewis can do." He affected a soothing, paternal voice, but it sounded odiously false and menacing.

"Stop there or I'll . . ." She paused, a blunder.

"You'll what?" he challenged her.

She never had time to answer. He reached out quickly to grab the knife. Without thinking she thrust it at him, stabbing him in the hand.

He recoiled instantly, clutching his wounded hand with his good one. He moaned loudly, hoarsely, a sound that was almost not human, staring alternately at his hand and at Alison.

"Look what you've done!" he shouted wildly. "Jesus Christ, look what you've done!" He stood there, rocking back and forth, blood dripping from his hand. It was as if he were trying to accustom himself to the notion that he could be attacked, that he was vulnerable, that he could bleed.

"You blew it, Alison," he said in a sickly, childish whine that bore absolutely no resemblance to the deep, resonant voice that had so attracted her just a few weeks ago. "I came here to prove something to you, to finish what we started back in New York. But you blew it, just like your friend Linda. Now you'll pay just like she did."

Alison felt herself gag. "*You* killed her," she said. "How could we have been so wrong?" She was too stunned to realize the implications this revelation held for her.

"I stopped her, that's all. I had to stop her before the whole fucking world knew Rob Lewis couldn't get it up. I didn't come here to hurt you, only to get what was coming to me, to show you what kind of man Rob Lewis is. And then you did this." He held up his injured hand, the blood trickling down his forearm. "No one hurts Rob Lewis and gets away with it. No one." He took a step toward her.

"I'll do it again," Alison warned, feeling a surge of strength. She began to inch her way around him to the door, slowly, warily.

All at once he let go a horrible, guttural cry of rage and lunged at her wildly, oblivious to the knife.

The deli was crowded with people buying last-minute items for Saturday dinner. Joe D. found the heavy cream and cheese, picked up a pint of ice cream for dessert, and got on line to pay.

Two women in front of him were talking about the Linda Levinson case. People in Seaside Harbor still talked about little else, though the focus of attention had shifted from

Linda herself to Eric Farber. As incredulous as people had been that Linda could be murdered, and in Fire Island yet, they were *stunned* that Eric Farber could be the killer.

"I had a crush on him, I swear to God," said one woman, holding a head of lettuce and a cucumber. "He seemed perfect."

"Looks are deceiving, Trish."

"Boy, did he have the looks, though."

"Next guy I go out with, I don't care if he's so ugly he stops clocks. And I'm going to do a reference check on him that'll make Dun and Bradstreet look like amateurs."

Joe D. willed the line to move faster. After paying he headed to the liquor store for wine, trying to forget the reason he'd come to Fire Island in the first place only a month ago. Trying to forget Linda Levinson and the violence and pain she'd triggered.

He couldn't forget, though. Something was gnawing at him, and he stopped suddenly in the middle of the walk to figure out what it was. Meeting Lewis on the beach—was it this that was bothering him? All that pent-up violence in a place like Seaside Harbor was dangerous, like a wild animal loose in a campground; the town had so few defenses, especially from someone who, superficially at least, fit in so well. It had turned out that Lewis was not Linda Levinson's killer, but he could have been: Joe D. felt certain he was capable of such an act.

Something else was eating him. It had to do with seeing Rob on the beach earlier that day, but it wasn't simply the hatred he'd felt from Rob, the contempt. It was something Rob had said, something about Linda. But what was it? What had he said that, hours later, still floated around the perimeter of his consciousness, a black cloud barely glimpsed on the far edge of the horizon?

He continued on his errand. Rob Lewis was a bomb looking for an excuse to detonate, he thought. Linda Levinson was almost the excuse, but someone else got to her first.

Chapter

ALISON didn't have to *use* the knife against Lewis. Instead, she just held it firmly in front of her, terror fortifying her grip. Paralyzing her.

He hurled himself madly at her. The knife pierced his shirt on the left side of his abdomen as his hands grabbed her neck. The force of his body pushed her back against the kitchen counter and drove the knife deeper into his side, but the cut had no apparent effect on him. His hands clamped about her neck—a passerby might have assumed they were kissing, she swooning against the counter as he pressed his body passionately against hers—but he was so close to her she couldn't pull the knife back to get in another jab.

For Lewis, with his big strong hands, cutting off Alison's oxygen supply was as easy as squeezing toothpaste from a tube. She realized, not immediately but soon enough, that he was choking her to death.

Choking her to death! The realization galvanized her body. Every muscle united in a desperate and furious effort to push Lewis away from her, but it was useless. In addition to his own strength, fueled by a rage that equaled Alison's own determination to survive, Lewis had gravity on his side, for Alison was bent backwards over the counter, which jutted painfully into her lower back, and Lewis, still gripping her throat, still completely flush with her body, was practically on top of her.

She managed finally to free her right hand, not completely but enough to pull the knife back an inch and give it a shove forward. This time she knew it had gone more deeply into him—it felt like piercing Styrofoam. His grip loosened for a split second. She managed one deep gasp of air before his hands clenched back around her throat. Why wasn't the knife wound having more of an effect? For one surreal instant she had a horrible vision: Lewis was already dead but his hands were frozen around her throat in a death grip as his body hung heavy and lifeless from her neck.

The solitary gulp of air her monumental effort had won her was not enough. Lewis's determined rage had petrified him: he was a mass of hard, unyielding, unfeeling stone bearing down on her—heavier, heavier. From his mouth emanated deep, hideous, mechanical sounds—the gurgling of a pump, the whir of a generator, the grinding of gears. She felt herself becoming dizzy and weak.

Joe D. purchased two bottles of California Chablis recommended by the liquor store's proprietor. He felt his stomach growl impatiently as he headed home, walking quickly lest the ice cream melt on the way.

He could hear the surf, also growling, from the other side of the narrow island. He didn't think he'd miss the beach much now that summer was officially over. Too many bad associations this summer, too many bad memories. Alison was the one good thing to come out of all this, the only good—

Bad memories. Joe D. stopped, suddenly dizzy with bad memories. No, dizzy with a single memory. A recent memory. Today, on the beach. Something on the beach.

"*. . . organizing a stock fraud, murdering poor old Linda Levinson, ripping up her clothes and getting his rocks off on her after she was already a corpse . . .*"

That was it, what had been bothering him all evening. No one outside of the police knew that Linda's clothes had been torn off her *after* she was dead. No one . . . except her killer.

"Alison!" he shouted in the direction of her house, taking off like a sprinter.

Finally, finally, Lewis shifted some of his weight off the knife, relieving the pressure on his left side. She pulled the knife out and went for his face. She felt his hands still clamped around her throat and knew she had perhaps a second or two left to live. But the knife was wet and slippery with blood, and her hands were weak, almost limp. The knife slipped and fell to the floor.

Her left hand still pinned under his right side, she used her right hand to attack his face. The angle was awkward and her strength was evaporating fast, but she managed to poke one of his eyes with her thumb. Lewis released her neck at last. He put his bloodied hand to his injured eye, howling with pain. Alison considered making a run for the door, but Lewis stood directly in front of it, and if he tried to stop her he would surely be successful, for her strength was all but gone now. Instead she dropped to the blood-splattered floor to retrieve the knife. No sooner had she gotten hold of it, however, than he stepped on her hand **299** with all his weight. She managed to extricate her hand—it burned with pain—but his foot held the knife on the floor.

Alison started to get up as Lewis leaned over and picked up the knife. She threw herself at him, hoping to knock him off balance and make a run for it, but even injured he was immovable. He grabbed her, threw her roughly to the floor, and got on top of her, pinning her arms painfully with his knees. "Look what you've done to me!" he shrieked. "Look what you've done to me!" He was sobbing as he said this, huge, deep sobs that began in his injured abdomen and gained force in his heaving chest and finally emerged from his wide-open mouth in audible blasts of grotesque fury. *"I hate you! I hate all of you. All of you."* He reached for the knife and raised it over her. Unable to defend herself further, aware that she had lost and aware, too, of the price of that loss, Alison let out an ear-splitting scream of rage and fear.

The scream may have saved her, for it startled Lewis, and he hesitated for a single second before lowering the knife. In that second Joe D. hurled himself against Lewis from halfway across the room, knocking him off Alison. Lewis's head hit a cabinet with a loud crack. He was stunned; after a moment's pause to recover from the blow he crouched to defend himself, still holding the knife.

"C'mon, Lewis. C'mon," prodded Joe D. "I'm waiting for you."

Lewis lunged at Joe D., the knife raised above him. Joe D. grabbed his raised arm with one hand and used his other hand to punch Lewis's gut with everything he had. The blow was audible from across the room. It sent Lewis back against the cabinets a second time. The knife dropped.

"C'mon, Lewis," taunted Joe D. once more. "Come and get me."

He charged a second time, but with less force than before. Joe D. stopped him with a second blow to the stomach, then sent him crashing back against the cabinets with a thud.

Lewis had had it. It was obvious he was losing blood fast; he managed to pull himself to his feet but pitched from side to side. His head started to roll limply in a circle. He crumpled to the floor slowly, defeated.

"Look what she did to me!" he sobbed, his uninjured hand moving from his swollen eye to his pierced abdomen to his other, injured hand. "How could she do this to me?" He looked plaintively at Joe D., as if he actually expected an answer. "How could she do this? All I wanted was a second chance. How could she hurt me like this? They always hurt me, always." His speech degenerated into uninterrupted babble.

"Alison, are you all right?" Joe D. asked hoarsely.

She turned from Lewis and buried her head in Joe D.'s chest. "Oh God," she said. "Oh God."

Joe D. called a hospital on Long Island, requesting a helicopter. Lewis continued to babble deliriously, his voice growing softer and softer as the minutes passed. He looked at Alison, his eyes vacant, as if he didn't know who she was, or thought she was someone else, and lifted his arms to her. "Don't leave me," he said. "Please don't leave me again."

"You'll be all right, Rob," said Joe D. in a soft voice that lacked conviction. "You'll be all right."

Chapter

LABOR Day may have been the official end of summer but the weather was having none of it. Tuesday was an unbearably hot day; the weatherman reported 98 percent humidity, which to Joe D. sounded like the whole world should be under water. He had the day off and slept late. In the afternoon he drank beer in front of a portable fan in his apartment and ran through the Linda Levinson case over and over again, searching for the overlooked detail that would make sense of it all, lend meaning and significance to what now seemed utter senselessness and waste.

The Linda Levinson case! Even thinking of it as the Linda Levinson case made him laugh bitterly aloud. It wasn't really her case at all, he thought sadly, except that she had had the misfortune to be the tragic point of intersection of three fucked-up lives: Golland's, Farber's, and Lewis's. Now she was dead and so were Golland and

Farber. Only her murderer survived; his wounds would heal, thought Joe D., though his mind was probably too far gone.

His own part in the affair he tried not to think about. Tried with little success. How could he have been so wrong?

Oh, to hell with it, Joe D. thought, not for the first time. No matter which way you look at it I fucked up. And it almost cost Alison her life.

All day Sunday and all day Monday, he and Alison had gone over it together. And had reached the same non-conclusions.

"It made such perfect sense," Alison had said. "We already knew Farber was a thief, we knew he was black-mailing Golland. He had motive, opportunity. With Lewis, the motives were purely psychological, harder to get a real grip on. And who would have believed that there were *two* people with *two* completely unconnected motives for killing Linda, when the idea of even one person wanting her dead was incredible? I know this is difficult for you to believe, after all that's gone on, but she really wasn't a bad person. Awfully mixed up, as it turns out, but a decent person. It makes me wonder what else goes on here in Seaside Harbor, where everyone seems so 'normal,' so similar."

"But don't you see?" Joe D. had said. "All three of them—Golland, Lewis, and Farber—wanted desperately to be normal, to fit in. For Golland and Farber, *normal* was making as much money as quickly as possible, even if it meant marrying it or stealing it. For Lewis, it meant scoring big with women, but he couldn't hack it, and as the pressure to score grew more intense he just got angrier and angrier until he finally blew his lid. There's tremendous pressure here to fit in, to belong, to be just like everyone else. There's sexual pressure, too, which might be the same thing. I was an outsider here, so I know what that pressure feels like."

"But it's not just Seaside Harbor," she protested.

"Of course not, but in other places you can hide, get lost in a crowd or just shut your front door and do your own thing. Not here. There are no doors here to shut, when you think about it, and everyone's so alike in so many ways that if you're different in just one way you can be made to feel pretty miserable. I think that's what finally drove Lewis crazy."

They had parted at the Waterside ferry dock Monday afternoon. It had been awkward—their relationship seemed as ill-defined as ever, and so the significance of the parting was unclear. The boat had been crowded with weekenders hauling their belongings back to the city now that the summer was over; an air of depression and regret suffused the air like humidity.

He put off calling her until four. He dialed the main number at Bloomingdale's. After fifteen rings—he counted them—an operator answered and transferred him to Alison. "Oh, hi. Look, it's chaos here, you wouldn't believe what I'm going through. I'll call you later." She clicked off but it was a few moments before he hung up on his end. Her voice was almost unrecognizable: tight and distant, like she was clenching a pencil between her teeth while talking. He resisted calling her all evening, afraid he'd hear that same voice and hoping, too, that she'd call him. At ten o'clock he got in his Trans Am and drove into the city. The Goldberg Variations in his tape deck helped, but not much.

He heard her open the peephole cover and smiled into it. She opened the door.

"Joe."

He pulled her to him and kissed her. It felt all wrong. "I shouldn't have come, right?"

She looked up to him, sadness clouding her eyes. "I wish you hadn't," she said softly.

They were standing just inside her front door. He noticed a glass of wine and an opened book on her coffee table; the curtains were drawn and the air conditioner hummed reassuringly. There was even an impression in the sofa where she must have been sitting moments ago, sipping her wine and reading her book. The effect was insular, self-contained.

"Alison, I love you, I want to be with you. What's the matter with that?"

She shook her head.

"You can't deny that I love you simply by shaking your head, Alison. Don't you feel anything for me?"

"You know I do."

"Then why do I feel like an intruder, like the summer's over and I'm supposed to disappear?"

"I just don't see it—us—working out, and I can't let myself get more involved with you when in the long run—"

"What's bugging you is you love me and that frightens you. I'm right, aren't I?"

She shook her head vigorously.

"You know it's not that I'm just a cop, or that I'm a Catholic, or that I don't have a college degree. Oh no. What bugs you is you really like me, as a matter of fact you love me and you can't stand it. Now, if I were some shithead keeping you up nights crying alone into your pillow here in this . . . this *cocoon,* while I was out with someone else or just with the boys, you'd really go for me, right? You'd be so happy to see me, you'd just jump for joy when I showed up, expected or not. Except that I'd never show up because I'm such a shithead. That's it, Alison, I know it is. You're going to be alone for the rest of your life **305** because you'll never let yourself love anybody who might just love you in return. Or maybe you'll do what Linda Levinson did, convince yourself you love some guy who is so wrong for you he's almost irresistible."

"How dare you bring up Linda that way?" she said with little force, tears forming in her eyes.

"Why not? You think Linda was in love with a man who happened, by chance, to be married? Wrong, wrong, wrong. She was in love with him *because* he was married. He was safe! You don't throw seven years of your life away on a guy by mistake. I think Linda was afraid she would find real happiness without Golland and she couldn't face it. You're the same, Alison. If something feels good, it must be wrong."

"Get out, please, just get out." Alison was crying now, her arms folded across her chest as they always were when she was upset.

He looked at her for a moment, turned, and left her apartment. When he didn't hear the door shut behind him, he turned. Alison was standing in the doorway.

"I'm sorry," she said quietly, almost shyly.

He walked over to her. "Alison, look at me." He held her chin up with one hand and put his other hand behind her. "I love you."

She smiled her half-smile that he adored.

"Tell me you love me, Alison. I need to hear it. Or tell me you don't love me. One or the other." She pulled his head down and kissed him on the lips. "I need you, Joe D."

"That doesn't count, Alison. I want you to tell me: either you love me or you don't love me. Just say one or the other."

Again she pulled him to her and they kissed. Silently she led him into her bedroom, where she slowly began unbuttoning his shirt. Joe D. was reminded of their first night together and realized how little progress they had made. No, how little progress *she* had made, for he had fallen deeply, irreversibly in love, while Alison had resisted it from the start like a disease to be fought and overcome.

"Love me, Joe D.," she whispered, pulling him down onto the bed. "Love me." And he did, wishing only that he had the strength to demand love in return.